As Tammy began to sing "Without You I'm Nothing," old memories threatened to overwhelm her and tears stung her eyelids. When she heard a low, pained groan, she knew instinctively it had come from her mystery man. She also knew instinctively that he would leave, and moments later, she felt the aura of his presence fade into the dark silence. She wondered why that particular song had affected him so profoundly. Had he lost someone close to him? Had the experience left him bruised and feeling empty? She knew only too well how that felt.

ECHOES OF YESTERDAY

BEVERLY CLARK

Genesis Press Inc.

Indigo Love Stories

An imprint of Genesis Press Publishing

Genesis Press, Inc.
P.O. Box 101
Columbus, MS 39703

ISBN: 1-58571-131-4
Manufactured in the United States of America

First Edition

Visit us at www.genesis-press.com
or call at 1-888-Indigo-1

PROLOGUE

"I'll bet you anything your mystery man is here tonight just like clockwork." Mikki Howard spoke matter-of-factly to her boss, Tammy Gibson, as they waited in her dressing room at the Café Moonlight for Tammy's turn to perform.

Tammy knew exactly to whom her companion was referring. She didn't know the man's name or anything else about him. But as Mikki had said, he appeared like clockwork to hear her sing, occupying a seat at the shadowed end of the bar. He hadn't missed a single one of her performances since she started singing in the San Francisco Bay area six months ago. No matter where she sang, he was there.

Although she couldn't see him, Tammy could feel his presence. Who was this man? She'd commanded Mikki to find out, but he'd managed to deftly elude her. Harry Houdini himself could not have topped this man's disappearing expertise. Mikki had questioned the bartenders. All any of them could tell her was the man seemed spellbound by Tammy's singing. And, they added, the only time he ever spoke to them was to order his drinks.

The fact that he remained so aloof irked Tammy. What was it about her that fascinated him so much? It wasn't as though she was an R & B superstar. She'd recorded several albums, but none had made it to the charts. But since she had a pleasing voice, she'd had no problem getting singing engagements in night-clubs. And although she enjoyed performing in them, she yearned for more, much more. Her goal was to solidly establish herself in the music business. What she needed was a songwriter of some worth, one she could share a rapport with, one who really understood her singing style and would be willing to work with her. So far that hadn't happened, and, lately, she had begun to think it never would.

After graduating from Julliard, Tammy had gone on to take private coaching lessons in voice control. A few music critics likened her voice to a cross between Lauryn Hill, Toni Braxton and Mariah Carey. Her singing range and sensuality astounded and entranced many; obviously and irrevocably her mystery man.

My mystery man!

Now where had that come from? He wasn't her anything. No man was her anything, not since David.

Why was he being so enigmatic? Why was he so interested in her? Surely he wasn't one of those obsessed fans who ended up hurting the object of their adoration, or maybe even killing them. She remembered what had happened to Selena a few years back. No, she didn't think he was like that. At least she hoped he wasn't.

Tammy banished the thought of him, closing her mind to everything, focusing on her coming performance, letting the excitement build inside her as it always did just before she was introduced.

Mikki guided Tammy over to a cleverly constructed pedestal that allowed a blind performer more freedom of movement without calling attention to her handicap. Tammy insisted on minimizing that aspect from all of her performances. She wanted people to focus on her singing talent, not pity her because she was blind.

Tammy heard the noise level in the club gradually die down as the band started its intro. She felt the familiar flutter of butterflies in her stomach. Then the bars from an old favorite, Jeffrey Osborne's "On the Wings of Love," started to play. From that point on, she lost herself completely in the song and her music.

He sat, as usual, in the shadows at the end of the bar. Tammy Gibson totally captivated him with her earthy voice, which not only touched his heart, but encompassed his very soul. He felt a special connection to her.

Ever since he'd heard her sing in a club in San Jose six months before, he'd been consumed by an overpowering need to see her face, to hear her voice over and over again. He recognized that the feelings he had for her went beyond admiration, passing into obsession.

If the media ever discovered his identity, he knew they would hound him once again. Although it had been years since he'd been the focus of their attention, they wouldn't hesitate to splatter his name and picture across the front pages of the tabloids. And that he definitely wouldn't let happen. Despite his concern over that very real possibility, however, he still sought her out every weekend.

As Tammy began to sing "Without You I'm Nothing," old memories threatened to overwhelm her, and tears stung her eyelids. When she heard a low, pained groan, she knew instinctively it had come from her mystery man. She also knew instinctively that he would leave, and moments later, she felt the aura of his presence fade into the dark silence. She wondered why that particular song had affected him so profoundly. Had he lost someone close to him? Had the experience left him bruised and feeling empty? She knew only too well how that felt.

CHAPTER ONE

"If we don't hurry, we're going to be late, Tammy," Augusta called up the stairs.

"I'm almost ready," Tammy answered as she finished her makeup. Joan Gordon, one of the instructors at the Braille Institute where she had attended classes years ago, had taught her how to apply it.

Tammy smiled. She'd come a long way from that rebellious teenager Augusta had taken into her heart and home thirteen years earlier. Her foster mother had taught her a lot about living, loving and sharing. And her foster father, Derek, had taught her that being blind need not be an obstacle to making of her life what she wanted it to be.

For a while, Tammy and her foster parents had been separated. Augusta and Derek had moved from Philadelphia to San Francisco, and Tammy had stayed behind to attend Julliard. After finishing, Tammy had pursued her singing career in New York for a few years, and then moved to Los Angeles.

After her two albums bombed, she moved to San Francisco to be near her family. Augusta was Chief of Surgery at Cedars Hospital, and Derek was head administrator of the San Francisco Braille Institute's chapter of the Junior Blind. Tammy doted on her foster brother, Derek Junior, whom she lovingly nicknamed D.J. To her way of thinking, her life was complete. She had her singing, her music and her family.

What more could anyone ask for? She told herself she didn't need or want anything or anyone else.

Augusta entered Tammy's bedroom.

"I'm glad your sense of style has changed from your days at the Institute. For a while there I thought you were a lost cause. You remember how hard I tried to get you to take an interest in your wardrobe?"

"Don't remind me." Tammy laughed. "Back then I didn't care if I wore a chartreuse skirt with an orange blouse and shocking purple stockings. I was a real pain in the butt. How did you ever put up with me?"

Augusta squeezed her shoulders. "Because I loved you. And because you reminded me of myself. I also knew you were hurting. You're not still hurting, are you, Tammy?"

"Of course not. Why do you ask?"

"You seem—I don't know—kind of down, I guess."

"I'm fine. In fact, I'm looking forward to going to the fund raiser dinner tonight. We were lucky to get Stevie Wonder for our guest speaker/entertainer on such short notice."

"He's known for sponsoring and contributing to any legitimate programs to help blind children. I knew if it was at all possible, he'd come. We'd better get a move on or we'll be late," Augusta chided over her shoulder on the way out of the bedroom.

Tammy wrapped her fingers around her cane and unfolded it. A sudden wave of loneliness washed over her. No matter how many times she told herself it didn't matter whether she had a man in her life, she knew deep down that she wanted what Augusta and Derek had. She wanted a man to love her the way Derek loved Augusta, and she also longed for a child of her own.

Tammy, Augusta and Derek entered the formal dining room at the Grant Entertainment Hall. For one inexplicable moment, Tammy felt uneasiness assail her. Why she felt that way, she couldn't say. Over the years she'd attended dozens of fund raiser dinners similar to this one. The San Francisco branch of OHBC (Organization to Help Blind Children), for which the dinner was given, was one of her pet projects. She had dedicated many hours to keeping the center operating.

"Tammy, I'm glad you're here," came the voice of Stevie Wonder as he and his companion approached.

Tammy eased her lips into a fond smile. "Stevie, it's good to hear your voice. You remember my parents, Augusta and Derek Morgan."

"Yes, I do."

"It's good to see you again, Stevie," Derek said, shaking his hand.

"I'm glad you could make it tonight," Augusta added.

"It's always a pleasure to converse with a lovely lady such as yourself, Dr. Morgan," Stevie complimented her.

"You know you're one of my favorite people in the whole world."

"Flattery will definitely get you somewhere, lady."

Augusta laughed, obviously charmed by the man.

Stevie cleared his throat. "Tammy, you remember my companion Vincent."

"Yes. How are you, Vincent?"

"I'm doing good. I can't wait to hear you sing."

Stevie took Tammy's hand in his. "The committee has suggested we sing a duet."

"Good suggestion. Let's do it."

Tammy handed Augusta her purse and cane, wrapped her arm around Stevie's, and Vincent guided them over to the piano.

After finishing her duet with Stevie, Tammy sang an original song, "Mystery Man." As she poured her heart and soul into the song, her mind drifted to the man who had inspired her to sing it.

When she finished singing, Tammy realized she was trembling. She and the mystery man had somehow connected even though he wasn't there in the flesh. Tammy shook her head to clear it. This was crazy. She was letting her imagination run riot.

Later, as Tammy was sitting with Augusta and Derek at their table, she heard Derek call out to someone named Sterling. When the man reached the table, Derek did the introductions.

"Augusta and Tammy, I'd like you to meet Sterling Phillips. His son Kevin is a student at the Junior Blind."

"I've heard a lot about you both," Sterling answered in a deep, slightly raspy voice that whispered across Tammy's senses.

For a few moments, Tammy was speechless. Then she said, "I hope what you heard was all good."

"I assure you it was," he replied.

"Sterling is a ballad and R & B composer," Derek revealed.

"Retired ballad and R & B composer, Derek," Sterling corrected him. "I haven't written anything in a long time. You have a fantastic voice, Ms. Gibson. It tempts me to compose again."

"Thank you," Tammy replied.

Sterling continued, "Derek has been telling me a lot about OHBC. So when he invited me to this dinner, I was eager to come. He also mentioned that you work twice a year with the Junior Blind at the Braille Institute as an instructor."

"That's true."

"I think you would be the perfect person to work with Kevin," Derek said to Tammy. "You see, in some ways, he reminds me of you when you came to your first sessions at the Junior Blind. You are still planning to help us during your hiatus from performing?"

"Oh, yes, definitely."

"Good. Then I'll expect you at our get-acquainted Thursday rap session. That way, you, Sterling and Kevin can get to know each other."

"I'll look forward to seeing you there, Ms. Gibson," Sterling added.

For some reason she couldn't fathom, the man and the intimacy in his low, raspy voice disturbed Tammy. She rose abruptly from her chair. "If you'll excuse me, I need to make a trip to the ladies' room. Augusta, come with me."

"All right." Augusta smiled at Derek and Sterling. "We'll only be a few minutes."

"What was that all about?" Augusta asked Tammy once they

were inside the ladies' room.

"I can't explain it. Something about Sterling Phillips makes me feel, I don't know, uncomfortable, I guess."

"He seems like a nice enough guy to me." Augusta gave Tammy a sidelong glance. "It's been a while, at least two years, since a man other than your mystery man has made an impression on you. Could it mean you're finally coming out of hibernation and getting over David?"

"There's nothing to get over. I've told you that. I put him out of my thoughts a long time ago."

"But the question is, have you managed to put him out of your heart?"

"Of course I have. It's just that Sterling Phillips—never mind." Tammy hurried into one of the stalls, nearly tripping in her haste to escape the subject of the conversation.

Sterling studied Tammy as she and Augusta moved away. She was slim, but with luscious curves in all the right places. It was her arresting face that caught a person off guard. Tammy had full, inviting lips that begged to be kissed, and her eyes were an unusual shade of chestnut brown. Many blind people chose to wear shades, but she refused to hide behind them. She wore her hair in a short choppy hairstyle similar to the actress Halle Berry's. And her skin was a dark, honey brown color...

"Your foster daughter is a very attractive woman," Sterling remarked to Derek.

"You won't get an argument out of me about that."

"She hasn't let being blind get her down, has she?"

"No. She hasn't. Tammy lost her sight as the result of a motorcycle accident when she was fifteen. It took real guts to triumph over that tragedy, but she did."

Sterling could tell that Derek didn't want to go into any intimate details, and he respected that. Besides, for reasons of his own, he didn't wish to pursue it.

"About your son. Kevin is a very troubled child. He's resentful and displays serious attitude problems. I can understand his frustration about being blind, but I have a gut feeling it goes much deeper than that."

"You think going to the Institute and being around other blind children will help him?"

"Yes, to a certain extent. But he needs you more than he's willing to admit or accept. I believe his attitude is in part connected to his relationship with you."

Sterling blew out a soul-weary breath. "You're probably right. You see, he's hardly spoken to me since the car accident. He blames me for his mother's death and his blindness."

Sensing an underlying sadness, Derek asked, "Were you the one driving?"

"Yes."

"And you feel guilty, don't you? Ah, guilt. I know the emotion well."

Sterling stared at Derek in surprise. "You do?"

"I'll have to tell you about it some other time. Augusta and Tammy are coming back." He smiled at them as they approached the table. "Here come the two loveliest ladies in the Bay Area."

"He knows to say things like that." Augusta smiled at Sterling and then winked.

Tammy was careful to sit as far away from Sterling as she could and managed to say as little to him as possible as the evening wore on.

Derek noticed and made a mental note to find out why.

Sterling also noticed. When the music began to play, he asked, "May I have the pleasure of this dance, Ms. Gibson?"

Tammy wanted to refuse. Dancing wasn't one of her better accomplishments, and she couldn't help feeling self-conscious while doing it. But to refuse would be rude. Her senses vibrated when she heard him get up, and her heartbeat quickened when he came behind her chair to help her to her feet. Awareness of him made her ache to know what he looked like. She was sure he would be good looking, and with that deep voice, probably sexy. When his fingers touched her elbow, as Sterling led her out on the dance floor, Tammy's senses went on red alert.

Sterling picked up on Tammy's wariness as they danced. He wondered if he was the cause or the dancing or a combination of the two. Her stilted movements revealed her discomfort. Whatever the reason, a definite tension was passing between them.

"Relax. I'm not going to hurt you. I'd be the first to admit that I'm no Gregory Hines when it comes to dancing, but believe it or not, I haven't trampled on any lady's toes in a while."

Tammy couldn't help laughing. "You dance just fine, Mr. Phillips."

"Your singing voice is really awe-inspiring, Ms. Gibson."

"Thank you." She gulped, unable to mask her reaction to the low, smokey timber of his voice when he said that. She reached for a change of subject. "I remember hearing one of the songs you composed, 'If Love Is There.'"

Sterling momentarily fell out of step, but quickly recovered and eased back into the rhythm of the dance.

Tammy couldn't help wondering why the mention of that particular song had distracted him.

"He is a very good looking man, isn't he?" Augusta said to Derek, taking in Sterling's lean, six foot plus frame, his almond brown skin, intense sable brown eyes, the straight nose, and the strong jut of his chin as he danced with Tammy. She sensed a sadness about him. Sterling Phillips was an unusually reserved man, she concluded. She couldn't help wondering why he was so tense around Tammy. And what puzzled her even more was that Tammy was acting equally uneasy around him. It would have led her to believe they'd met each other before if she hadn't known otherwise. But then again, maybe it was the attraction they were both trying so hard to resist, for whatever their reasons.

"You through?" Derek interrupted her evaluation.

"What?"

"You were giving Sterling Phillips a thorough going over, doc," Derek teased.

"I do that with everyone. You know that. It's a habit I haven't been able to break. Call it a leftover from once being blind."

"So what's the verdict?"

"I haven't reached one yet. Sterling seems all right, still..."

"The man is carrying around a lot of pain and guilt from

what I've managed to find out. I can definitely identify with those emotions." A faraway look came into Derek's eyes.

Augusta put her hand over his. "You still feel guilty about causing my blindness? That was a long time ago, baby. I got my sight back, and I'm operating again, thanks to you."

"But it was because of me you had to go through that in the first place. We were lucky Dr. Eekong was able to restore your sight so you could operate again. If only he could have done the same for Tammy."

"Yes, if only. The two most frustrating, overused words in the universe."

Just then the music ended and Sterling escorted Tammy back to the table.

"Augusta and Derek," Sterling began, "I really must be going." He said to Tammy, "It was nice meeting you, Ms. Gibson. Derek, I'll be in touch."

"What happened between you two while you danced?" Augusta asked Tammy after Sterling walked away.

"Nothing."

Derek studied Tammy's expression. The hell it hadn't. He didn't believe her for a minute. Something had happened between her and Sterling that she wanted to avoid talking about. He wondered what that something could be.

After Derek and Augusta dropped Tammy off at her house, she didn't go directly to bed. Instead, she went into the living room and eased her tense body onto the recliner. For some reason, Sterling Phillips had upset her equilibrium. Something about his voice was hauntingly familiar, but at the same time, frustratingly elusive. That was crazy. She'd never met him before. Surely she would have remembered. Still, other little things about him bothered her. It annoyed her that she couldn't wrap her thoughts around a single word to adequately describe the feeling.

What you mean is that you're deeply attracted to the man.

No. She wasn't. Tammy shook her head to clear it, then shifted her thoughts to her upcoming teaching assignment at the Junior Blind. She was curious to meet and get to know Sterling Phillips's son. From the little she'd been told, Kevin wasn't adjusting to his blindness.

She could definitely relate to that. Tammy recalled how hard it had been for her. It was probably even harder for a pre-teen boy. Maybe she could help him accept his condition, show him that being blind wasn't the end of the world.

Her thoughts left Kevin and back-pedaled to the fact that disconcerted her about Sterling: his first name was the same as David's first name. She wondered if Sterling's middle name could be David. That would be a real coincidence. She couldn't help feeling the way she did about the other Sterling. Upon learning that she would be blind following the motorcycle accident, Sterling David Dixon had let it influence him not to come see her at the hospital. After a while, she came to realize he had no intention of ever doing so, and she'd been devastated. Although being very young, they had been in love. She had believed they were truly soulmates. They'd shared the most intimate relationship two people could have. She sighed. That was a long time ago, and David was now relegated to a part of her past she never wanted to think about.

But no matter how hard she tried to blot him and what had happened from her memory, that devastating experience still had a vice-like grip on her ability to trust. She'd never admitted that to anyone, not even Augusta and Derek.

Tammy's thoughts returned to Sterling Phillips. She sensed that a lot was going on between him and his son. She wanted to help the child, but didn't want to get involved with the father. But if she worked with Kevin, she couldn't avoid contact with Sterling. What if Kevin picked up on the tension between her and his father? It could only have a negative effect. She couldn't in good conscience allow that to happen.

She might feel uncomfortable in Sterling Phillips's presence, but she would have to get past it in order to help his son. Her involvement with Kevin need not go beyond helping him adjust to the reality of his situation.

And just who are you trying to convince?

CHAPTER TWO

Sterling unlocked the door of his recording studio, turned on the lights, then slowly entered. Considering the amount of time he'd spent in this room, it was inconceivable that he should now feel like a stranger in a foreign country. He'd written over five hundred songs in here. His eyes settled on the sound booth and instrumentation enclosure for a moment. Then he shifted his attention to the corner window, where his desk sat, and then on to the piano. A dust canvas covered its smooth mahogany surface. The other pieces of furniture without a protective covering were blanketed in a layer of dust.

In the last three years Sterling hadn't allowed anyone, himself included, inside this room. He walked over to his desk. The last song he had started composing still lay where he'd left it. "Where Do We Go from Here" was a song about betrayal, anger and bitterness. At the time, they were exactly what he'd felt toward his wife. But following Kayla's death, he'd ceased feeling those particular emotions. Guilt and pain had replaced them.

He reached inside a cabinet beside the desk where he kept a paper shredder, flipped the on switch, picked up the yellowed sheet music then sent it through the machine's razor-sharp teeth. If he could only rid himself of the guilt and pain as easily.

The last year of his marriage to Kayla had been a living nightmare. Kevin had been the only reason they'd stayed together. In the end, Kevin hadn't been enough.

Hatred hadn't always been what he and Kayla had felt for

each other. He thought they'd loved each other in the beginning. But later, Kayla grew to resent the time he spent composing his music. He had thought having a child would keep her occupied, and it had for a while. But when Kevin started school, she had time on her hands and began complaining that Sterling didn't care about her.

He was so into his music he hadn't listened. He admitted now, in hindsight, that he had neglected his wife. Even so, he'd felt betrayed when he had found out Kayla had had a string of lovers. Kayla had accused him of betraying her with his mistress: his obsession with composing music. No woman could ever compete with that, she'd declared, and she didn't intend to try.

Sterling stepped over to the linen closet adjacent to the bathroom, grabbed a towel and wiped the dust from his desk, then walked over to the piano and slid the canvas off. He stood for a few tense seconds, staring at it before finally sitting down on the bench. He uncovered the ivory keys. Beads of sweat popped out on his forehead and above his upper lip. Did he have the guts to begin again?

His fingers shook when he reached out to touch the keys. A sudden pain knifed into his brain, and he pulled his hands back, letting them drop lifelessly onto his lap. He closed his eyes, took a calming breath, rose to his feet, walked back to the desk then picked up his composition pad.

Thoughts of Tammy Gibson came storming back, and, with them, all the old pain. After all these years, he'd never thought he would see her again.

Tammy hadn't recognized his voice because it had been altered in the accident that had claimed the life of his wife and blinded his son. Tammy was the same, yet she was different: more mature, definitely more attractive. She now exuded a confidence she'd never possessed when he'd loved her at fifteen. She had been a volatile wild spirit, ready to try anything. She seemed different now, toned down, but he sensed that her free spirit was still there, just buried beneath the surface.

A song he'd written for her years ago, "I'll Always Be There for You, You Can Count on Me" popped into his mind. That was a laugh; he'd never been there for anyone he cared about when they'd really needed him. He'd been a selfish bastard back then and later an indifferent husband. And over the last three years, an ineffectual father. It wasn't surprising that his son treated him with so little respect.

Sterling strode over to the sliding glass door leading into the garden and looked out. He'd had a chance to be the kind of father his son needed, but he'd blown it, and Kevin wanted nothing to do with him. He blamed him for his mother's death. Sterling grimaced. Hell, what could he say? He blamed himself.

Sterling returned to his desk and sat in the chair behind it, opened the drawer and retrieved a pencil. The words never came. At the moment, he felt so much and yet couldn't put it down on paper. The flow wouldn't come. Years before he'd had to bridle the flow, because he couldn't set the words to music fast enough.

Seeing Tammy at the fund raiser and hearing her sing "Mystery Man" had made him ache to compose again. He hadn't come close to feeling anything like it for three years. Now that he was feeling it so much, something was blocking the flow. He knew it was guilt.

He shouldn't inflict himself on Tammy or any other woman.

After discovering Kayla's betrayal, he'd lost the desire to share anything remotely intimate with a woman. But Tammy's beautiful voice, her very presence and the memories she'd evoked threatened to melt the icy barriers he'd erected around his heart. She had reached deep inside him and grabbed hold of something that was essential and elemental.

Sterling rose from his chair and headed for the door. Without looking back, he switched off the light, then quickly closed the studio door and locked it.

That night, Sterling relived in his dreams the horror that changed his life forever.

He'd seen the patches of black ice on the street, but he was going too fast to stop or swerve to avoid any of them. He was helpless to prevent what was about to happen.

"Tammy, hold on tight, baby!" he yelled to his girlfriend over the noise of the engine.

"Oh, David, I'm scared!"

Before he could offer any words of comfort or reassurance, the front wheel of his motorcycle started to wobble. He felt himself losing control, and in a panic, slammed his foot down hard on the brake and frantically squeezed the hand brakes to slow the momentum, but that only made it worse. The scream of the tires as the motorcycle skidded across the asphalt assaulted his ears, and the smell of scorching rubber nauseated him.

Suddenly, a department store window loomed in front of him.

"Oh, God!" They were going to crash into the building if he couldn't bring the bike under control.

He tried in vain to maneuver his bike away from it, but moments later the bike hit a dip, catapulting him and Tammy over the handle bars, sending them both crashing through the huge glass window. David pitched harmlessly into a display of towels and bedding, but Tammy was not so lucky. She was flung head first through the glassed-in perfume counter.

As if through a haze, he heard the voice of a man yelling to call 911. David crawled over to Tammy. She was unconscious and lay half inside the display counter. When he lifted her out, he saw that her face and the upper portion of her body was covered in blood.

Oh, God!

There was so much blood!

He started shaking uncontrollably at the sight of so much blood.

"Tammy!" he cried. When she didn't respond, tears streamed down his face. *Is she dead?* his tortured mind screeched over and over.

Minutes later, he heard the loud wail of sirens. He must have blacked out, because the next thing he saw and heard was the paramedics.

"Kids," said one, shaking his head. "Jim, you check the boy."

"Speed demons, the lot of them. He was probably going too fast when he realized he couldn't stop. Will they ever learn?"

A policeman approached David soon after the paramedic finished examining him.

"How old are you, son?"

"S-Seventeen."

He didn't hear the rest of what the man said. All he could do was stare in horror as the paramedics worked over Tammy, then watch as they strapped her onto a stretcher, finally sliding her into the ambulance.

At the hospital, he was treated and then admitted overnight for observation. When he asked about Tammy, the nurse told him she was in critical condition and had to be rushed to the operating room.

Later that next day, he stood outside ICU, listening as two doctors discussed Tammy's case.

"She's only fifteen."

"It's too bad she wasn't wearing a helmet. In my opinion, teenagers shouldn't be allowed behind the controls of any vehicle. We've lost nearly as many as we've managed to patch up and save."

His heart leaped into his throat. *What are they talking about? Tammy will be all right! She has to be!*

When the doctors headed down the hall, he walked over to the nurses' station, informing them that he was Tammy's brother. The nurse escorted him inside to see Tammy. Her head and left arm were heavily bandaged. The other arm and the upper part of her body was in a cast.

He broke down and cried at the sight of her. Guilt came crashing down on him like an avalanche. He was responsible. So deep in the dregs of his own misery, he jumped when he felt a hand on his shoulder. He looked up. It was one of the doctors that he had overheard discussing Tammy's case.

"How is she, doctor?" David asked.

"Extremely critical," came his grim reply.

"Why is her head bandaged like that?"

The doctor frowned. "She had severe head trauma and damage to her optic nerve. I'm afraid she's going to be permanently blind, son."

Pain like he'd never felt before ripped him apart.

"Permanently blind!" his voice cracked.

"You aren't her brother, are you, son? You were the one driving the motorcycle, weren't you?"

"I didn't mean to—"

"It doesn't matter. You were reckless and irresponsible, and because of that, you've cost this girl her sight, possibly her life."

Guilt demolished him. After the doctor left, he looked at Tammy lying on the bed, wrapped in bandages, barely holding onto life, and he wanted to die. How could he ever face her after what he'd done?

The next night, he went to see Tammy one last time. She was heavily sedated and didn't know he was there. He took her hand in his and kissed it, then kissed her lips. He laid her hand across her stomach then headed for the door. He looked back at her. Pain and guilt tore through him. The best thing he could do was get out of her life and stay out, he told himself.

Sterling awoke shaking violently, his heart thudding heavily in his chest. That soul-wrenching experience had nearly destroyed him. Tears slid down his cheeks, and he covered his face with his hands. He hadn't had that particular nightmare in a very long time.

He lay back and tried to fall asleep again, but there was no use. He swept the comforter aside and scrambled off the bed. Sleep would not visit him tonight.

Sterling found himself heading in the direction of his studio. He reached for the key up over the door, let himself inside, strode over to his desk then eased into the chair behind it. Glancing at his composition pad, he reluctantly picked it up. Deep emotions bombarded him. He retrieved a pencil from the desk drawer and began scribbling frenziedly.

> The tears in my soul won't let me sleep
> Because the pain in my heart is much too
>   deep…

An hour later, he finished the song and scrawled the title "Tears in My Soul" across the top of the first sheet. It was as though a whole other person had taken possession of his mind and body. Finally, the flow began to ebb, relinquished control. Sterling had never felt anything quite like it before. What did it mean? Could this be the start of something? Hope began to rise inside him.

Glancing at the song he'd written, Sterling could almost hear Tammy singing it.

Did he dare approach her about recording it?

Even if she agreed, what would happen when she discovered the real identity of the person who'd written it?

Sterling closed the composition pad. Tammy had known him as David Dixon. He had gone by his middle name back then. He had honestly believed that the name Sterling didn't fit him, that it was a quality of character he'd never deserve. But when he embarked on his song writing career, he'd wanted his new undertaking to be one of a pure, sterling quality, so he decided to go by his first name and change his last to Phillips.

He was no longer that stupid, reckless boy who'd driven his motorcycle like a bat out of hell, without a thought to his safety or that of other people. Living life on the edge had lost its appeal after the accident. Seeing Tammy lying torn, bleeding and broken, possibly dying, had changed him forever.

Sterling walked over to a cabinet and took out the albums Tammy had recorded and slipped them into the CD player.

Listening to her, he could tell she was serious about her singing career. He sat analyzing the songs for several hours. They were all right, but they failed to showcase the inner beauty of her voice.

He and Tammy had had a special rapport when they were teenagers. Many days they had sung together for their own enjoyment. A sudden thought came to him. He could help launch her into superstar status. And in this small way, he could start to redeem himself and salve his guilty conscience.

He would have to write enough songs to float an album. He breathed out heavily. But what if the song he'd just finished was merely a fluke and he was he incapable of delivering more? But when that sudden burst of hope threatened to vanish, an inner strength kicked in. He sensed that an irrevocable change in him had occurred, and there would be no turning back.

CHAPTER THREE

It was the last night of Tammy's singing engagement at the Inner Harbor before her hiatus officially began. She didn't have to wonder whether her mystery man would be there. His appearance was a foregone conclusion. She'd begun to take his presence for granted. When the engagement ended, she would miss him. What was she saying? He was probably just a temporarily obsessed fan who would eventually move on to worship some other performer. Deep down, though, she didn't really believe that. Something intense and indescribable dwelled inside the man. What it was, she hadn't figured out yet, but a kind of invisible bond seemed to connect them.

"Tonight is my last night at the Inner Harbor," Tammy announced to her audience before singing "Mystery Man." When she heard a familiar male groan of inner pain escape, she knew it had come from him.

She didn't remember ever feeling this connected to anyone, not since David. As much as she wanted to deny it, the pull of attraction between her and this man was undeniable. Who was he? Why was he here? Why hadn't he personally communicated with her? Why had he chosen to stay in the shadows? What did he want from her? She knew instinctively that he did want something.

After the last set, Tammy returned to her dressing room. The scent of flowers greeted her and Mikki the moment they entered. "These roses are so beautiful!" Mikki exclaimed. "There are white ones as well as red ones."

"Who sent them?" Tammy asked.

"As if you need to ask," Mikki muttered under her breath.

Tammy heard her companion walk over to the flowers and sniff before opening the envelope. Then she read the card aloud:

"Your voice is mesmerizing—

Like the fire in a white diamond.

Enchanting—

Like the passionate color of a blood red ruby."

"There's no name on the card. Aren't the words romantic, poetic even? I'll bet you anything they're from your mystery man."

"You don't know that."

"Come on, Tammy. You know good and well they're from him."

"I'm tired, Mikki. Help me undress so I can go home."

"You really need to get a life."

"There's nothing wrong with my life. I like it just the way it is."

"You should be going out and having fun instead of staying stuck in the house. There's more to life than work. Any number of eligible men you know would jump at the chance to take you out, if you ever gave them one."

"Mikki!"

"I'm only speaking the truth."

That night in her bedroom, Tammy eased her fingers over the Braille-dotted page of the book she had been reading. After going over the same sentence for the fourth time, she stopped and felt around for her bookmark. Finding it, she clipped it to the page then put the book down on the nightstand. She slid her fingers across the nightstand to the vase. Mikki had insisted on bringing the roses home and putting them in water before going to her own room.

The cool, wet-silky texture of one rose and its delicate fragrance conjured up the shadowy image of David, the boy she'd once loved. He'd given her a single red rose one evening after they'd slipped away to be together. She had loved him with all her young heart. Despite what she kept telling herself, the pain of his abandonment still had the power to hurt her. That experience, along with the hatred she felt toward her father for walking out on her and her brothers and sister, had shaped her negative perception of men in general. Derek was the only man she completely trusted and respected.

Where was David now? And why was she thinking about him—again? It was probably because of the two men who had so recently entered her life.

With the mystery man, it was the roses. Eventually, he would lose interest and stop coming to hear her sing.

And what about your attraction to Sterling Phillips?

What about it? Nothing could ever come of it. It was only because he had the same first name as David she had even noticed him. Other than that, no connection existed between them.

If you want to believe that.

She shook her head, flinging that last taunt from her mind. Once her teaching assignment at the Institute ended, she wouldn't have to deal with Sterling Phillips. Only when both Sterling and the mystery man were gone from her life would it return to any semblance of normalcy. Mikki would call it settling back into its usual state of boredom.

❋

For the first time in the three years since she had begun teaching at the Institute, Tammy was anxious about facing her Junior Blind class. She knew why. In the Thursday rap session with Kevin Phillips, he had sent attitude vibes reverberating through the room like the fierce winds signaling the onslaught of a hurricane. It brought back memories of her own attitude years ago.

Tammy understood only too well this boy's protective mechanism, but wasn't sure how to neutralize it—at least not yet. Augusta and Derek had never given up trying to reach her, and she could do no less for Kevin Phillips. She felt a unique kinship with this bitter young boy.

When Tammy first began teaching at the Institute, she'd had Derek set up the classroom the way he'd set up Augusta's at the Institute in Philadelphia, even down to having a piano delivered. In the past she'd found music to be a universal language and used it to reach deeply troubled kids. Advice from Stevie Wonder had helped ground her teaching strategy.

She'd made it her business to find out what interested the kids before they lost their sight. For those who had been blind since birth, she helped them find a focus and reach for a realistic goal.

Though she wasn't always successful, she also wasn't one to give up easily. She remembered quite well how difficult she'd been and the patience Augusta and Derek had shown. Despite her efforts to remain the queen of attitude, Augusta and Derek had eventually broken through her defenses. God knows she had tested their patience and compassion to the limit.

The sound of the kids shuffling into the classroom intruded on her reverie. Tammy eased her fingers across her Braille-dotted roll call book. When she called their names, each child answered, with the exception of Kevin Phillips. That defiant gesture was so reminiscent of her own behavior years ago that she had to smile.

"I'm sure I was assigned ten students. Does my tenth student have laryngitis?"

No answer.

"Kevin Phillips, are you present?"

Still no answer.

"I guess I'll have to inform his parents that he didn't show up today."

"I'm here," he said sarcastically.

"Why didn't you answer before?"

"Maybe I just didn't feel like it."

"What do you think will make you feel like it next time, Kevin?"

"Nothin'. I don't wanna be here, period. Nothing you or anybody else can say or do will make me feel any different."

"Not even your father?"

"'Specially not him.'"

Tammy heard him rise to his feet and unfold his cane.

"The class has just begun, Kevin."

"You think I care? I'm leavin'."

As Kevin opened the door, he stumbled into Derek.

"Where are you going?" Derek asked, "Class just started."

"I don't care. I'm gettin' the hell out of here, that's where."

"We don't use that kind of language around here."

"Maybe I decided I don't wanna be here."

"Son, I—"

"I'm not your son."

Derek ignored the tone in his voice. "How are you ever going to—"

"What? Learn how to be blind? I don't need you or her to teach me how to do that," he answered bitterly. "I already know."

Derek started to say more, but Tammy spoke.

"Let him go. If he wants people to pity him, let him walk out that door. Maybe begging on street corners and in airports is what he wants to do with his life."

"I can't play football, baseball or any other sport," Kevin cried defensively. "I'm never gonna see again, so what's the use in coming here?"

"You can learn to cope, Kevin. You think it was any easier for me or any other blind person? There are other things you can do."

"Name one of 'em."

"We have to talk about it and see—"

"See?" He laughed harshly. "That's never gonna happen. I'm outta here."

"Kevin." Derek started after him.

"Let him go, Derek." Tammy called a recess and instructed the kids to go out into the garden. She sighed. "Kevin

ECHOES OF YESTERDAY

Phillips is more of a hard case than I was, and he doesn't have the excuse of being raised in the ghetto."

"Is he too much for you, Tammy?"

"No. Right about now what I said is working its way into his brain. He'll probably come back just to get one up on me."

Derek laughed. "You sure know how to read them, don't you?"

"I guess. I've noticed with boys it's more of an ego and pride thing than it is with girls."

"So what are you planning to do next?"

"That's my secret."

"Like your mystery man."

"He's not my mystery man. And he's not a secret."

"Who he is, isn't? By the way, have you spoken to Sterling Phillips since the rap session?"

"No."

"Any particular reason? You usually get talking to the parents out of the way from the jump."

"Well Kevin's case is different."

"In what way?"

"Derek, let's drop it. Okay?"

"Why don't you like Sterling? Does he remind you of David?"

"No, he doesn't," she answered sharply. "Why do you and Augusta keep harping on David? I've forgotten all about him."

"When pigs can fly. You haven't completely gotten over the pain of his rejection and abandonment and probably never will. Tammy, you need to admit to yourself—"

"I don't want to talk about this. It's time to call my students back in."

When Kevin failed to attend his classes the next two days, Tammy began to worry about him and decided to call his father.

"Mr. Phillips, this is Tammy Gibson. Is Kevin sick? I was wondering how he was."

"As far as I know, he's not sick. If anyone should know how he is, it's you."

"He has to attend classes for me to know that, and he hasn't been here the last two days. It's the reason I'm calling."

"You're saying he hasn't been there at all? He's been dropped off there each morning as usual, and picked up every afternoon on time. If he hasn't been going to class, then where has my son been going?"

"I don't know. All I know is that he hasn't been to class."

"Where could he possibly be going?"

"I have no clue, but I think you'd better make it your business to find out."

"Now just wait a minute."

"Either you're interested in your son or you're not."

"You don't know a damn thing about how I feel. And you certainly have no right to judge me."

"I'm not judging you, Mr. Phillips."

"I think you are. I care about my son and don't you forget

it."

"Look, I didn't mean to imply that—"

"I'll find out where my son has been going and make damn sure he comes to class."

Tammy held the phone away from her face at the bang that exploded in ear when he hung up. She certainly had handled that all wrong. She'd never spoken to a parent like that. Why had she done so with Sterling Phillips?

"Where in the hell was Kevin?" Sterling muttered as he paced the length of his living room over and over again as he waited for his son to get home. Anything could have happened to him. Why had he been ditching his classes? Sterling's shoulders slumped. Even when Kevin got home, he wouldn't tell him, if he chose to talk to him at all.

Sterling felt awkward around Kevin. Even though he was his son, sometimes it was like being around some strange, alien child.

As he stood looking out the living room window, Sterling saw the limo drive up and waited for his son to come inside. When he heard the key turn in the lock, he tensed in anxious anticipation. As Kevin made climbed the stairs, Sterling cleared his throat.

"Where have you been?"

"At the Institute."

"Don't give me that bull. Ms. Gibson called to tell me that you haven't been there for most of this week. Where in the hell have you been?"

"It's not like you really care."

"Son, you know that's not true."

"Do I?"

"Let's not go there, okay?"

"If you really wanna know, I went to the cemetery to visit my mama's grave."

Pain twisted through Sterling's gut. He hadn't been able to make himself go there since the funeral. Kevin had asked him to personally take him several times, but Sterling had refused and had their chauffeur, Marcus, drive him that first year.

"How long have you been going there by yourself?"

"Since the last time I asked you to take me, and you said no."

"That was two years ago. You mean you've been going there on your own all this time?"

"I learned how to go on the bus. You would have never found out if you hadn't made me go to that dumb old blind school."

"Let's get back to why you haven't been going to your classes."

"Why do you keep acting like you really care what I do? You don't care about me. And you didn't care about Mama when she was alive."

"I've always cared about you, Kevin. You're my son."

"Mama was your wife, and you didn't care about her."

"You're wrong, son, I did."

"No, you didn't. You hated her. I heard you arguing with her just before the accident."

"People say things they don't really mean when they're angry."

"You meant it all right. I heard you slap her. I'll always hate your guts for that. You're probably glad she's dead."

Sterling put his hand on his son's shoulder. "Kevin, you don't understand and can't remember everything that happened that night."

"But you do. I don't have anything else to say to you." He jerked away then started up the stairs.

"Well, I have something to say to you, young man. I want to know the real reason you've been ditching your classes. And I want to know now."

"It's not gonna do me any good. They can't help me to see again, so what's the use in going."

"Kevin, you need to learn how to take care of yourself."

"I already know how to do that."

"No, you don't. You just think you do. Your teacher said—"

"I don't care what she said. I'm not going back, and she can't make me."

The challenge in Kevin's voice said more: that even his father, especially his father, couldn't make him go either. How did he handle this with his son? Sterling wondered.

"You haven't given it a chance. Once you learn Braille, you can read, and once you learn how to use your other senses, you can—"

"What? Play football? Baseball? Don't you get it? I can't see, and it's all your fault. You did it. And you killed my mother."

Sterling groaned and tears stung his eyes at the hate and bitterness radiating from Kevin's voice. For his own son to say something like that hurt him to the core. He wondered if he would ever forgive him for any of it. He had vowed that he wouldn't let Kevin's attitude stop him from getting him the help he needed.

He'd given him more than enough time to pull himself together. Maybe that was the problem; he'd given him too much time.

Kevin was all he had. It didn't matter that his son said that he hated him. He intended to see that he got the best help available. He owed him that.

"Whether you think I'm responsible or not, you're going back to the Institute. And your ditching classes stops. From now on if you want to go to the cemetery, or anywhere else, you'll ask permission, and I'll see that you get there after your classes are over. You understand me?"

Kevin didn't answer.

"Do you understand me?" Sterling repeated in a voice brooking no argument.

"Yes," Kevin conceded through clenched teeth, then angrily made his way up the stairs, stumbling, nearly losing his balance. He grabbed hold of the special railing Sterling had had installed.

Though he ached to reach out and hug his son, Sterling restrained himself. He watched until Kevin made it to the top of the stairs, took the folding cane from its shoulder bag case and disappeared from sight.

The next morning at the beginning of class, Tammy heard Sterling tell his son he would be picking him up after his last class. She also heard the sulky, bitter sound in Kevin's voice when he answered his father, and she regretted anew talking to Sterling the way she had. He evidently had a lot to deal with where Kevin was concerned.

She thought again about all that Augusta had put up with from her all those years, how she and Derek had never faltered in their crusade to reach her.

"Mr. Phillips, I'd like a word with you before you go. Would you step out into the garden?"

"All right," he said, following Tammy after she had settled the class down. Sterling closed the sliding glass door behind them. "What do you want to talk about?"

"I want to apologize for what I said."

"It's not necessary."

"I think it is. I was way out of line. Look, we need to set up a meeting to discuss Kevin and what to do to reach him. When would be a good time for you?"

Sterling wanted to laugh. He had all the time in the world since he no longer did any composing. That wasn't quite true. He had written that one song. He cleared his throat. "Anytime you say."

"How about this coming Friday afternoon? Kevin will be in his mobility training class with Derek. That should give us plenty of time to talk."

"I'll be here."

CHAPTER FOUR

As he stood gazing out the sliding glass door of his studio, Sterling contemplated his scheduled meeting with Tammy. He wasn't sure how he was going to handle being alone with her. He'd been lucky so far in his dealings with her and hadn't given away his feelings. The time she came at him about Kevin had given him the excuse he needed to distance himself. If he stuck to just talking about Kevin, then maybe he'd be safe.

Who was he kidding? Every time he was anywhere near Tammy, his heart rate sped up and he felt as if he were about to go into cardiac arrest. The feelings he had for her were nowhere close to being over. He had loved her when she was fifteen, and he loved her still, and probably would until the day he died.

He laughed. She would never believe him if he told her that. He couldn't blame her after all that had happened to her because of him. Recognizing the complexity of the situation with Tammy, he sought refuge in thoughts of his son and his problems.

Kevin was drifting farther and farther away from him. He smiled, thinking of the good times he'd had with his son before the accident. There hadn't been nearly enough of them, and he regretted that. He'd been too wrapped up in his music to give himself and his son the quality time they'd needed to bond and really become close. Was it too late?

Sterling turned away from the tranquil garden scene and his troubling thoughts and glanced at the piano. He felt the urge to sit down and play. A slow, intense melody had resounded inside his head for the past few days. The words, "I care about you, can you ever care about me again," echoed through his mind. He could no longer resist the temptation to sit down at the piano. As if his fingers had a mind of their own, they started playing the persistent melody that would not leave him alone.

It was three o'clock in the morning before the flow left him. Sterling gazed at the pages of music he'd composed. he scribbled the title across the top sheet: "Can You Care About Me?"

He'd completed another song. He could still feel the after-effects of the sudden rush of excitement just thinking about Tammy gave him. In his mind, he could hear her singing the words to the songs he'd written.

Still too charged up to sleep, Sterling went into the kitchen and made a pot of coffee. Later that day, he would go to the meeting with Tammy to discuss Kevin. Maybe she could help him to help his son.

He frowned. She didn't have a very high opinion of him as a father. Or maybe he'd just overreacted to her comments and taken them the wrong way.

❈

"Which one do you want to wear?" Mikki asked Tammy.

"What did you say, Mikki?"

"You haven't heard a word I've said, have you?"

"I'm sorry, my mind was on something else."

"Like your mystery man?"

"No. I haven't thought about him for a while."

"Then what or who is occupying your mind?"

"The maize-colored outfit will be all right."

"Since you didn't answer my question and changed the subject, you've really got me curious. Who is he?"

"I was thinking about a boy in my Junior Blind class, Mikki."

"Oh. I thought—"

"I know what you thought. Would you please stop with the matchmaking campaign? I'm not interested in finding a man and cultivating a relationship. Okay?"

"That's what you say now."

Tammy threw her hands up. "Mikki! Look, I've got to get to the Institute. Would you just hand me the dress. Please." Tammy heard her companion's sigh of disappointment as she moved to do as she asked. Mikki was an incurable romantic.

Today wasn't anything about romance. It was about a troubled boy who had lost his mother as well as his sight and was still in denial. It was about the breakdown in communication between a father and son. She hoped to help bridge the gap. First, she had to resist the physical attraction she felt for Sterling Phillips. More than just chemistry was at work between them. She had to ask herself why her reaction to him personally had been so charged with prickly tension from day one.

As the children filed out of the classroom, the tension began to build in Tammy. When she heard Sterling's voice, she trembled with awareness. This was crazy. They were, after all, only going to talk about his son.

"We can get started whenever you're ready, Ms. Gibson."

Sterling cleared his throat. "Would you mind if we called each other by our first names?"

"No, of course not." Something about the way he'd said her name vaguely reminded her of someone, but who that someone was eluded her. That wasn't possible. She was just being paranoid. Tammy reached for a measure of objectivity. She was going to need it to effectively help Sterling and Kevin.

"We have to get Kevin to face his problems and learn to go on from there. I better than anyone know how hard it will be for him. I had to do it as a teenager when I lost someone very dear to me."

Pain knifed through Sterling at her words, and he smothered the groan threatening to escape his control. "I know you're right, but where do I begin?"

"We'll have to work on getting you two closer together. The lines of communication between you and Kevin have shredded, but hopefully haven't completely been severed. How was your relationship with him before the accident?"

"All right."

"Just all right, not close?"

"Now if you're going to start—"

"Please, don't you get an attitude."

"I'm sorry." He breathed out sharply. "I guess I'm just overly sensitive. Kevin and I were never as close as we could have been because… I have to confess that I spent most of my time composing and not enough time being a father. But I want you to know that I love my son, and I'll do anything I can to help him."

"I can't ask better from you than that, Sterling. The desire and willingness to do something about it is half the battle. It's obvious how much you care about your son. I'm sorry if I made you think otherwise."

"How do we help Kevin?"

"We've got to make him see that his life isn't over because he's blind. I know for someone his age that's hard. Besides sports, is he interested in anything else?"

"I don't know. He won't talk to me. He hasn't really talked since the accident. What little rapport we had before that is gone, and I don't know how to get it back."

"You're a composer, aren't you?"

"Yes." She already knew that. Sterling frowned, wondering where she was going with this.

"Has he shown an interest in music?"

"Not in a long time. Kevin is so resentful and bitter about so many things." Sterling wasn't sure if Kevin's attitude stemmed more from his blindness and his mother's death or his bitter feelings toward his father.

Tammy sensed that Sterling was beginning to see the intricacies of Kevin's problem. She could also sense his frustration and helplessness. And her heart went out to him for what he was obviously suffering.

She realized that in helping Kevin she wouldn't be able to avoid getting closer to his father. That realization made her feel vulnerable because Sterling evoked more than sympathy in her. He evoked emotions she didn't want to feel. What was she saying? The only thing between them was their mutual concern for his son. Anything past that...

"I conduct a music jam on Tuesday nights at seven. Why don't you bring Kevin, and we'll go from there."

"If I can get him to agree to come with me. He has more than your average knowledge of music and can play the piano. I saw to that. If he's still interested, though, he hasn't shown it."

"Maybe we can revive his interest. You know that music can heal as well as entertain."

He had to agree with Tammy about that. Hearing her sing worked like a restorative on him; her voice was a therapeutic balm for his battered soul. Maybe it could work a similar miracle on his son.

"You're still here," Derek said to Tammy as he walked into her empty classroom and over to where she sat in front of the piano. "I heard you playing."

She pulled the lid over the keys. She had just finished a melody to a new song she'd written. "I was thinking about the meeting I had with Sterling."

"How did it go?"

"I'm not sure. Sterling is deeply concerned about his son and is desperate to help him."

"Did he tell you why Kevin stopped coming to his classes?"

"No, we didn't discuss it. Evidently, he and Kevin did because Kevin is back in class. The thing is to convince him that he needs to keep coming, not just because his father insists that he do so."

"You're a genius, you'll figure it out."

"I knew there was a reason why I've always loved you all these years."

"You're the closest thing to a daughter I have."

"I consider you my true father, Derek. How's D.J.? I haven't seen much of him lately."

"Talking about somebody getting lost in their music, that boy certainly does. I think Augusta is right; he's permanently hooked."

"There's nothing wrong with that, Derek, even though I know you wanted him to get interested in Morgan Electronics."

"Only if it's what he wants. I want him to do what makes him happy. What about what makes you happy, Tammy?"

"I'm fine. I keep telling you and Augusta that."

"About that I have my doubts. All right, I won't preach. I know how much you hate that. I've got to be getting home. Why haven't we seen you there? You know you're always welcome."

"I've been kind of busy since I've started teaching at the Institute. I'll come for a visit real soon. I promise."

"If you don't, I'll be your conscience and torture you until to do."

"I know you will." Tammy smiled when she heard the door close. So D.J. was already focused on what he wanted. Maybe if she got him and Kevin together, they could be friends. First, she had to reach Kevin and cultivate her own rapport with him. Would that also mean cultivating a rapport with his father? Probably, since she couldn't separate the two. If she wanted to help Kevin she would have to deal with his father.

Why did Sterling Phillips have this strange ability to arouse her nurturing instincts and, if she were truly honest, her more romantic ones as well?

Tammy's students interested in music came to her Tuesday jam session. She let out a disappointed sigh when Sterling and Kevin weren't among them. She had hoped... As she got everyone started in their own pursuits, Mikki announced that Sterling and Kevin had arrived.

Excitement thrummed inside Tammy at the sound of Sterling's voice. She immediately picked up on his uneasiness and Kevin's rebelliousness. She didn't need to see to be aware of the fragile truce between father and son.

Tammy smiled. "You're just in time to join us."

Sterling eyed her. Dressed in jeans and a sweater, she looked a lot younger than her twenty-nine years. If he didn't know she was blind, he would think she could see by the way she gracefully moved about the room. He shifted his gaze to the set-up of the room. It reminded him of the old-fashioned music rooms he'd seen in pictorial history books of the Victorian era. A warm, casual, relaxed atmosphere filled the room, making it nothing like the usual run-of-the-mill, impersonal music rooms.

When his initial uneasiness began to ebb, he realized that was her aim. This mature Tammy was light years ahead of the old. She was all woman. Hardly a trace of the girl he'd known remained.

Tammy made her way over to Kevin and Sterling. "Kevin, I'm glad you and your father could make it. Would you like to join our group?"

"I said I'd come, but that's all."

"Well, it's a start. What kind of music turns you on? R & B? Hip-hop? Rap?"

"You mean you'd let me do rap if I wanted to?"

"Sure, why not? Several of the kids do their own jams. I let them express how they feel in their own way. You want to try it?"

"I don't know if I believe you."

"Fair enough. We'll just have to make a believer out of you, won't we? DeAndre is ready to do his thing. Hit it, DeAndre."

Sterling observed his son's reaction as DeAndre conveyed his pain, anger and frustrations in his Rap. He wondered what was going through Kevin's mind. He also observed Tammy and saw an intense, genuine caring expression on her face. She cared deeply for all of her students.

When DeAndre finished, Tammy invited the other kids to do their thing. Jasmine strummed her guitar and sang a ballad Tracy Chapman style. On his guitar, Carlos played a Spanish tune he'd written. Kioki played an arresting, exotic piece on a harp. Jed played a country music ballad, accompanying himself on the guitar.

Sterling noticed the grudging interest that spread across his son's face, before shifting his attention to Tammy. She was accomplishing in one evening what he hadn't in three years. But then, he hadn't really tried. His guilt had stood in the way of getting close to his son and mending their relationship. The ache he felt in his heart at all he'd lost or let slip away was close to a physical pain.

Tammy walked over to Sterling and put a hand on his shoulder. "I think we've made progress tonight. What do you think?"

"It's a little early to tell, but from what I've observed so far, you may have cracked the ice."

"I want to ask you a favor. Would you play something?"

Sterling was startled by the request. "I don't know."

"You're a composer. Surely you can put together an impromptu gig for us. I occasionally compose music and songs myself, so I know a melody is always floating around inside your head."

Sterling smiled. She was right. Whether he wrote them down or not, a melody of some kind always lingered in his mind.

He decided to do one of the songs he'd written for Tammy.

After a few runs, Tammy picked up on the chorus and joined him. Sterling looked around the room and noticed that everyone, including his son, was enchanted by what they were hearing.

When they finished, the kids clamored for Sterling and Tammy to do an encore performance. And they did.

When the final notes ebbed into the silence, Tammy was struck by the rightness and intimacy of her voice and Sterling's blended together in song. That early attraction she'd tried to convince herself didn't exist was working like magic, lingering in the air like incense.

The kids and Mikki clapped, breaking the spell. Kevin didn't clap, but Sterling saw the interested expression that lighted his face though he sought to hide it behind a shade of indifference. Their singing had obviously impressed his obstinate son in spite of himself. Together, he and Tammy had made progress, although he wouldn't go so far as to shout it from the rooftops. But maybe he would in the near future.

Later, as Mikki and Tammy straightened up the room and cleared away the remains of the snacks they'd prepared, Mikki commented, "So that's Sterling Phillips, the famous R & B composer. I remember when he used to write songs for all the top singers a few years back. I often wondered what happened to him. After the awful accident that killed his wife, he just dropped out of the music world. Something about his looks and voice immediately snag your attention. A certain sensuality."

"There you go romanticizing again."

"No, I'm not. I see he's snagged your attention and you can't even see what he looks like."

Tammy smiled. Ten years ago she would have come back at Mikki for making a comment like that. But now it just rolled over her head.

"He came here because he thought I could help his son, Mikki."

"I'd say you helped more than his son. Maybe—"

"Don't say it, Miss Matchmaker of the Century. Let's finish the cleanup so we can go home."

"What do you bet he comes to your next jam session?"

"Mikki!"

"All right. I'll shut my mouth, but mark my words, he'll be there. And it won't be for just his son's sake. "

CHAPTER FIVE

"So what did you think about the jam session?" Sterling asked Kevin on the way home that night.

"It was all right, but it wasn't all that," he answered noncommittally. "Why do we have a chauffeur drive us every place? Why don't you drive?"

"I've told you that I just don't like driving anymore."

"Because your driving is the reason Mama is dead and I can't see?"

Sterling glanced in the mirror at his driver and saw the pitying look in Marcus's eyes and looked away. "Kevin, I—"

"Forget it."

Sterling's nerves were always frazzled after one of these episodes with his son. "You think you'll want to go to any more jam sessions?"

"Why you asking me?"

"Kevin."

"It's what you and Miss Gibson want. It won't change anything. All the jam sessions in the world won't make me see again."

Sterling's hopes sank at his son's comment. "I know that, but maybe they can help you adjust."

"It won't bring Mama back. She hated your music and the songs you were always writing. She said you cared more about them than you did us."

Sterling realized that his wife had warped his son's mind with her own misery in ways he'd never imagined.

"That's not true, Kevin."

"'Cause you say it?"

Sterling didn't attempt to prolong the conversation. Soon after they arrived home, Kevin started up the stairs to his room. Sterling shook his head. His son was filled with bitterness. He wished he could expel it. One of the eye specialists he'd taken Kevin to, a Dr. Ben Hastings in Philadelphia, had said that he couldn't find a physical reason for Kevin's blindness. In his opinion, he was suffering from a condition called hysterical blindness, as a result of the trauma surrounding the accident. Was it possible Dr. Hastings could be right? What would it take for Kevin to conquer the pain and sense of loss at his mother's death and possibly see again? Dr. Hastings had said he'd done all he could for Kevin, and the rest was up to him. He'd also recommended that he contact Derek Morgan to help Kevin, should his diagnosis be wrong and he didn't get his sight back.

That Derek and his wife were close to Tammy, he was forever grateful. He could tell after meeting them and seeing her interact with them, that they cared deeply for Tammy. She'd needed that after the accident, because he'd been a coward. If only he could turn back time. But he couldn't. What he could do was help Tammy with her singing career. Maybe doing that would go a long way toward righting the wrong he'd done and easing the pain he'd caused. Maybe then he could make peace with himself.

Sterling woke up on the couch in his studio the next morning. He'd been completely wiped out after feverishly composing yet another song. The flow had grabbed hold of him, not releasing him until he'd scribbled the last note. He didn't remember falling asleep, but evidently he had.

He picked up the sheets of music and sounded out the notes and the lyrics in his head. Like the last four songs he'd written, they were perfect for Tammy. It was as though the Almighty Himself were guiding the progress of the album with the addition of each song needed to properly launch Tammy into the higher ranks of the music world.

Sterling glanced at the clock. It was almost time to drop Kevin off at the Institute, and he still had to shower and change.

Kevin.

What was he going to do about him? He had resisted any help from Sterling or Tammy, but for a few minutes at the jam session, he had displayed a positive reaction to being with the other kids. Maybe Tammy's idea of getting him involved with the jam sessions was a solution of sorts. Maybe not a cure-all for Kevin's problems, but a solution to some of them. To solve the really big problems, Sterling needed a miracle. Could Tammy possibly pull it off?

Sterling grimaced at the way his son ate his breakfast. He needed to learn how to manage his meals better so he wouldn't knock things over or pour salt into his food instead of pepper. Sterling had arranged the table to make it easy for Kevin, but it hadn't done any good because he had chosen not to cooperate and deliberately rearranged things to cause spills and other disasters. At times like these, Sterling felt the weight of fatherhood and the frustration of failing in his responsibilities. Seeing how Kevin acted out his anger, bitterness and frustration at what he believed Sterling had done to him was torture to watch.

"Are you ready to leave for the Institute, Kevin?"

"Would it matter if I said I didn't want to go?"

"No."

"Let's get it over with."

There was nothing else Sterling could say. His only hope was that his son would resign himself to what he had to do if only because he realized his father had no intention of backing down.

"Kevin," Tammy called to him. He didn't answer. She'd thought they'd gotten past this form of rebellion, but evidently not. "Are you becoming more familiar with the alphabet?"

"It's just a bunch of stupid little dots that don't make any sense."

"If you concentrate on the differences between each touch card, it'll get easier with each new addition. Eventually, you'll be able to distinguish one set of dots from the other by touch. Then you'll be ready for more advanced Braille."

"You and my father have it all figured out, don't you?"

"We only want to help you be more independent and learn to take care of yourself, Kevin."

"I already know how to do that. I don't need to learn any stupid dot system."

"It's a form of communication. When you learn to read in

Braille, it will broaden your world."

"I still won't be able to see. Can't you get that through your head?" He angrily swept the cards off the work table.

"I understand better than you think, Kevin. I've been where you are now. You think it was any easier for me to accept being blind? It was hard, but I did it, and so can you."

"Maybe I don't want to."

"I think you do. Besides, you have no other choice."

Ignoring the last part of what she said, he defiantly replied, "You can think anything you want to. It doesn't mean I agree with you."

Tammy realized that Kevin was being particularly obnoxious and disagreeable. He was testing the limits of her patience to see how far she would let him go. She smiled, he wanted her to throw her hands in the air and give up on him. He just didn't know her if he thought that would work. She knew all the tricks he'd tried and then some.

"It's what you think that's important, Kevin. It's your life and you can make what you want of it."

"So you say. That's never gonna be true and you know it."

"I don't know it and neither do you. You haven't even tried, so how can you know anything?"

There was no comeback. Tammy knew there wouldn't be. What could he say? Deep down he knew everything she said was the truth.

It had been several weeks since Kevin's return to class. He'd come to two of the Tuesday jam sessions, but as yet hadn't participated. Tammy sensed Sterling's disappointment in the long silences. Kevin knew the effect he was having on his father and was reveling in it. At the last session, Sterling had just dropped his son off and hadn't stayed. She intended to find out why. The next morning Tammy called him and suggested having a meeting in her classroom that afternoon while Kevin was in Derek's class.

Sterling paced. "I thought if I weren't around, he might join in."

"Well, he didn't. Are things really that bad between you?"

She heard the hesitation before he answered.

"Yes. Sometimes he tunes me out all together," Sterling admitted.

Tammy felt a deep empathy for Sterling. He was obviously tortured by his son's behavior and attitude toward him. If there were a way to reach Kevin she would find it. Suddenly she thought of Stevie Wonder. If anyone could impress Kevin with what a blind person could accomplish, it was Stevie. She hoped he wasn't too busy or out of the country. She knew if it was at all possible, he would answer her appeal and come to San Francisco or at least give her a call.

"I have a plan, Sterling. But I'll have to get back to you about the details as soon as I've ironed them out. In the meantime, don't give up. Okay?"

"It's hard when your son hates you."

She found his hand and placed hers over it. "I imagine it must be. He doesn't really hate you, though. We'll find a way to reach him. He's learning mobility training with Derek, and he's the best. That training will help Kevin become more confident."

Tammy hesitated a moment, but decided to wade right in. "Did you find out where Kevin was going when you thought he was coming here?"

Sterling moved his hand from under hers. "He was visiting his mother's grave. You see, I refused to take him, so he's evidently been going there by himself for the last two years. Where was I when he was doing all this? I keep asking myself. I was there yet I wasn't. I was drifting in a sea of personal misery and completely oblivious to my son's misery."

She heard the anguish in his voice and winced.

"I guess your opinion of me as a father has probably dropped ten degrees below zero."

"Don't, Sterling." This man was as needy as his son, maybe more so. There was so much pain in him as well as some other emotion she could only guess was guilt. She found his hand.

"Stop stressing yourself about this. It won't do you or Kevin any good."

The touch of Tammy's soft, slender hand on his aroused Sterling. He gazed into her lovely face and wanted to kiss her ripe full lips, caress her throat, her collarbone, the peaks of her breasts and ease his hand lower to her hips and squeeze her soft buttocks. He wanted to do what he had not done in over thirteen years: make love to her. But he knew it was impossible. He didn't dare hope that things would ever be that way between them again. By walking away, he'd seen to that.

"Sterling."

"I know you're right." He glanced at his watch. "Kevin's class will be over in a few minutes, I'd better be going. I hope what you have in mind works."

"So do I."

After hearing him leave, Tammy sat thinking. She had two men in her life. The mystery man and Sterling Phillips.

But neither man was her lover.

Not yet, an inner voice echoed.

"A penny for your thoughts. From the look on your face, a dollar would be more like it. Talk about deep thinking... I've been calling your name for the last five minutes. Where were you, girl?"

"Augusta!"

"Don't look so surprised to see me. You're my daughter and my husband does happen to be the administrator of this institution." She laughed. "Were you thinking about anybody in particular, like say, Sterling Phillips?"

Tammy flinched.

"I was right! You *were* thinking about him. Is something going on between you two that I should know about?"

"Augusta!"

"Well?"

"No. We've been working together to help his son. That's all."

Augusta wanted her daughter to do more than think about her work at the Institute or be absorbed in her singing career. She wanted her to find somebody to love. She needed someone besides her family.

"I dropped in to invite you to dinner on Sunday. We're having some friends over. Can you come?"

"Sure. What time?"

"About seven."

"I'll be there."

"Bring Mikki with you. A certain young man she's crazy about is going to be there. She'll know the one I mean."

Tammy shook her head. "You and Mikki are incurable romantics."

"Love doesn't make the world go round, but it sure makes the ride worthwhile. Don't you know that?"

"A certain mother of mine has told me this no less than a million times."

"I'm off to look in on my handsome husband. See you Sunday."

CHAPTER SIX

As she dressed for the evening, Tammy couldn't help wishing that Sterling and Kevin were going to be at Augusta's dinner party. Her brother D.J. would be there. Interaction with someone his own age might help Kevin.

What about the interaction between you and Sterling? a little voice whispered in her mind.

Tammy had to admit that she would enjoy being in his company again.

"You almost ready?" Mikki asked.

"Yes."

"Are you all right? You seem preoccupied. Thinking about anybody in particular?"

"Mikki."

"I saw how you were acting around Sterling Phillips at the last jam session. You like him, don't you?"

"Yes, I like him."

"I think it's more than like. I think it's the best thing that could happen to you. He likes you, too. I can tell."

"Now don't start."

"I'm not starting anything. You did that yourself."

Tammy gave up trying to convince Mikki otherwise. After all, there was an element of truth in what she'd said.

Tammy sat talking to Mikki and Wiley Johnson, the young man Augusta had invited to the dinner. She couldn't help teasing him about his name.

"I've been called Wile E. Coyote forever." He laughed.

"And you don't mind?" Tammy asked.

"It wouldn't do me any good if I did. If I got offended every time someone called me that, I would stay mad at this fine young thing sitting next to me."

"I do it because I know he has a sense of humor and can laugh at himself," Mikki confided. "And I like that."

Tammy's mind wandered away from the rest of the conversation, lighting on Sterling and his son, as if thinking about them could make them appear. A few minutes later, the doorbell pealed and she heard Sterling's voice. At the deep masculine sound, her heart rate accelerated.

After Augusta showed Sterling and Kevin into the living room, Sterling searched the room for the one woman he hoped would be there. When he saw Tammy, desire surged through him like an electric current. He couldn't help it; he wanted her badly.

"D.J., come and meet Kevin," Augusta called to her son who was standing by the buffet table shoving an appetizer into his mouth.

D.J. walked over to them.

"I'd like you to meet Kevin Phillips. Kevin, this is my son, Derek Junior, better known as D.J."

Sterling noticed that D.J. wasn't put off by or uncomfortable with Kevin's blindness as a lot of kids were, but then his foster sister was blind. He suddenly remembered Derek telling him that Augusta had also once been blind. That was a story he would like to hear.

"Tammy, guess who's here," Augusta called to her daughter as she, Derek, D.J., Sterling and Kevin moved to where she sat.

"You know Sterling and Kevin Phillips," Augusta went on.

Tammy smiled. "Augusta didn't mention that you would be here, Sterling. But I'm glad you and Kevin could make it."

"So am I," Sterling answered.

Kevin didn't respond.

Rising to her feet, Mikki said, "I've got something to discuss with Wiley Coyote here."

"What did I tell you, Tammy?" Wiley quipped, letting Mikki lead him over to the windows.

"You want to go up to my room and listen to some real music instead of this elevator stuff?" D.J. asked Kevin.

"You sure you want me to? I'm blind," Kevin said baldly.

"So?"

Sterling could tell that Kevin was surprised by D.J.'s attitude.

D.J. took Kevin's hand, urging him along. "Let's go."

At a loss for words and what to do, Kevin let D.J. guide him out of the room.

Sterling smiled as he watched them go.

"D.J. helps me with outings and field trips for the Junior Blind sometimes," Derek explained. "He's used to being around blind kids Kevin's age."

"Derek, I need your help in the kitchen," Augusta said, pulling him in that direction.

"My foster mother wasn't very subtle, was she?" Tammy laughed when she and Sterling were alone.

"No, but I don't mind if you don't."

"I don't, not really. I think Kevin responded positively to D.J. Don't you?"

"Yes, I believe he did. D.J. is an amazing young man."

"He's that all right. And I'm not saying it because he's my brother. I think it would be a great idea if I invited him to one of our jam sessions. I had thought that someone older and who was blind could better help Kevin. I overlooked the obvious."

"Judging from Kevin's reaction to your brother, you could be right."

Sterling wanted to talk about a subject other than his son's problems. He wanted to get to know this older, more mature Tammy.

"I know you're a composer. Would I be out of line in asking why you don't write songs anymore?" Tammy asked.

Sterling was quiet so long she thought he wasn't going to answer.

"Actually, I have started writing again," he confided.

"You have? For whom?"

"No one in particular."

Tammy rose to her feet and held out her hand. "Augusta and Derek have a music room. We can go in there while everyone else is occupied. You can sing or play one of your songs."

"I don't know…"

Sterling felt uneasy for a moment, then decided to do it. If he ever wanted her to sing any of his songs, this might be the perfect opportunity to put things in motion, so he let her lead him into the music room.

Tammy knew every inch of the house because she'd stayed with Derek and Augusta when she first moved to San Francisco.

She'd later met Mikki at a dress shop where Mikki worked part-time. They became fast friends and decided that it would benefit them both if they shared a house. Since Mikki had aspirations to work in the music business it had all worked out.

Tammy felt a new kind of excitement being in Sterling Phillips's company as she closed the door behind them.

Sterling took a moment to admire the room. It had plenty of windows, was huge and was done in soothing beige, brown and champagne colors. In one corner stood a bandstand, complete with drums, and an electric keyboard. A grand piano sat near floor-to-ceiling, sliding glass doors that looked out over the bay. He could see the terrace had steps that descended to the beach. This time of the evening, the city lights were twinkling in the distance.

He frowned. Tammy would never see them or anything else. All because of him. He would have to help her realize a different kind of beauty through her music. He hoped the songs he'd already written and those he would write in the future would be instrumental in accomplishing that.

Tammy seated herself on the couch.

Sterling walked over to the piano and sat down on the bench and started playing.

Tammy found herself humming the melody. "I like it. Have you written any lyrics to go with this masterpiece?"

"Yes."

"Please, sing a few bars for me."

"I don't have a voice like yours."

"I've heard you sing, and you're not half bad."

"Thanks a lot." He sang:

"You're someone special

A pearl with the power to rock my world…"

As she listened, Tammy wondered if he had a special woman who rocked his world. She couldn't help wondering what it would be like to be that special someone he loved.

She shook her head. What was the matter with her? Where was all of this coming from? Was it the song? Or was it that she hadn't been involved with a man in so long? She'd dated on and off over the years, but her only deep relationship after David had ended in disillusioning disappointment. After that, she'd never wanted deep. Never even gave deep a second thought, until the last few months. It had all started with the mystery man and extended to Sterling Phillips.

It was as though the music, the words and his voice had merged, arousing thoughts and feelings she had believed long dead and buried. When the music stopped, she sat silently, contemplating all that had happened in the space of a few minutes.

"Are you all right, Tammy?" Sterling's voice held concern.

"I'm—yes, I'm fine. It's just that the lyrics, the music…"

Sterling knew exactly what she meant. He'd felt it, too. The distinctive intimacy in the music and the words. And add to that, being alone together. It was as though she somehow knew he'd written the song; especially for her.

For them.

"I really loved the song."

"I can make you a tape and bring it to the next jam session if you want me to." When he did that, it would be the first step toward redeeming himself, repaying a debt that had haunted his soul night and day for the past thirteen years. Maybe he'd find peace in her forgiveness. If she ever forgave him. He wanted a release from the guilt that tortured him. To hope for her love was probably projecting too much, but hope was all he had.

All through the rest of the evening, Tammy felt the bond the song had forged between her and Sterling, drawing them ever closer. There was no use denying it, nor trying to escape it. It was beyond their control.

In what direction would this lead them? Certainly not into a platonic friendship. With him an intimate one was the only category left. She didn't know if she could handle anything past friendship. Beneath the surface, she was still afraid of getting emotionally involved. She'd tried convincing herself that she had outgrown that feeling, but she'd evidently been lying to herself. All it took was one evening in Sterling's company in an intimate setting to dispel that fallacy.

Derek had been right when he had said that she wasn't completely free of the past. Hadn't healed from the damage David had done. The pain and hurt were still there, though deeply entrenched.

As the evening wore on, Sterling sensed a change in Tammy. She was slipping back into her reserved mode, and that bothered him. He wanted their earlier intimacy back.

During dinner, Sterling noticed how helpful D.J. was with

Kevin, giving him low, discreet directions as to where things were on the table. To his surprise, Kevin didn't verbally lash out at D.J. as he sometimes did at his father and other sighted persons. Maybe Tammy was right. D.J. could very well be the key.

"I'm glad you and Kevin could come, Sterling," Augusta said as he and his son prepared to leave.

"So am I. You'll all have to come to our house for dinner one day soon."

Augusta noticed the meaningful gaze Sterling aimed at Tammy and wondered if something was going on between them. She hoped so. And judging from the look on Derek's face, he hadn't missed a thing. Augusta smiled at Tammy and then shifted her gaze back to Sterling. Maybe there was hope for them getting together. If so, she'd help it along any way she could. Both Tammy and Sterling needed someone in their lives. Why couldn't it be each other? Yes, she liked that idea; she more than liked it, actually.

Tammy heard the inflection in Sterling's voice at his invitation. It wasn't a simple invitation; it hinted at more.

Could he possibly want more? The thought that he might scared her yet excited her all at the same time. These contradictory feelings where he was concerned were driving her crazy. On the one hand, she wanted to be in Sterling's company. On the other, she feared the direction a relationship other than an impersonal one would lead to. She had to consider Kevin. She really did want to help him. Neither relationship with the Phillips males was coming along as she'd originally intended. She remembered a saying Derek had shared with her once. "Life is what's happening while you're busy making other plans."

Derek walked over to Tammy. "You can't freeze Sterling off without hurting Kevin or yourself."

"Derek is right, Tammy," Augusta added. "Believe me, I know that. I once tried to deny my feelings for Derek. I was completely miserable, and so was he. You should remember that. You suffered through it along with me. What we want is to see you happy. Give yourself a chance. I know you're attracted to Sterling, and he's attracted to you."

"Now that you've both figured everything out, I think I'll go home. Mikki," she called to her companion who was deep into conversation with Wiley.

"Tammy…"

"Augusta, I know you mean well, but I don't want to talk about it anymore."

"You were warming up to Sterling when Wiley and I left you two alone. What happened?" Mikki asked Tammy during the drive home. "I hope you didn't go into one of your ice queen modes." Tammy didn't answer.

"What's wrong with you, girl? Sterling Phillips is fine to the bone. Even though you can't see him, that sexy voice of his alone should send fire sizzling through your veins. If I weren't crazy about Wiley, I'd give you competition."

"Mikki."

"Don't worry, he's not really my type, but he is yours. You better get on it."

"I told you I wasn't interested in a relationship."

"You're interested in him no matter what you keep telling yourself and me. He's perfect for you, Tammy. I hope you realize that before it's too late and somebody else scoops him up."

Tammy knew it was no use talking to Mikki, so she didn't even try. She just remained quiet the rest of the way to her house.

CHAPTER SEVEN

Tammy noticed a marked change in Kevin after he and D.J. became friends. Though he was hostile at times, still defiant and bitter at others, his friendship with her brother had somewhat mellowed his attitude. He was making steady progress in learning Braille, and Derek had mentioned that he also seemed eager to master his mobility training.

Kevin's attitude toward his father hadn't changed, though. She wished she could get to the core of his resentment. Kevin, however, refused to discuss anything personal with her. Sterling was the only other option, and she didn't want to get into it with him just yet.

Sterling had come to the last few jam sessions, but hadn't contributed. Instead, he sat quietly, observing what was going on. Tammy had the feeling he was observing her as much as he was his son. She could picture him doing this in her mind's eye. He hadn't brought the tape he'd promised to bring either. She knew he was waiting for her to ask him to.

The intimacy of the song wasn't something she could handle right now. It made her feel too vulnerable. She knew she was only putting off the inevitable, but she left his unspoken challenge simmering on the back burner. Though her need to hear him play the music and her to actually sing the words was like an itch she felt an urgent need to scratch, she didn't dare move to satisfy the urge.

Since when had she become a coward? She'd lived a large portion of her life in the ghetto of Philadelphia where one survived on one's courage. So what had happened to hers? It seemed to have deserted her. She reached for the phone and punched in her voice-phone address book, asked for Sterling Phillips' phone number, punched in send, then waited. The phone rang and rang before the answering machine picked up. Sterling wasn't home. She wondered where he could be.

"You sounded like you really needed to talk when you called earlier," Derek said to Sterling as they entered the Morgan's living room. "Sit down. How about a cup of coffee? Augusta had to rush to the hospital to do an emergency heart operation, so if you want coffee, I'm afraid you'll have to take a chance on mine."

Sterling smiled. "I don't want any, but thanks. Coffee has begun to bother me lately, giving me heartburn." He rubbed his chest.

"Oh? Maybe you need to make an appointment with my wife," Derek said jokingly.

"I don't know if I need a doctor, but I do need to talk, Derek. When I mentioned guilt feelings, you said you knew how I felt. I got the feeling you really did, that your words went beyond showing empathy for a friend."

"You're right, they did." Derek walked over to a picture of Augusta on the fireplace mantle and rubbed his finger across it. "I caused this beautiful lady a lot of pain. I thank God that she still loves me."

"Why wouldn't she?"

"You see, before I met her, until I literally crashed into her life, I was a self-centered bastard. She was a person out there making a difference, saving lives as a heart surgeon while I... I used to like fast women and even faster cars. One day I went speeding down a residential street just as a little girl guided her bike into the crosswalk. I was going too fast to stop and would have run her down had Augusta not zoomed her car in front of her. To save a child, she put her own life in jeopardy. My car hit Augusta's, and the momentum sent her car crashing through a thrift store window."

Derek exhaled hard before going on.

"The child wasn't hurt, but Augusta was blinded in the accident. I can tell by your reaction you have some idea of the anguish and guilt I felt."

"Oh, yes." Derek had no idea how well he knew that feeling. He probably thought Kayla's death tortured his mind, when in fact it was what he'd done to Tammy. He could still conjure up the motorcycle accident in vivid detail, and he shuddered at the memory.

Derek continued. "After the accident, I saw how worthless my life had been. I wanted to do something for Augusta besides paying her doctor bills, so I went to the Braille Institute and insisted that they teach me how to help the blind. I learned Braille and some other things I thought would help Augusta. My one burning desire once I learned that she wasn't doing anything to help herself was to help her learn how to take care of herself. It was the least I could do."

Derek smiled. "You see, I didn't tell her who I was. I pretended to just be a man who helped the blind. Of course, I fell madly in love with her. When she found out the truth, she refused to have anything to do with me. I thought I'd lost her."

"How did you get her to forgive you?"

"I didn't do anything. Her love for me was stronger than her hatred at what I'd done."

"How did she regain her sight?"

"A doctor in Africa had developed a new technique for treating damaged corneas and other eye conditions. I arranged through a friend for Augusta and Tammy to go to his clinic in Nigeria. Augusta's sight was restored, but, unfortunately, they couldn't do anything for Tammy."

Sterling's heart ached for the disappointment Tammy had to have obviously suffered. "How did Tammy take it?"

"She was disappointed of course. Though she tried to hide it for Augusta's sake, I knew it cut deep."

"How did Tammy become your foster daughter?"

"When Tammy came to the Institute, she was a bitter, angry, disillusioned girl. From the moment they met, Augusta was determined to help her. Believe me, it wasn't an easy task she set for herself. I recognize certain similarities between what's happening with Tammy and Kevin and what happened between Tammy and Augusta years ago."

Derek gazed thoughtfully at Sterling. "I get the feeling that their relationship isn't the only one you want to talk about, not that you don't care about the relationship between Tammy and your son. You care for Tammy the woman, don't you?"

Sterling heaved a soul-weary breath. "Yes, I do. I think I'm falling in love with her all over again."

"Again?" Derek looked puzzled.

"My real name is Sterling *David* Dixon."

Derek gave a low whistle.

"Exactly. I wanted to leave the pain and the guilt behind and start fresh, so I changed my last name to Phillips and went by my first name when I started composing. As you have no doubt already guessed, I've never been able to completely put it behind me. You probably feel like punching my lights out for what I did to Tammy."

Derek laughed. "I have no right to do that or to judge you. It would be like the pot calling the kettle black, don't you think? I know there's a story waiting to be told. Why don't you tell me about it, Sterling?"

"You're handling it better than I thought you would."

"Don't mistake me. You weren't far from wrong about my reaction to what you've just told me, but I'm wise enough and human enough to understand there are two sides to every story. Now tell me yours."

"I was an irresponsible boy back then, Derek. It took me a while to find myself and once that happened, I regretted, more than you could ever know, a lot of the things I'd done, the decisions I'd made."

"I can understand regret, pain and guilt. I've experienced enough of it to last a lifetime."

"After what you told me, I can imagine you have. Seeing Tammy broken and bleeding that night changed me forever. Knowing what my recklessness had cost her, I couldn't face her."

"So you never went to see her?"

"Oh, I slipped into her hospital room, but I couldn't bring myself to let her know I was there."

"What happened after that?"

"I went away to Julliard and studied music and became totally absorbed in it, trying desperately to block out what had happened. While I was going there, I met my wife Kayla. We were attracted to each other and one thing led to another. She became pregnant and we got married. We realized later that we really didn't have much in common, only sex and the baby. And that wasn't enough to float our marriage.

"Music became my obsession, and I spent most of my time composing. I had phenomenal success from the start. Over the next ten years, I wrote over five hundred songs. As you might have guessed, I neglected my wife and my son in the process. Kayla resented it and sought comfort in the arms of other men. Our lives turned into a living nightmare, Derek. Believe me, I paid for that success. We had money, but we weren't happy."

Sterling paused to gather his composure.

"The night of the car accident, Kayla and I argued. We were on our way home from an awards ceremony. I'd won several Grammys and wanted to celebrate. Kayla didn't want any part of it. We'd picked Kevin up from her aunt's, and I intended to drop them off at home and go on to one of the celebration parties. Kevin was asleep in the back seat when it started raining.

"Kayla threw her latest affair in my face. The next thing I can remember is feeling pain explode in my head. That must have been when the accident happened. In the accident, I suffered a concussion and I lost my memory of what happened minutes before the accident. All I could remember was hearing Kayla and Kevin scream. Then everything went black. The next time I opened my eyes, I was in the hospital, Kayla was dead and Kevin was blind."

"Was there nothing they could do for Kevin?" Derek asked.

"I've had the best eye specialists in the country and in Europe examine him. They can't see any physical reason for his blindness. Dr. Ben Hastings in Philadelphia believes that Kevin is suffering from hysterical blindness, that the trauma from the accident and his mother's death was too much for him to handle."

"If his condition is psychosomatic, then maybe he can get his sight back."

"Dr. Hastings said that could happen. He also said it was totally up to Kevin. He believes that because Kevin blames me for Kayla's death, it's a contributing factor to his continued blindness."

"Didn't you try explaining to Kevin that you couldn't remember what had happened?"

"Oh, yes, but he refused to believe me. He's convinced that I hated Kayla and wanted her to die."

"I see." Derek didn't say anything for a few moments. "You do have problems, man. The two people you care about have or believe they have good reason to hate your guts. I don't know what to tell you. I've noticed that you don't drive."

"I haven't been able to get behind the wheel of a car or any moving vehicle since the accident. I've had counseling. The therapist said my phobia about driving is much like Kevin's hysterical blindness."

"What we do to ourselves," Derek remarked thoughtfully.

"Yes. How do you think Tammy will react once she knows the truth?"

"I don't know. She's attracted to you, but she's wary of any close relationship with a man since—"

"Since I broke her heart and destroyed her trust."

"Don't beat yourself up about that, Sterling. We all make mistakes. We grow up. We all feel pain. You have to find a way to tell Tammy the truth."

"I was afraid you'd say that. I'm hoping to redeem myself by making her a superstar. Since she's come back into my life, I've been composing again. I've written songs for her that I believe could put her at the top of the R & B charts."

Derek smiled. "I also sought redemption by helping Augusta learn how to deal with her blindness. I have to tell you, I wasn't completely successful. When she found out I'd been deceiving her, she went off. I tried everything to convince her that I loved her, but she was too hurt and refused to believe me. This is really echoes of yesterday for me. I'm afraid you're going to experience the same kind of pain I did. Maybe if you could…"

"What?"

"I don't know if making her a superstar will soften her where her personal feelings for you are concerned. She's never gotten over David. If she could fall in love with the person you are today, then maybe."

"You think I should try a little wooing?"

Derek grinned. "It couldn't hurt."

"I'll do it if she'll lower the barriers long enough to let me in."

"If you need any help, Augusta and I will do all we can."

"You think Augusta will feel like doing that once she learns who I really am?"

"She'll be angry at first, but yes, I think she'll come around once she knows that you really care for Tammy."

"I sure hope so, because I do. Man, I need all the help I can get."

"Don't wait too long to tell Tammy the truth. I made the mistake of doing that with Augusta and almost lost her. In the meantime, if you need to talk, I'll be here. I want to see my girl happy. And you, too, Sterling."

"Now that Kevin has become fast friends with your son, maybe I can make some headway with your daughter. Wish me luck with Tammy."

"You got it."

When Sterling got home that evening, he heard music. He followed the sound to his studio then opened the door where he found Kevin listening to one of his tapes.

"I haven't heard any of these songs before. It's you singing on it, isn't it?"

"Yes."

"Mama hated your songs. She hated your music. She said they took you away from us."

"I admit that in a way she was right. But, Kevin, she never understood what composing meant to me."

"She said it meant more to you than we did. She said it was the only thing you ever really cared about."

"Kevin."

"I thought by learning to play the piano when I was little, I could make you care about me."

"I always cared about you. You're my son. I love you."

"No, you don't. Because of you, Mama is dead. I heard you arguing with her that night. You hated her."

"I didn't. You don't understand. Let me explain."

"I don't want to hear it." He rose from the chair behind the desk, unfolded his cane, started to stalk out of the room, but he stumbled.

Sterling reached out to steady him. He felt Kevin stiffen, then jerk away.

"Kevin, we need to talk."

"*We* don't need to do anything." With that, he left the studio.

Tears stung Sterling's eyes. Was it hopeless to believe that he and his son could ever become close? Derek was right. He had to do some serious breaking through if he wanted to reach the two people he loved most in the world. How did he go about repairing the damage he and fate had done to them?

CHAPTER EIGHT

From where he stood in the doorway of her classroom, Sterling watched Tammy organize her desk. God how he admired this lovely gutsy woman. She'd gone through hell and survived.

"Are you going to come in, Sterling? Or stand there gaping at me all day?"

"How did you know it was me?"

"Your cologne is very bracing, Mr. Phillips. The kind a woman can't possibly ignore."

Sterling strode into the room. "I hope you find me half as bracing."

"Did you come to discuss Kevin's progress?" Tammy asked, putting things back on neutral ground.

"I'm interested in that, yes, but it's not the reason I'm here. Have dinner with me this evening."

Tammy hesitated.

"I won't bite. I promise. I'm not the big bad wolf."

She laughed. "I guess I'll have to take my chances and hope you're telling me the truth and won't eat me."

Sterling flinched at her innocent use of the word *truth*. He couldn't tell her a certain truth just yet or he'd be rejected and possibly reviled before he could get to first base. If he could just get her to fall in love with him again…

"I don't have your address."

After giving it to him, Tammy smiled. "I wondered if you'd ever ask me out."

"You're a beautiful woman. Why wouldn't I?"

"I'm glad you think so."

"Don't tell me no other man has ever told you that."

She shrugged her shoulders in a you-decide-whether-it's-true manner. He was making it impossible to keep things light. "What time will you be picking me up?"

"How about eight o'clock?"

"I'll be ready."

"I'm so glad you're finally seeing the light," Mikki exclaimed to Tammy.

"It's only dinner, Mikki."

"There's dinner and there's dinner with Sterling Phillips."

"He's just a man."

"But what a man. Where's he taking you?"

"He didn't tell me."

"It doesn't matter, anywhere he takes you will be special. The blue silk dress looks good on you. I'll have to do something with your hair."

"You're priceless. It's not as though I can't do it myself."

"I know, but this is a special occasion."

"You're certainly not modest." Tammy laughed.

"Why be modest? If you can stand out, do it."

Tammy shook her head. Mikki was something else. Her thoughts returned to the evening ahead. She could feel the excitement bubbling inside and chided herself. After all, she was only having dinner with the man. It didn't have to mean that she would become intimately involved with Sterling. After her year-long relationship with Brent Stevens fell apart, she'd promised herself that she wouldn't get intimately involved again. It hurt too much. Yet, here she was going out with Sterling Phillips. She couldn't let it evolve into anything deeper.

Who are you trying to convince, girl? You were drawn to him from the start, and nothing's changed.

No, it hadn't. Theirs was an attraction she couldn't ignore or pretend didn't exist. On the other hand, maybe his dinner invitation was just a good will gesture for helping his son.

Now you know...

Yes, she did know. He was as attracted to her as she was to him, and he evidently wanted it to develop into something more. What something more was he thinking to make it? Maybe he was the one making too much of this dinner. Maybe she shouldn't have agreed to go.

"The man is here—and in a limo! He's got style," Mikki exclaimed, breaking into Tammy's reverie.

The muscles in Tammy's stomach fluttered as fast as the wings of a hummingbird as she waited for Sterling to come to the door.

Sterling's eyes traveled appreciatively over Tammy. His Tammy was breathtaking in her sapphire silk dress. It clung to her body in all the right places. He shifted his gaze to her lovely face and lingered there.

Those dark, ripe cherry lips were so kissable he wanted desperately to indulge his fantasy and taste them. No, he wanted to do more than that. He knew a taste wouldn't be nearly enough. He wanted to savor her like a fine wine.

If he could just put how she looked and how she made him feel into words and set it to music… Maybe he could. Anything was possible when he had her for inspiration.

"Your carriage awaits, my lady," he said softly.

"My carriage, huh?" Tammy answered. "Where are you taking me, Mr. Phillips?"

"The Olive Tree."

The Olive Tree was an intimate restaurant with a near-to-genuine Italian theme. Tammy recalled hearing Augusta describe it as being as romantic as those she'd dined in when she and Derek were vacationing in Rome. The word *romantic* teased Tammy's senses. Did Sterling have wooing her in mind?

"Let me get your stole," Mikki interjected. On her way out of the room, she whispered in Tammy's ear, "You go, girl."

Tammy felt like strangling her for her temerity. But Mikki was just being Mikki.

Sterling smiled, imagining from Tammy's expression that her companion had said something provocative. Home girl was the kind of woman who spoke her mind. He had a feeling that Mikki wanted something to happen between him and Tammy, as did Derek and possibly Augusta. With so many people in his corner, he had a shot at winning this wary lady's heart. He wasn't going to get ahead of himself, though. Too much hinged on his ability to be patient and go slow. Not only that, he had to tell her the truth before he dared hope for something more.

"You look lovely tonight, Tammy."

"Thank you." It was just a simple compliment, but it made her feel like Miss Universe.

Mikki returned with Tammy's stole. Sterling took it from her and placed it around Tammy's shoulders.

"You ready?"

"Yes." She could feel the warmth of his hands through the fabric of her stole, and her heart started racing.

Sterling smiled at Mikki then escorted Tammy out the door and down the walk to the waiting limousine. When they arrived at the Olive Tree, Sterling guided Tammy to the entrance, where a man dressed in a bright Italian costume stood. When they were seated, Sterling described to Tammy the clothing of the waiters and waitresses and the ambiance of the restaurant, starting with the live olive tree residing in the center of the foyer near a marble fountain.

Tammy could hear the sound of bubbling water spilling from the fountain and tried to imagine how it looked. She'd seen pictures of the fountains of Rome in an encyclopedia at school before she lost her sight.

Sterling sensed her mood. She was evidently calling on old memories from when she could see. He had a lot to make up to the lovely woman beside him.

He wanted this woman so badly, he ached with it. Over the years, he'd channeled all of his energy into his work, but it had only been a substitute. Now he knew that what he really wanted was a life with Tammy. She was his soul mate. He really hadn't had a life without her. He'd been merely existing all those years.

Tammy sniffed in the scent of lemon, tomato sauce, olive oil and pasta, and listened to people talking, laughing, clinking glasses. Soft, romantic music played in the background, contributing to the relaxed and refreshing atmosphere. Sterling had obviously picked this restaurant for just that reason.

The waiter came to take their order.

"The shrimp scaloppini is excellent," the waiter suggested.

"Tammy?" Sterling asked.

"Sounds wonderful."

"We'll have that."

"What would you like for dessert?"

"None for me, thank you."

The waiter smiled. "I'll send the wine steward to your table." Then he left them alone.

After they decided on the wine and the steward walked away, Sterling took Tammy's hand in his.

"Would you care to dance, Ms. Gibson?"

Tammy was about to refuse because dancing wasn't something she did well.

"It's my favorite jazz piece, slow, easy and mellow."

"Sterling, I—"

He rose to his feet and pulled her to hers.

"No excuses."

Tammy found that she couldn't resist, didn't really want to. His deep, sexy voice mesmerized her; and his lean, warm hands on hers inflamed her senses. How could one man's touch affect her so?

Out on the dance floor, they moved in complete synchronicity, as though they'd danced together forever.

None of Tammy's earlier awkwardness at the fund raiser was evident, Sterling observed. As they danced, he found himself thinking of all they could have had together. It made him sad. But that was all water under the bridge. They had the here and now to get it right. He would do his damnedest to make it real for them again.

"Sterling, I know you're a composer and you have a son, but I don't know anything else about you."

"What do you want to know?" he asked.

"Where is your home?"

"I'm originally from Philadelphia."

"So am I. That's interesting."

She had no idea how interesting it really was. His Tammy was sharp. He knew he would have to watch his answers until the right time came for him to tell her the whole truth.

"I went to Julliard and studied music after I graduated from high school."

"I went there, too. Those were some of the best years of my life." Tammy smiled in fond remembrance. "I had a family that cared about me. You see, I was for all intents and purposes an orphan until Augusta and Derek took me into their hearts and their home. And my favorite singer, Jeffrey Osborne, took me on as his protégée. My only regret is that I haven't lived up to my potential."

"You just haven't had the right person writing the songs for your incredible voice. I have a few ideas about that, but we won't discuss them tonight. Tonight I just want to enjoy your company."

"Are you really enjoying my company, Sterling?"

"Most definitely. I think we could be good together if you gave us a chance."

"Now, Sterling, I—"

He stopped her words with a kiss. She gasped and a little moan escaped her control. She hadn't meant for this to happen.

Don't fool yourself, girlfriend. You wanted it to happen all right.

That revelation jolted her.

Their kiss was so electric that Sterling felt it down to his toes. What they had in the past in no way touched what was developing between them now, at this very minute.

What Tammy had fought against happening had happened despite her efforts to stop it. And that scared the hell out of her. She stiffened. Just then the music stopped and Sterling guided her back to their table. She wanted to go to the ladies' room, but didn't know the way. She would have to ask for assistance. Even then, she wondered if her legs would support her. Talk about being weak in the knees... Sterling made hers tremble like an earthquake.

"Our dinner has arrived," Sterling said, his voice sounding scratchy.

She wondered if their encounter had affected him the same way it had her. Only once since David had she felt this kind of attraction. She remembered all too well how vulnerable she had been when she had given in to Brent Stevens's desire to deepen their relationship. It had been a big mistake. She didn't want to keep making the same mistakes over and over again. If there was going to be more to the relationship with Sterling, she wanted to take it slow, but judging from their reaction to each other, she doubted that would be the case.

Sterling observed how expertly Tammy ate her meal. She moved her finger down the side of her cup to judge the level of coffee by the heat. She used the spoon and the fork to secure her shrimp. It amazed him how she compensated for her lack of sight. He hoped that Kevin would one day become as proficient.

Going out with a blind woman might be a turn off for some men, but it wasn't for him. He admired Tammy all the more for her courage and determination to adjust and learn to live with her situation. And she did so with grace and confidence. He wanted this special woman back in his life, and he would do whatever it took to bring it about.

As the limo headed for Tammy's house, she realized that Sterling had gone all out in hiring a driver just to take her out to dinner.

"I agree with Mikki. I like your style in picking me up in a limo."

Sterling swallowed hard. "All to please a lady," he said glibly.

Could she be wrong, or had she detected something in the way he'd said those words? Was she just being paranoid? Sterling had made tons of money in his career and could afford to pick up his dates in a limo.

Sterling walked Tammy to her door. When she reached for her keys, he stayed her hand, took her into his arms, lowered his head and kissed her. Her arms went around his neck in a what-comes-naturally gesture. The moist heat of his mouth and the caress of his tongue set her senses aflame.

"Oh, Sterling," she moaned.

As he continued to kiss her, he moved his hard, aroused maleness against the cradle of her femininity. God! He was on fire and his body was threatening to incinerate.

"Tammy, girl…" His voice faded into groans of pleasure.

The porch light came on, immediately dousing their ardor.

"Uh-oh," Mikki said. "I didn't mean to interrupt."

"It's all right, Mikki," Tammy said, gathering her scattered senses.

"I'll call you, Tammy. And good night to you both." With that, Sterling strode to the waiting limo.

"If what I saw is any indication, you've got yourself a real honest-to-god relationship brewing."

"Mikki."

"I know, it was only dinner. That's a start. But what a start."

Tammy could hear the smile in her friend's voice.

"We'd better go inside. It's getting chilly out here."

"I guess, considering how the two of you came close to burning this porch down a few minutes ago."

Tammy started to say something, but decided it wouldn't do any good. Mikki was a romantic and was sure she knew what was going on. What exactly was going on between her and Sterling? She wished she knew.

You know, you're just not ready to admit it to yourself, an insistent inner voice chided.

Sterling gazed out the limousine window as Marcus headed for home. People saw this limo as a luxury. He saw it as a necessity. His insides froze at the thought of driving. How could he explain his phobia to Tammy without telling her the circumstances that had precipitated it? But he'd have to explain if he continued to go out with her. She'd want to know why he never drove.

He could tell her that he had been an accident waiting to happen whenever he found himself behind the wheel of any vehicle.

He could say, "By the way, Tammy, it was my fault you can't see your own face in the mirror. Oh, and my wife is dead and my son is blind because of my irresponsible driving."

When the time came, he'd worry about that. After all, one dinner date did not a relationship make. It would take time and patience.

Sterling rubbed his chest. He shouldn't have had any coffee after all the spicy food he'd eaten. Now he was suffering heartburn big-time. He reached inside his pocket for antacid tablets. Heartburn seemed to be his constant companion lately. If it persisted, he'd have to see a doctor. Or he could just be more conscientious about his diet.

"Will that be all for this evening, Mr. Phillips?" Marcus asked.

"Yes, Marcus. After you've parked the limo in the garage, take the rest of the night off. In fact, make it a long weekend. You can use the Navigator."

"Thanks, Mr. Phillips."

"Just make sure you're back in time to drive Kevin to school Monday morning."

"Don't worry. I will be."

As he headed up the walk to the house, it occurred to Sterling that he would be without transportation. Oh, well, if he needed to go somewhere over the weekend, he could always call a taxi. In any case, he would worry about that later. Right now the excitement of going out to dinner with Tammy this evening kept replaying over and over in his mind. Just being with her made him happy, an emotion he hadn't felt in years.

After entering the house, Sterling went straight to his studio, pulled off his jacket and tie, rolled up his sleeves, turned on the recorder and then sat before the piano. As if by magic, his fingers flew over the keys and the notes formed a melody.

Well into the night, he worked feverishly to perfect the song. When he finished, he dragged himself over to the couch and sprawled on it, exhausted. He felt drained of all energy, but at the same time, revitalized. What he'd written for Tammy was some of his best work. Having Tammy come back into his life had inspired his creativity.

Oh, what they could accomplish together.

Maybe.

Once she found out who he was, would she still want to be with him? She had every reason to hate him and despise his touch while he had every reason to love and help her.

It occurred to him that if he bound her closely to him and his son, she wouldn't want to be apart from them. He would encourage a more personal bond between her and Kevin. Then with the songs…

You can do all those things, but if the love isn't there, then what?

She was already attracted to him. And God only knew how much he loved her. Still, once she found out the truth… Maybe by that time it wouldn't matter.

You're only fooling yourself if you believe that.

Maybe he was, but what other hope did he have to cling to?

Tell her the truth now so you'll know where you stand.

Did he dare risk it? No, he needed more time to prepare her.

And how do you propose telling her when the time comes?

He didn't have the answer to that question.

You'd better find one soon.

He was on an upper and wouldn't let down thoughts ruin what he was feeling at this moment. He'd gone out with Tammy. He'd kissed her sweet lips, and she had responded with all the fire he remembered.

He wanted a new beginning with Tammy, and he was going to do everything in his power to have that second chance at happiness with her.

CHAPTER NINE

"Hello?"

"Tammy, it's Sterling. I'm having a small dinner party at my house on Sunday, and I'd like you to come."

"Sunday? You said small. How small?"

"Derek, Augusta, and of course, D.J."

"Yes, I'll come. What time?"

"Six o'clock. I'll send a car for you. Marcus should arrive at around 5:30."

"You don't have to go to all that trouble."

"It's no trouble." He cleared his throat. "The other reason I called is that I need to set up a meeting so we can discuss Kevin."

"When?"

"What about Friday afternoon, while Kevin is in mobility training with Derek?"

Tammy heard more than just concern in Sterling's voice. What was going on?

"Friday will be fine."

After hanging up with Sterling, Tammy walked over to her stereo and searched through her CD collection. They were all marked in Braille with special labels. Although she'd adjusted to being blind over the years, at times she wished with all her heart she could see.

At times, girlfriend?

All right, since Sterling Phillips had walked into her life.

She was curious about what he looked like. She also wouldn't mind seeing her mystery man.

She'd be back doing her club dates in a matter of weeks. She hadn't thought about him much since meeting Sterling. As the days went by, Sterling was becoming an increasingly important part of her life. And not just because of his son. A gentleness about Sterling reached out and touched the tender, vulnerable side of her, and the deep sadness in him wrenched her heart.

The man had obviously suffered a great deal and still did. It had to hurt every time he looked into his son's sightless eyes. But it had been an accident. Accidents happened. And nine times out of ten, it was never all one person's fault.

She'd forgiven David the accident. But what she couldn't forgive him for was not coming to see her afterward. To know that when he'd learned she would be blind he'd turned his back on her. She sighed. His betrayal had wounded her to the bottom of her soul.

Although it had happened a long time ago, she sometimes wondered where David was and what he was doing with his life.

He'd no doubt forgotten all about her.

"We Can Work Things Out" by Crecia began to play. It was a song Sterling Phillips had written seven years ago, but it still sounded good. The song told of a relationship gone wrong. The love was still there and the hope that the man and woman together could work things out. The plea in the singer's voice touched Tammy in a way she hadn't expected. She'd played that particular CD many times, but it had never affected her quite like this.

Something deep inside entreated her to consider a possible

relationship with Sterling. But she still carried around so much emotional baggage. Would it be fair to burden him, or any man, with that on top of her blindness?

If you want a chance with him, you'll have to risk it, that persistent inner voice of reason whispered.

She wasn't sure she was emotionally equipped to handle a significant relationship with Sterling.

One thing is sure, you'll never know unless you try.

"Another dinner date with the man. Yes!"

"Mikki, it's not exactly a date," Tammy told her. "Besides, we won't be alone. Augusta, Derek and D.J. will be there, not to mention Kevin."

"If he's invited your parents and brother, that means he's really interested in you, girl."

"It doesn't have to mean that at all."

"I bet you anything it does. He's courting you right and tight."

"Mikki, please."

"You know it. If I could just get Wiley to move as fast."

"You're making too much out of a simple dinner party."

"You're not making enough out of it, if you ask me. Handsome hunks like Sterling Phillips don't come around everyday. When they do, you'd better grab 'em."

"What do you mean, hunks like him?"

"He's drop-dead gorgeous, talented, rich, famous. Need I say more?"

"I'm sure he's all those things, but—"

"You mean you haven't 'seen him with your hands?' One of the first things the Institute teaches is how to form mental pictures of people by using your senses, especially touch. You can't be afraid of touching him, not after the way you were kissing and hugging the man a few weeks ago."

"Mikki!"

"What was it like? With those deliciously full lips of his, he looks like he'd be a good kisser."

"He is—I mean..."

"I know what you meant." Mikki laughed.

Tammy could just picture the knowing, mischievous grin on her companion's face.

"You're probably hungry for more," Mikki went on, "but you just won't admit it to yourself."

"You're impossible, Mikki Howard."

"Not impossible, perceptive and dead on."

Yes, way too perceptive, Tammy concluded. She left Mikki straightening up the living room and went up to her room to get ready for bed. An hour later, Tammy lay awake, unable to sleep because her thoughts kept drifting to Sterling. What did he want to discuss about Kevin?

She had noticed that Kevin seemed almost withdrawn since she'd gone out to dinner with Sterling. She wondered if he somehow felt threatened by her. Had he voiced objections to her going out with his father? Could that be what Sterling wanted to talk about? If that concerned him, though, he wouldn't be inviting her to his house for dinner. Would he? She'd just have to wait until tomorrow's meeting to find out.

❋

On Friday, Tammy sat behind her desk at the Institute, anxiously waiting for Sterling to arrive for their meeting. That morning, Kevin's attitude had bordered on out-and-out rudeness toward her, attitude he hadn't displayed in a while, not since he and D.J. had become friends. Evidently, something was going on with him.

"Sorry I'm late," Sterling apologized as he strode into the classroom.

"It's all right." Tammy smiled. "Sit down and tell me how I can help you with Kevin."

"I want you to consider working with him privately after you're done with your teaching assignment at the Institute. I know you'll be resuming your nightclub dates, but he really needs your help."

"I don't know, Sterling."

"Kevin doesn't really know you, and I want him to. You'd be so good for him, Tammy. He misses not having his mother, whether he'll admit it or not."

"I can't be a substitute for her."

"I don't expect you to be. That's not what I meant. What I'm trying to say is that he needs a woman's softness and gentleness in his life." Just as I do, he silently added. "Say you'll think about it. Please?"

"All right." Of all the things she'd imagined he might say, this surprised her. Maybe this was the kind of relationship he'd had in mind all along, one that wasn't really personal. A streak of disappointment jetted through her. She'd been telling herself she didn't want a serious relationship. Now that it looked as if she'd get her wish, she realized that she did want a serious relationship.

Sunday afternoon, Sterling was standing in his living room talking with the caterer about the dinner party that evening when he saw Kevin enter the room and flop down on the love seat. He quickly concluded the conversation with the woman and sent her out to the kitchen then walked over to his son and sat down next to him.

"You didn't come down for breakfast. Are you feeling all right, Kevin?"

"I just wasn't hungry, okay?"

Sterling hated it when his son turned defensive like this over the most innocently asked questions.

"Kevin, I—"

"I think I'll go to the kitchen. I am hungry now." He pushed himself up from the love seat and unfolded his cane.

Sterling watched as he left the room and realized that Kevin had become so familiar with the room he no longer stumbled into things. Derek had done a good job with him. Thanks to his patience and caring, Kevin was more mobile and more confident.

Confrontations with his son always drained his spirit. He headed down the hall to his studio. It had become his haven once again, a place where he could recharge his batteries. But it was different this time around. He wasn't using it to tune out his unhappiness and advance his career. Now it had another purpose. If things worked out the way he wanted them to, he and Tammy would be spending a lot of time in here.

As she dressed for the dinner party, Tammy wondered if Sterling expected an answer to his offer this evening.

She'd pondered all he had said. Should she take on the job of tutoring Kevin? Did she want to be drawn into his and Sterling's private life with all its pain? If she decided to take Sterling up on his offer, would she be able to alleviate any of the problems, or would she be simply creating more problems for them all?

Tammy wondered about Kevin's attitude lately. She was curious to know why he'd suddenly become so hostile toward her. It was as if they'd returned to square one.

"You almost ready?" Mikki asked.

"Yes, just about."

"Seems to me you've gone to more trouble to look good than you usually do when going out."

"Now, Mikki, don't start."

"I'm not starting anything. You're doing that all by yourself, girlfriend."

"I shouldn't be late getting home."

"I don't mind if you are. It would please me if you and Sterling—"

"It's not like that between us. How many times do I have to say it?"

"No times. All I know is what it could be if you let it."

"You're impossible."

"I know. The limo should be driving up any minute."

Tammy had a sudden attack of nerves as she realized the evening meant more to her than she had wanted to admit to herself. Her family would be there. Could Mikki be right in her claim that Sterling was officially courting her?

As she climbed into the limo a few minutes later, Tammy wondered about the significance of sending a car for her. Maybe Sterling knew he wouldn't have time to pick her up himself. But a limo? He could have arranged for a taxi just as easily, or she could have had Mikki drop her off.

When the limo reached Sterling's house, the driver helped her out of the car then escorted her up the steps to the front door. Tammy hesitated then rang the bell. Sterling himself answered the door.

"Just in time, pretty lady. Your family is already here." He cupped her elbow and guided her inside to the living room.

Tammy heard the voices of her parents before she reached them. Sterling guided her to where they sat.

He smiled appreciatively at Tammy's simple form-fitting, black slip dress. She looked exceptionally beautiful tonight, but then she always did.

His plan had to work. He frowned, gazing up the stairs. D.J. and Kevin were up in his room listening to music.

Kevin had been in a mood all day. When Sterling stopped to think about it, he realized he'd been that way for the last couple of weeks. Kevin hadn't seemed very receptive to the idea of Tammy personally tutoring him when Sterling brought up the subject. But then, he could have misread his son's reaction to the news. Maybe Kevin just needed more time to get used to the idea.

"Sterling, man, these hor d'oeuvres are the bomb. But when do we get to the main course? The smells floating in from the kitchen are wreaking havoc with my digestive juices," Derek quipped.

"I guess you can tell where his mind is," Augusta confided to Sterling. "On his stomach."

"That's because she doesn't feed me at home," Derek whispered in an aside loud enough for all to hear.

"Derek Morgan!" Augusta exclaimed.

Tammy laughed at the exchange. Her parents' kidding with each other eased the awkwardness she felt.

It isn't awkwardness, you're feeling, girl; it's awareness of Sterling Phillips that has your nerves pulsing on overload.

The evening seemed to be going well, Sterling thought. But the burning question was, when Kevin came downstairs, would he behave himself?

Finally, Kevin appeared, and they all sat down to dinner. Sterling noticed how much his table manners had improved. He gave the credit to D.J. for his patient coaching. Just when it looked as if he were home free, Kevin burst his bubble.

"Miss Gibson, my daddy wants you to tutor me. You gonna take the job?"

"Do you want me to, Kevin?" Tammy answered.

"You gonna take the job?" he persisted, ignoring her question.

"Kevin," Sterling warned.

Tammy could hear the edge of battle in the voices of both father and the son. "Only if you want me to, Kevin."

"You think 'cause you been going out with my father you can come on in and take over."

"I don't at all. I only want to help—"

"That's what grown-ups say when it's not really like that."

Kevin readied to leave the table and knocked over his water glass. The cold liquid ran across the table and dripped onto Tammy's lap. She gasped and shot to her feet. Sterling groaned.

"D.J., I think you'd better—" Augusta started to suggest.

"I'll see about Kevin, Mama," he answered, finishing her request and following his friend out of the room.

"I'm sorry, Tammy." Sterling took a napkin and blotted away the wetness on dress.

"Accidents happen. Maybe it's not a good idea for me to tutor Kevin."

"I don't agree," Derek interjected. "You better than anyone know what he's going through, Tammy. I'm sure you remember how confused and threatened you felt when Augusta and I met and became involved, then decided to get married. You thought she was trying to edge you out of my affections. Kevin sees you as a threat to his relationship with Sterling and his mother's memory, and he's attempting to put a stop to it."

Derek turned to Sterling. "During my counseling sessions with Kevin, I've found out how much he really wants to be close to you, Sterling, but there are a couple of other things he has to learn to face. One, that his mother isn't coming back, and two, that it doesn't help to punish his remaining parent.

"I believe that he needs a buffer between you and himself." Derek shifted his gaze from Sterling to Tammy. "Once Kevin realizes that you're both sincere about wanting to help him, his attitude is bound to change. When that happens, there's a good chance he might get his sight back. He has so much anger and bitterness bottled up inside of him. Not just toward you, but toward life in general for all he has lost."

"I should have realized that," Tammy answered thoughtfully.

"So will you accept my offer?" Sterling asked.

"Yes, but if Kevin doesn't accept me—"

"I understand." She just didn't know that he would take her on any terms he could get her, despite his son's attitude.

After Derek, Augusta and D.J. had gone home, and Kevin up to his room, Sterling and Tammy sat on the couch in the living room talking.

"So do you think Kevin will accept me?"

"When I talked to him before he went to bed, he said he'd give it a try."

"He said it grudgingly, though, didn't he?"

"Nearly everything Kevin agrees to do is done grudgingly. We'll work it out."

Sterling gazed into Tammy's lovely face and couldn't resist lightly gliding a finger down her cheek. Its silky-softness aroused him, and his breathing grew labored.

"Sterling, I think we should—"

He silenced her words with his lips on hers. A tingling sensation sizzled through her body. As he deepened the kiss, Tammy felt herself melting and leaning toward him. She heard Sterling groan as he drew her closer to his body. The rub of his chest against her breasts made her nipples harden and peak in a pleasure-pain sensation that blazed a path of fire down to her femininity.

"Oh, Tammy girl," he uttered roughly.

"Sterling, I—we…" Her voice faded into a moan.

He hadn't intended to move this fast, but being near Tammy sent his senses flying out of control. He kissed her again and again like a man who had been deprived of love his entire life. He eased the strap of her dress off her shoulder and caressed her nipple. Her gasp of pleasure encouraged him further.

"We'd better slow things down, Sterling."

"I don't think I can."

"We have to." With the last ounce of her will power, she pushed him away.

"I care about you, Tammy."

"You sure it's not gratitude?"

"No, it damn well isn't. What I feel for you is not gratitude or anything close to it. I want you for yourself, Tammy Gibson, for no other reason. I'm glad that you agreed to help me with Kevin, but aside from that, what I feel for you is genuine."

Tammy didn't know quite what to believe, what to say. She was attracted to this man and could no longer deny it. She eased her fingers to his face and moved them across his strong lean features, to study him. His lips were sensually full, his nose long, rounded on the end and easing up into a high bridge. He had prominent cheekbones and a wide, intelligent forehead. Her fingers delved into his hair and found it soft and curly. She agreed with Mikki's assessment: he was a hunk.

Sterling watched Tammy's facial expressions as she felt his face. Derek had told him when he had gone for an orientation before admitting Kevin as a student, that the blind formed their own opinions about people with their senses, touch playing an integral part in the process. He wondered what she was thinking as she studied him. What was her impression of him?

"You won't refuse to go out with me, will you, Tammy?"

"No, I won't," she answered softly.

"Then you do have feelings for me?"

"You know I do."

He sure hoped so. Sterling smiled and then squeezed her hand and pulled her to her feet. "It's getting late, I'd better be getting you home."

Moments later, when she heard Sterling giving instructions to his driver to bring the limo around, Tammy was surprised. She had assumed that Sterling would drive her home.

Sterling made a guess as to what she was thinking. "I don't drive anymore...not since—since the accident," he confessed.

Tammy realized, for the first time, how deep the trauma of the accident and his guilt ran. He obviously blamed himself for his wife's death and his son's blindness to the point of self-inflicted punishment. He was truly one of the walking wounded.

"I don't want your pity, Tammy."

"And you won't get any. There are certain things that only you can resolve. Have you sought counseling?"

"Yes. I've been told pretty much what you've said, that it's up to me if I ever get behind the wheel of a car again." He cleared his throat. "Marcus is waiting to drive you home." He took Tammy's hand and urged her toward the front door.

"You don't have to come along."

"I'm coming with you. And I don't want an argument."

And that was that. She was learning what a stubborn, determined man Sterling could be.

CHAPTER TEN

Sterling walked Tammy to her front door, pulled her into his arms and kissed her. He wanted her to think about him tonight as he knew he would her.

"Sterling, I don't know if we should do this."

"You haven't changed your mind about tutoring Kevin, have you?"

"No, not that. Us, I—we…" Her voice trailed away.

"I know we don't know each other that well, but I want to remedy that." He tilted her chin and kissed her again.

Tammy's stomach muscles fluttered like a swarm of punch-drunk butterflies, and an involuntary shudder of need shook her body. She'd never felt anything like this for any other man.

Sensing her confusion, Sterling ended the kiss and moved a step back. He didn't want to pressure her. He wanted her to come to her own realizations about him, form her own opinion about their relationship. It was a relationship, whether she was willing to acknowledge that fact or not.

Sterling took her keys and unlocked the door. "I'd better be going."

"When do you want me to begin the tutoring sessions with Kevin?"

"How many weeks do you have left on your teaching assignment at the Institute?"

"Four. I begin my nightclub engagement at the Black Pearl the last weekend of the month."

"How about a week after that? It should give you time to work out a study program. In the meantime, we can ease the way by doing things with Kevin, letting him really get to know you."

He said *we*, she thought, which meant the three of them would be spending time together, like a real family. The word *family* and the thought of togetherness with Sterling and Kevin delighted Tammy. Augusta, Derek and D.J. had been her only family for so long.

"Sounds like a plan."

"Then we'll shoot for that. Goodnight, Tammy," he said softly, waiting for her to go inside before he left.

"Goodnight." Tammy closed the door, and once inside, she leaned against it and listened to his footsteps as he strode out to the waiting limo.

Sterling Phillips was a complex man, Tammy concluded as she made her way up to her bedroom. And he was determined to court her. Despite what she wanted to call it, courting was exactly what he was doing. Was he doing it under the guise of getting to know his son? Or was it prompted by his feelings for her? She had to find out which one it was before they proceeded any further. He said he cared for her, but men said a lot of things in the heat of passion. So did some women, she had to admit.

She sensed that Sterling wasn't devious, just determined. Feeling drawn to a man was one thing, but to consider a serious relationship with one was something else again. Her past was proof of that. Since David and other than Brent, no other man had really sparked her interest until now. Sterling Phillips reached her on so many different levels. And she hadn't begun to explore all of them.

Did she really want to? Dare she chance being hurt—again?

Isn't loving, caring and living, taking a chance? that persistent inner voice of reason asked.

What she'd been doing for the last ten years wasn't really living. She loved Augusta, Derek and D.J., but that was a safe unthreatening, unconditional kind of love. She cared for them, that was easy. But to have a deep man-woman relationship with Sterling...

Sterling studied Kevin as he ate his breakfast the next morning, wondering what he was thinking, how he was feeling.

"You still gonna keep on seeing Miss Gibson?" Kevin asked.

"You have a problem with that?"

"That's you. It doesn't make me any difference."

"Difference to what, Kevin?"

"It's not like you're gonna stop seeing her if I ask you to."

"Why would you ask me to do that?"

"She's not Mama."

"I know that, son. I like her for the unique, wonderful person she is. I thought you liked her, too."

"She's all right, I guess," he said grudgingly. "D.J. told me a lot about her life. That she lived in the ghetto and how she lost her sight."

Sterling's insides clinched painfully at his son's revelation. He cleared his throat. "Is it because you think she's trying to take your mother's place that you're less than eager to have her tutor you?"

"She said she didn't want to do that, but I don't know."

"Give her a chance to prove it to you, Kevin."

"I said I would."

"Yes, you did." Sterling smiled, and an inner feeling of relief spread through him. Maybe Derek was right and things would work out. Last night, Sterling had spoken to Augusta, and she'd agreed that Tammy needed someone in her life, but warned him not to hurt her again or he'd have to answer to her. He had to admire the gutsy lady. His Tammy was every bit that gutsy.

Tammy invited Sterling to a class picnic that she and Derek had arranged for the Junior Blind students. D.J. and Augusta came along to help out. Ben Hastings and his wife, Myra, and their daughter, Olivia, who were in town visiting with the Morgans, also came.

Tammy heard the rude expression of indifference in Kevin's voice when D.J. introduced him to Olivia and frowned. Her brows rose in surprise when she heard Olivia's comeback.

"What's your problem? D.J. calls you his friend. I don't know how he puts up with you."

"You're saying that 'cause I'm blind," Kevin shot back.

"No, I'm saying it because of your attitude. You don't know how to be nice to people."

"Liv, you don't understand," D.J. interrupted.

"Don't apologize for him."

"I can do that for myself," Kevin answered. "I didn't mean to hurt your feelings."

"Prove it," Olivia challenged.

"How?"

"By acting like a real person."

Tammy smiled.

"You heard?" Augusta asked.

"Liv is something else, isn't she?"

"She sure is," Myra answered. "Just like her father. But don't tell him that. His head is big enough as it is. He thinks that all our daughter's good qualities come from him."

Tammy shook her head. Myra Hastings was still the same.

She missed her sense of humor and sharp wit. After Augusta and Derek had moved to San Francisco, Tammy had spent weekends and holidays with the Hastings when she attended Julliard.

She disagreed about Olivia taking everything after her father. She had her mother's straightforwardness in speaking her mind.

"Is this the women's coffee clutch, or can a lowly male join?" Ben Hastings interposed into the conversation.

"Of course you can join, Ben," Tammy said graciously.

"This man has to be a part of everything I do," Myra said in a loud aside. "When I was pregnant with Liv, he would have carried her and had my labor pains if it had been possible. Said I was too puny to do the job. I showed him."

"She sure did and still is showing me what she can do." He leaned over and kissed the tip of her nose. "How's it going, Tammy?"

"I'm afraid to ask what you mean."

"Sterling has been singing your praises since we got here. Something going on between you two?"

"Ben!" Myra admonished.

"It's all right, Myra. Nothing is going on."

"Yet," Augusta added.

"We're just friends," Tammy insisted.

"For now," Augusta amended.

"I get the picture. She's in denial the way you were about your feelings for Derek before you finally admitted that you loved him."

"I'm not in love with Sterling Phillips," Tammy protested.

"I wish she were," Sterling answered from behind Tammy. "But I'm working on it."

"Sterling!" A gasp escaped Tammy's lips.

Augusta took Myra's and Ben's hands. "I think we'd better leave these two alone."

Tammy wanted to call them back after what had just been said.

"Don't feel embarrassed, Tammy," Sterling said in a sympathetic voice. "I know how it is with well-meaning friends and family."

"I'm not exactly embarrassed."

"Yes, you are. I don't know why you're fighting it."

"Fighting what?"

"What's happening between us. And don't say nothing is, because you know better. Just give me a chance. Give us a chance."

"Sterling."

"You don't have to say anything. I think time, well-meaning

friends and my own determination to win you over will eventually wear you down."

"You don't give up, do you?"

"No, I don't." Tammy just didn't know the lengths he was prepared go to have her love him again. He needed her the way a plant needs the warm, strengthening sun rays. He'd been in the dark way too long. Only her kind of light could brighten his world. "I'm enjoying this outing, and I think Kevin is, too." He glanced at his son, D.J. and Olivia. "He, your brother and Ben's daughter seem to be having an intense conversation over by the swings."

"They are. I think Olivia has made quite an impression on Kevin because she's not afraid to tell him what's on her mind."

"He needs that. So many people, especially kids his age, tend to walk on eggshells around him, not knowing how to react to his blindness."

"I can relate to that. I went through a similar period."

"I know you did, and that's one of the reasons I think studying with you will be good for Kevin." He was sure the plan to bring them closer would work. He would cultivate the patience to see it through and not rush his bases.

In just two weeks, Tammy would be coming to his house to tutor Kevin. He and his son had gone to her last two Tuesday night jam sessions. At one of the sessions, Kevin had finally agreed to play the piano. It brought tears to Sterling's eyes when he heard the pain and grief ebb from Kevin's heart through his fingers. Tammy had put her hands on Sterling's shoulders.

Evidently, his pain had touched her and moved her to offer comfort.

Sterling realized that he was learning about the different facets of love. Love was joy, pain, compassion, giving, long-suffering, trust and so many other emotions. One basic element it involved was trust. He knew he had to tell Tammy everything. But was she ready to hear it? It was vital that he prepare the way before telling her who he was.

Tammy sensed that something was going on with Sterling, and that it had nothing to do with his son and more to do with their personal relationship. She finally had to admit that that was what they were having. Over the last few weeks, Sterling had been attentive and warm. And considering his desire for her, patient.

What about herself? She couldn't help feeling more and more vulnerable with each encounter, and that scared her.

A few minutes later, Tammy heard D.J. and Olivia ask Kevin to walk with them. He refused. After they'd walked away, she made her way over to where he sat on a swing. This park was on the Institute grounds, and she knew every inch of it and had insisted that her students learn it as well.

"Why didn't you go with D.J. and Olivia?"

"Maybe I just didn't want to."

"What is it about me that you don't like?"

"I never said I didn't like you."

"Maybe not in so many words, but it comes out in your attitude. I'm really not out to take your mother's place if that's what's worrying you. I just want to help make your life bearable, Kevin.

I know how hard it is. I've been down that road."

"That's what D.J. told me. Did you really grow up in the ghetto?"

"I did, and it wasn't any picnic." She smiled at her unintentional play on words.

"Daddy said that's where he grew up, too." Kevin paused before going on. "About being blind. How can you be so—so…"

"Accepting? I'm not. I hate being blind. At times, I want to see so badly, I feel like exploding."

"I feel that way all the time. I get so mad I could break something."

When Tammy put her arm around his shoulder, he didn't pull away. "I know, Kevin. It's all right to get mad, but after you get over that feeling, you go on with your life."

"I don't see how."

"I'll help you."

Sterling overheard and blinked away the moisture threatening to escape his control and continued to listen as Tammy offered words of comfort to his son. He had complete confidence in her ability to do so. She had inspired him to compose again, to find joy in living. When she mentioned that she hated being blind, his insides twisted. His Tammy was a strong woman, a survivor. She hadn't let her condition defeat her. He suddenly felt the need to slip away and be by himself for a few minutes.

"I saw you talking to Kevin. Is everything all right," Derek asked as he walked over to Tammy then wrapped her arm around his.

"He feels so lost right now, Derek. I hope I can help him."

"I'm sure you'll give it your best shot. I'm going to miss you at the Institute."

"You know I'll be back next semester."

"Still pursuing that dream of fame and fortune."

"Recognition and respect, Derek."

"I stand corrected."

Tammy laughed. "You're really something, you know that?"

"And don't you forget it."

"It's not like you're going to let me."

From his place beneath a nearby oak tree, Sterling glanced at Tammy and Derek as they walked. He could feel the love flowing between them. He hoped to one day have another kind flowing between himself and Tammy. Right now it was all one-sided on his part, but he hoped to change that very soon. He pulled a cassette tape from his pocket and moved over to the picnic table and slipped it into the tape player sitting on top of it.

The kids and grownups alike flocked around the picnic table to listen. Sterling watched the rapt expression on each face, especially Tammy's. He could see that the music really touched her. After the tape finished playing and the audience moved away, he saw tears in her eyes. He brushed the wetness from her cheek with his fingers.

"I've written words to it," he said gently. "And I think they would fit your voice perfectly."

Was he saying he'd written them just for her? Or had she misunderstood? True enough, the music had intrigued her, making her yearn to know the words, to actually sing them herself. It was as though Sterling were weaving a spell around her with his music and his desire. Was she really ready for this?

He saw the indecision on her face and smiled. He was getting through to her. He could feel it, and he was elated by the revelation, but he wouldn't let himself get too excited, not yet. He still had a long way to go.

While everyone was eating, Augusta studied Sterling. She watched how he occasionally rubbed the area beneath his rib cage and then popped antacid tablets into his mouth.

"Are you feeling all right, Sterling?" she said, walking over to help clear the picnic table.

"It's just a little heartburn. It'll pass."

"You sure that's all it is?"

"I know you're a doctor, but please don't practice on me today."

She held up her hand. "I left my medical bag in the car. I'm just concerned about a friend. We are friends, aren't we, Sterling."

"I hope so. I know Derek has probably told you what we discussed."

"About you being the David of Tammy's past, you mean? Yes, he told me."

"I was just wondering how you really feel about me. I know

you said that you didn't hold the past against me."

"And I meant it. I don't. If you and Tammy can find a way back to each other, you won't have a problem with me. It's only if you hurt her that I'll beat you down."

"Fair enough."

"The music you played earlier was, as D.J. would say, way cool." She smiled. "You have a good singing voice. On the one piece you didn't sing, I had the feeling there were words to go with the music. Am I right?"

"Yes, and I want Tammy to sing them, hopefully record them and a few others I've composed for her."

Augusta frowned. "What you feel for Tammy isn't all about redemption and guilt, is it?"

"No. I want her to forgive me for what I did years ago, but it's more than that. I want to reclaim her love."

"You really do love her, don't you?"

"With all that's in me. I hurt her once, but I'd die before I'd ever do it again."

"I believe you. Derek and I will help you all we can."

"You don't know how glad I am to hear you say that."

Derek inserted himself into the conversation. "You two have been over here a long time. I didn't miss the good part, did I?"

"You already know the good part," Augusta answered. "Sterling is in love with Tammy."

He glanced at Sterling. "I'm a great advocate of love."

"I'm proof of that." Augusta smiled then gave her husband a quick kiss on the lips.

"You two have what I one day hope to have with Tammy."

"Hang tough, Sterling. We're all rooting for you, man."

"Thanks Derek."

CHAPTER ELEVEN

"I believe your mystery man is here tonight, judging by the bartender's description of a man sitting at the bar," Mikki whispered in Tammy's ear just before her first set at the Black Pearl nightclub.

"You're such a romantic, Mikki. Do you pump every bartender or waiter at every place I sing?"

"Of course. It's the only way to find out anything since he prefers to remain so aloof."

Tammy knew Mikki was right. Her mystery man was there, and although she could feel his presence, it was at times like these that she wished she could see him, or even study him with her fingers as she'd done with Sterling.

Sterling sipped his drink slowly, letting the pleasure of hearing Tammy sing take him.

"She's very good, isn't she?" the man sitting next to him commented.

"She's fantastic."

"Rumor has it that a mystery man comes to every one of her performances." The man glanced around the people-packed nightclub. "I wonder who he could be."

Sterling's senses went on red alert. Who was this man? He remembered seeing him before, but at the moment he couldn't recall where. He returned his attention to the woman who owned his heart and always would.

"Want another mineral water, sir?" the bartender asked Sterling.

"No, I'm fine."

"That's all you've been drinking?" the man seated on the stool next to him inquired. "I could have sworn it was something stronger. She really turns you on, doesn't she? I guess you're high on her, and you don't need alcohol to help you out. That's interesting. Do I know you from some place?"

Sterling tilted his glass, dousing the man's lap, and then apologized. While the bartender was helping blot the wetness from his pants, Sterling eased away from the bar and headed for the door. He turned, staring at the man, wondering, again, who he could be. Then he took one last lingering look at Tammy. This would be the last time he went to any of her singing engagements. His presence was becoming too conspicuous. He would just have to work harder on getting her to sing for him in his studio.

Tammy knew the moment *he* left. Who was this mystery man? She was beyond curious about him now. She sensed that he wasn't a danger to her, at least not in a physical sense.

When she returned to her dressing room, flowers stood in a vase waiting for her. She could smell their fragrance and knew instinctively they were from *him*.

Mikki followed her inside. "A dozen red roses. He's been here all right. Am I good or what? I almost got to see his face, but before I could reach the bar, he left. Still there was something familiar about him."

Tammy sighed. Would she ever find out the identity of her mystery man?

The day of Tammy's first tutoring session with Kevin arrived, and she was a little nervous. He'd been a student of hers at the Institute for weeks, but now she'd be working with Kevin one-on-one at Sterling's house.

Would Sterling stick around while she did it?

You know deep down you want him to.

"You ready for me to drop you by Mr. Phillips' house?" Mikki asked, interrupting the flow of Tammy's thoughts.

"Yes."

"I wonder if the hunk is going to sit in while you instruct his son."

"I'm sure he will. It is his house and his son."

"I'd say you were looking forward to more than just tutoring his son."

"Mikki!"

"Okay, I'll shut my mouth, but you know I'm right."

Fifteen minutes later, Tammy knocked at Sterling's front door.

"Tammy!" Sterling exclaimed when he opened the door. "I

was going to send the car for you."

"It wasn't necessary. I had Mikki drop me off. I hope Kevin is ready."

"He's in his room. I don't know what kind of mood he's in, though." Sterling escorted Tammy into the living room. "Let me take your work bag," he said, easing it from her hand. "I'll go get him."

"Not just yet. I want to accustom myself to your house. Will we be studying in this room?"

"If you want to. We have a family room you could use."

"I like this room."

Sterling felt relieved. The family room hadn't really been used since Kayla's...the accident. Kevin never went in there either. When they first moved into the house, it had been the center of activity, but then he got busy with his career and Kayla started doing her thing with whomever, whenever. They had rarely been together enough to use it.

Sterling watched Tammy explore the pieces of furniture with her hands. It was as though she were touching him, coming to intimately know him. He felt she really belonged here, belonged in his life. If she'd let him, he would convince her of that.

Just then, they heard Kevin coming down the stairs and waited until he made his way into the living room. Tammy wondered how to begin. At the Institute, her relationship with Kevin had been on a more impersonal basis because he preferred it that way. Now, in his own home, that would change, putting them on a more personal footing.

"Kevin, Tam—Miss Gibson is here. You ready to begin your

tutoring session?"

"I guess." He shrugged as he entered the room.

"Where would you feel comfortable studying?" Tammy asked.

"I don't care. In here is all right."

Sterling wondered what his son was thinking. "You sure, Kevin?"

"We could go in the family room," Kevin suggested in a mocking tone of voice that he knew would aggravate his father.

Kevin's words made Tammy aware of just how strained the relationship between father and son really was. This hostility he projected toward Sterling had to stop. They needed each other, and she intended to make sure they both realized just how much and help heal the breach between them.

"We haven't used that room since—" Sterling began. He couldn't go on because his throat suddenly clogged with emotion.

"Since you kill—since Mama died," Kevin finished quietly.

Tammy heard Sterling's sharp intake of breath at his son's cruel words and empathized with him.

"If it'll make you feel more comfortable, Kevin," Tammy reassured him, "we can use the family room. I don't have a problem with it." Tammy wondered if Kevin were testing her true intentions by suggesting they use the family room or whether he was just doing it to get at Sterling because he held him accountable for his mother's death.

This was no easy job she'd taken on, Tammy realized. The whole situation was a minefield riddled with emotional booby traps that could explode and blow them all away if not approached with caution and neutralized.

Sterling led Tammy to a game table and took the dust cover off, explaining that it could be converted into a convenient work area. To offset the first few awkward moments in the family room, Tammy took the contents from her work bag and spread them out on the table.

Sterling looked on as Tammy started the session. She was patient and encouraging. When he saw that Kevin seemed to be warming to her, he excused himself and headed for his studio, relieved to be out of the family room. He hadn't realized that Kayla had so many of her things still in it.

He wondered why his son had suggested using the family room. Was it just to punish him? Or was it that he wanted to feel close to his mother? He wondered if he should remove Kayla's things. It wasn't as if Kevin could see them. But Sterling could, and they bothered him. He came to a decision. He'd put them in storage. If Kevin later decided he wanted them, they'd be there. He wished his son could know how much he regretted not having made the time for his wife and son.

Tammy and Kevin stopped studying to eat lunch when the housekeeper brought in a tray of sandwiches and lemonade. Tammy wondered where Sterling had gone. He'd only stayed a few moments. She would have to change that and get him more involved.

"You like my father, don't you?" Kevin suddenly asked, interrupting her thoughts.

"Yes, I do."

"How much?"

"Why do you ask?"

"Forget it."

"No. I'd like to know."

"You said you weren't trying to take my mama's place."

"And I'm not."

"That's what you'd be doing if you and he—you know."

"Kevin, listen to me. I care about your father, and if anything happens between us, that's a whole different thing. His marriage to your mother was their business while she was alive. Because I've been seeing your father doesn't mean that I'm out to take her place. I could never do that. She's your mother and always will be, and no one can ever take her place in your heart.

"You know that Augusta Morgan is my foster mother. As much as I love that dear lady, she'll never take my real mother's place, and she doesn't want to. She's earned her own place in my heart. I hope you'll allow me to earn a place in yours."

Sterling stood in the doorway listening to Tammy express her feelings. Maybe his dream was not so impossible after all.

❋

After Kevin had gone upstairs to his room, Sterling invited Tammy to come into his studio to listen to some music and relax before having Marcus drive her home.

"I can have Mikki pick me up," she offered.

"You don't have to do that. I'll have Marcus drive you." He walked over to the audio producer. He'd enhanced the tape she'd listened to at the picnic and added special orchestration. "I have something I want to play for you, Tammy. You remember the tape I played at one of your jam sessions, then again at the picnic?"

"Yes," she said curiously. "Is that what you want me to hear?"

"Yes. I've made a few changes, and I'd like you to hear the words to the song."

"All right."

Sterling flipped a lever. As the music flowed into the room, Tammy listened to the lyrics. As if she'd heard them many times before, started repeating them. The sound track stopped a few moments before replaying the song. From the way Sterling had described his equipment, Tammy knew it was similar to what Stevie Wonder had donated to the Institute.

When Sterling was sure Tammy had memorized the words, he replayed the all-music version, and they sang it together. The words spoke of an eternal love that no one or nothing could destroy. He noticed that it brought tears to her eyes.

Sterling drew Tammy into his arms. When she lifted her face, he kissed her tenderly on the lips then deepened it as the seconds passed.

Tammy breathed in his mesmerizing cologne mixed with his own unique masculine scent. He tasted of passion, making her hunger for more. Her breasts tingled and peaked when his chest rubbed against them. An inner heat began to smolder in her veins, sending hot, aroused blood into her femininity. The brush of his tongue against the sensitive walls and roof of her mouth built the fire hotter and higher.

"Oh, Tammy, girl," Sterling murmured in her ear, easing her

down on the couch.

Tammy slipped her arms around his neck, participating fully in the beautiful moments of rapture they were sharing. She gasped when she felt his fingers slide back and forth across her nipples. Her breathing came in soft, staccato moans of pleasure that he muted with his lips.

"Sterling."

"Yes," he said thickly, all but insensate to anything but his desire for this woman.

"I—I think we'd better stop," she said shakily, pulling away from him. His passionate onslaught had kindled a desire that went beyond what she felt she could deal with.

Sterling groaned, taking a moment to gather his scattered control and impose calm into his throbbing lower body. He sensed that Tammy had handled as much as she could for now. He had planned to go slow with her, but so far those plans had been shot to hell. The situation reminded him of a song by Teddy Pendergrass called "Love TKO." He felt knocked out by love all right, down for the count, his brain reeling from the onslaught. This woman was the only one who could do that to him.

"I'll call Marcus and have him drive you home."

"Sterling, about what just happened. Do you think we should—"

He put a finger across her lips. "What happened between us was more than just desire or lust. I won't put any pressure on you. I want what is blossoming between us to develop into something special, Tammy. I sense that you're not ready for anything intimate. I can wait until you are."

"But—"

He kissed her lips. "No buts." He reached for the phone. Minutes later, they saw Marcus drive up. Sterling walked Tammy out, helped her into the limo then handed over her work bag.

"I would come with you, but…" He let his voice trail away.

"I know," Tammy said in a voice barely above a whisper.

"Think about me tonight." He slipped the tape into her hand and closed her fingers around it.

"You know I will."

Sterling straightened, watching as the limo moved down the drive, out the gate then disappeared around the hedges. He stood there for a moment before walking back into the house. The rub of his pants against his throbbing flesh reminded him of how close he had come to losing control. He knew in his head it was too soon for him and Tammy to have the kind of relationship he desired, but his body obviously held a different opinion. It would be hell convincing it that it couldn't have its way just yet.

Sterling couldn't remember the last time he'd felt this alive. He felt like a man who'd been rescued from a sinking ship. Tammy had done that for him. She was his life preserver.

He wanted her with every fiber of his being, but he would wait as long as he had to; she was worth waiting for.

CHAPTER TWELVE

Sterling thumbed through his mail with bored interest until he came to one of the entertainment newspapers he subscribed to. The headlines immediately snagged his attention.

**"LOCAL NIGHTCLUB SINGER
BEWITCHES MYSTERY ADMIRER
Who is this man? This reporter suspects that
he is a well-known personality and vows to
reveal his identity."**

Sterling's thoughts returned to the man at the bar. Could he be this celebrity reporter? He glanced at the article. The columnist was Hunter Bryant, but there was no picture.

All he needed was some news-hungry reporter dredging up the accident, spreading rumors about his personal life, and splattering the details across the front page of some tabloid. God, he couldn't go through that again. And it wouldn't stop there. They would dig and dig until they uncovered things in his past that would ultimately hurt Tammy. He could not let that happen. She'd suffered enough already because of him. He owed her some happiness.

Making her into a superstar would be a step closer to making her life happier. The thought consumed his every waking hour. He smiled as he remembered the expression on Tammy's face when he'd played the tape. He could tell that she loved the song. Somehow he would convince her to record it and the others as well. He now had enough material to float an album. These songs were some of the best he'd ever written and would put Tammy at the top of the R & B charts in record time. He knew all the right people to make it happen, and he intended to plug into every one of them.

It had been several weeks since their intimate encounter. Since then, Tammy had been subdued and left right after her sessions with Kevin. He knew she was fighting what she felt for him. Didn't she know it was useless? They were destined to be together. He ran away from that destiny years ago, making a disaster of his life and a desolation of hers.

He didn't regret getting involved with Kayla because that relationship had given him Kevin. But he did regret not being the kind of husband his wife had needed, pushing her into the arms of other men. She'd searched for the love and affection he wouldn't or couldn't give her. Tammy had always been there like an invisible third person in his marriage.

From the start, there had been something special between him and Tammy. Although they'd been reckless teenagers years ago, they'd connected in ways that only people who really love each other can. She'd been a part of him. He hadn't realized how much a part until it was too late to go back and change things.

Sterling was sure that Tammy thought her blindness was the reason he hadn't been to the hospital to see her after the accident, but that wasn't true. His guilt at what he'd done had kept him away. At the time, he had been too immature to handle it. He'd needed to grow up and experience life to realize what was really important. He'd had to go through a lot of pain and unhappiness in the process. Now he had a chance to get it right. He intended to try with all that was in him to win Tammy back.

You need to tell her the truth first, man, his conscience counseled.

He would tell her soon, but not just yet.

"You've been kind of quiet lately," Mikki said to Tammy as she helped her out of her royal purple evening gown following her last performance of the night at the Black Pearl. "Is it because your mystery man hasn't been here the last few weekends? Or does it have something to do with Sterling Phillips? Or maybe both?"

It *was* both. Her friend was way too perceptive. "Mikki, please, I'm not up to doing twenty questions tonight. I'm tired and sleepy."

"All right, all right. You can fool yourself, but you can't fool me. I can smell man trouble a mile away. In your case, men trouble."

"Why do you have to—I'm not going there with you, okay?"

"That's too bad because I *am* going there with you. I want to know what's up with you. I was here with you tonight and saw the look on your face when *he* didn't show up. He'd really begun to get next to you, hadn't he?"

"Just drive me home, Mikki. I really don't want to talk about this."

"You've got to talk about it with someone. If not me, then Augusta. I'm sure she'd understand; she's always been there from what you've told me."

As Mikki drove them home, Tammy considered her suggestion. Maybe she would give her foster mother a call tomorrow.

"Doctor Morgan here."

"Augusta, it's Tammy." Her fingers tightened on the phone receiver. "Are you free for lunch today?"

"Let me check my calendar. How about 1:30? It'll have to be a quick one in the hospital dining room, though. I have surgery scheduled for 2:30."

"That'll be fine."

"Is anything wrong?"

"No, not wrong exactly."

"Sounds serious to me. See you at 1:30."

As Tammy hung up the phone, she wondered if she was ready to talk about this even with Augusta. Tammy was so—she didn't know anymore what she was. How could she be so drawn to two men? She'd never met the mystery man, yet something about him made her continue to think about him.

Then there was Sterling Phillips and his haunting music with the beautifully compelling lyrics he said he'd composed just for her. And his obvious desire for her.

Tammy pushed the play button on the cassette player. When the music began to play, she started singing the words. It was like nothing she'd ever sung before. How had Sterling known so perfectly what suited her voice range? He seemed so intimately acquainted with her that it was uncanny. Not only that, he had the musical genius of a Babyface or an R. Kelly.

"I never heard you sing that song before," Mikki said, entering the living room. "That was past being the bomb, totally awesome. Your voice, those words and that music... It's the same music Sterling played at one of the music sessions, right? It sounded good before, but add the words and your voice, and it's transformed into something special."

"I agree. It was as though he wrote it just for me. I knew Sterling was talented, and this song definitely confirms it."

"If you record it, I guarantee you it'll be up there with Lauryn Hill or Mariah Carey in no time. Something about your voice sets you apart, and Sterling has picked up on it."

As Tammy waited in the hospital cafeteria for Augusta, she recalled what Mikki had said. Was it possible that she had that unique quality record producers would kill for? She'd thought so after recording her first album, but it hadn't set the music world on fire and neither had the second. Maybe with Sterling writing her songs...

"You been waiting long?" Augusta asked.

"No."

"I'm sorry I'm late, but it couldn't be helped." Augusta placed her tray on the table and seated herself across from Tammy. "So what's up with you?"

"I don't know quite how to get into this. You remember the mystery man who came to all of my club dates?"

"Yes. Did you ever get to meet him?"

"Unfortunately, no."

"Despite that, you're intrigued by him. Right?"

"I should have known you'd pick up on that. Anyway, he stopped coming to hear me sing, and I feel as though he's abandoned me. For a while, I thought he could be David. I know that sounds crazy."

"No, it doesn't. The thing with the red rose was like *déjà vu*. You associated that with David because he abandoned you. And you feel vulnerable. That's a normal reaction. It's called being human."

"But I never even met the mystery man to know whether he was David or not."

"Doesn't make any difference. He touched a part of you and made you start to feel again. Nothing strange about that. But that's not the only thing bothering you, though, is it?"

Tammy sighed. "No. I have feelings for Sterling Phillips. And he also makes me feel vulnerable. I've gotten more deeply involved in his life through his son."

"How are the tutoring sessions going?"

"Oh, they're coming along."

"But? It's more than just Kevin. I sensed that at the picnic."

"After the first session, Sterling took me into his studio and we…"

"I see. You're afraid to trust in the feelings you have for him, aren't you? I can definitely relate to that. I went through something similar with Derek. But for you it's more because of what happened with David. And what you were beginning to feel for the mystery man who also seems to have abandoned you."

"You should take up psychiatry as a sideline."

"I'm only drawing on my own experiences. Life at best is very complicated. It wouldn't be life if it were any other way."

"You got that right. So what do I do?"

"Cope with it, try to find happiness with someone you love, like the rest of us mere mortals."

"I can't do anything about the mystery man."

"No, but you can about Sterling Phillips. Give yourself a chance. Give him a chance. Don't automatically back away from him."

"But I'm not sure I can handle a relationship with him."

"You'll never know unless you take a chance."

"You don't pull your punches, do you? Thanks for the advice, Augusta."

"I'm your mother. I'm only doing my job."

"Who is this? She has a fantastic voice."

Sterling smiled at the enthusiastic response of Jeremy Ward, the president of R & B Records, to the tape he'd just played for him. "You're right, she does. I can't give you her name until she agrees to do the demo."

"You mean she hasn't already done one?" Ward asked, his voice incredulous. "With a voice like that she should already be under contract and working on an album." He gazed at Sterling thoughtfully. "I've heard her voice before, but I can't quite remember where or when."

"Don't strain your brain, Jeremy. If everything goes according to plan, you'll know the identity of this talented lady soon enough."

"You're interested in her beyond her recording your songs,

though, aren't you?"

"Don't go there, Jeremy."

"Okay, I won't. If you can talk her into doing a demo, I want to be the first producer to hear it."

"You will be, that's why I let you hear this sample. I believe you would be the right recording company for her, but we'll have to wait and see what develops."

After leaving R & B Records, Sterling went home. He knew Tammy would be studying with Kevin, and he intended to broach the subject of a demo after the tutoring session was over.

You want to do more than that, Phillips.

Yes, he did. He wanted a life with the woman he loved, but at the moment, it was like a mission impossible episode where the leader has to figure out a way to make his mission succeed against overwhelming odds. Sterling knew he would have to take one careful step at a time. To move any faster might ruin any chance he had with Tammy. She was too important to him, to his life and his son's to risk losing her.

Without actually hearing him enter the family room, Tammy sensed Sterling's presence. That familiar tingle of excitement whenever he was near strummed along her senses. Today was the day she would take that all important first step and find out exactly how deep her feelings for Sterling ran. And his for her As for the mystery man, she would have to put him out of her mind since he had obviously put her out of his. But the knowledge that he had still hurt.

"How's it going, Tammy?" Sterling asked.

"We're making progress, aren't we, Kevin?"

He shrugged.

Tammy felt the tension tighten between father and son and wished she could do something to loosen it. A son shouldn't feel such animosity toward his father.

"Sit down while Kevin and I show you how well he's doing with advanced Braille."

Feeling scorched by Kevin's hostility, Sterling was reluctant to remain, but decided to stay because he wanted so badly to make inroads with his son and be near Tammy.

He listened as Kevin read from a Braille book, noticing how encouraging Tammy was when he stumbled over portions of the text. Sterling's heart went out to his son who appeared to really be trying to master this new form of communication. If only the three of them could be a family, a real family.

"Okay, Kevin, I think you've done enough for today. I want you to study the assignment I've given you."

"But it's too hard."

"I know it's not an easy assignment, but if you keep working at it, you'll get the hang of it."

"I'll never get the hang of being blind," he said in a defiant tone he directed toward Sterling, clearly making known where he placed the blame for his condition. Kevin rose abruptly to his feet, unfolded his cane and left the room.

Sterling's heart sank. Would he and his son ever get past his obvious bitterness?

Tammy put a hand over Sterling's. "It takes time," she said gently. "He's only twelve years old and at a point in his life when everything is changing. He has to face more than the average boy his age will ever have to face."

"I know you're right. If he would only talk to me. I know he blames me for his mother's death, and believe me, I've tried to convince him that it was an accident, but he refuses to listen. I feel so damned frustrated."

"I can understand that. Maybe in time he'll come around. About the tape…"

"Yes."

"How did you know the song would be so perfect for me?"

"As I told you before, I wrote it for you. I listened to you sing and was inspired."

Tammy frowned. He hadn't heard her sing enough to know that, unless…

"Yes, I'm your mystery man," he admitted quietly.

"But—I don't understand why you stayed in the shadows and never made a move to introduce yourself?"

Sterling pulled her into his arms and silenced her question with a kiss.

"Since that first moment I walked into the Midnight at the Oasis Club in San Jose and heard your beautiful voice ringing out soulfully in song, I was captivated."

She pulled away. "But why did you feel that you had to keep your identity such a mystery? All this time I've wondered. I even thought he—you might be David Dixon. You see, we were so close until I lost my sight in the accident. I never saw him again and one night when the mystery man sent me a single red rose, I thought… You have no idea how relieved I am to know that it was you and not David.

"When I met you at the fund raiser dinner, I knew there was something so—I don't know—familiar about you, I guess. Why did you stop coming to hear me sing?"

"I'm sorry about that, but a man appeared one night and started asking a lot of questions. I believe he was a celebrity reporter, and I didn't want him digging into the details of my past, splattering them across the front pages of the tabloids." Sterling held his breath. Had he revealed too much?

"You don't have to explain anything else. I know how hard it must be for you, Sterling. But it was an accident. You didn't want any harm to come to your wife and son. Mikki filled me in on all the publicity and conjecture surrounding the accident."

Sterling let out the breath he'd been holding. It hadn't occurred to him that she might think the mystery man was...

It's only a narrow escape, a temporary reprieve. Tell her the truth, man.

He wanted to, but he just couldn't. Right now wasn't the time.

"About your singing. I've written other songs for you, Tammy. I think we could work well together."

Her stomach lurched. Surely this wasn't what he was leading up to, and he really didn't care for her the way she was beginning to think he did.

"Don't misunderstand me, Tammy. Your voice isn't the only draw. You've completely beguiled me. I care for you, girl."

"You don't know how relieved I am to hear you say that."

Tell her the truth now.

"I need to tell you—"

Tammy kissed him, damming up his words. "Now that I

know why my mystery man, you, disappeared from my life, anything else you have to tell me can wait. Just knowing you care for me and want to help me with my career is enough for now."

"But Tammy—"

She put a finger across his lips. "I know you have other problems, and I'll help you sort them out. And together, we'll help Kevin cope with his blindness."

Kevin wasn't the only one he was thinking about. He had to tell her the truth, but how? He was supposed to be a genius with words, yet he couldn't find the right ones to tell her what he must.

Don't wait too long, an inmost voice admonished.

He wished he could hush it up permanently. But for now he would ignore it.

"We'll go with the flow and see what happens," Sterling said gently. "But right now I just want to hold you and kiss you and enjoy being with you, baby."

"I want that, too."

Sterling held her close, burying his face in her hair. He loved this woman so much. He wanted to do so much for her. She'd made his life worth living again. She owned his heart and anything else she cared to claim. But would she want to claim it or any other part of him once she knew who he was? That was the burning question.

CHAPTER THIRTEEN

Sterling knocked on Derek's classroom door before entering.

"Sterling. How's it going, man?"

"Not so good."

"Sit down. I'm afraid all we have here is water. If you want to go to the staff lounge for some coffee, we can."

"That's all right, I don't want anything, just to talk. You got a minute?"

"I'm free until two." Derek gave him a sidelong glance. "You haven't told Tammy who you are, have you?"

"No. But I did admit to being her mystery man."

Derek shook his head. "You're full of secrets, aren't you."

"I never wanted it that way. I want more than anything to be honest with Tammy. It's just that I can't find the right time or the right words."

"Man, you sound like I did thirteen years ago. I was a procrastinator to the bone."

"I remember you telling me that. I knew that you of all people would understand. I want to tell her the truth, but I'm so afraid of losing her, Derek."

"It's gone that far between you two, then?"

"We haven't been intimate, but I'm deeply in love with her, man."

"Does she love you?"

"She's attracted and she cares, but as to love, I just don't know. And if I tell her now and she...well..."

"I understand. You're between a rock and a hard place. I definitely don't envy you. I've been there and know exactly how that feels."

"But Augusta forgave you, didn't she?"

Derek sighed. "She did, but Sterling, let me tell you I went through hell. If I had told her sooner, I could have saved myself and Augusta a lot of heartache. I can say that now because hindsight is 20/20."

"And don't I know it. I can't help thinking that if I had paid more attention to my wife, she might be alive today. But like you said, hindsight is 20/20. I don't want it to be too late for Tammy and me, Derek."

"I'm sure you don't. I can see this is really stressing you out."

"Yes, it is. I tried to tell her last night, but I just couldn't bring myself to do it. For the first time, she reached out to me. Before, I've always been the aggressor. And now that I've convinced her to work with me on a song, possibly an album—"

"You don't want to mess things up. I can understand that. You'll be working closely over the next few months, right? In that time she'll have the chance to really come to know the person you are today. She'll come to realize that the immature boy has grown into a responsible, caring man, one worthy of her love."

"I'm glad I came to talk to you, Derek."

"I wish I could do more than just offer advice. I wish I could present you with the perfect solution to your dilemma."

"You have no idea how much I've needed someone to talk to who really understands how I feel."

"I'll be here if you need me, Sterling."

"You're a good friend, Derek. I appreciate you, man."

"It cuts both ways. I might need you to do the same for me."

❋

Tammy played the tape and sang along with it. She and Sterling didn't sound too bad together. Hearing their two voices blended in harmony made her think about the times she and David had sung together. They'd shared a special closeness. She now shared that with Sterling. It was different with him, though.

How is it different?

David had been her first love. Back then they'd been so young, thinking that they knew everything. She was a different person now and Sterling was definitely not David.

But how do you feel about Sterling?

She realized that she had come to love him. Loved him deeply.

You're finally admitting this to yourself.

She'd loved him from the beginning, she had to confess. Because she'd been afraid of being hurt she'd fought it. But unlike the way it had been with David, her being blind didn't bother Sterling. When she was in his arms, nothing else mattered. Just being with him was enough. But did he love her? She knew he desired her, enjoyed her company, loved to hear her sing and was even inspired to write a song for her. He was also grateful to her for helping him with his son. But did he truly love her?

Tammy wanted to know, had to know how he felt about Tammy the woman aside from all those things.

How are you going to find out, girlfriend?

Considering how deep her feelings for him were, she'd have

to be sure of him before she risked her heart.

Love doesn't come with guarantees.

How well she knew that. She'd been so sure that David had loved her. She'd obviously been wrong. He'd shown his true colors after the accident by never calling or coming to visit her.

But that part of her life was over a long time ago, and she thought she'd moved on. But had she really? At least she'd thought she had. She still carried baggage from her relationship with David. She'd have to get completely rid of it before she could find true happiness with the man she'd come to love.

"You're humming that song again. When you gonna record it and make it a household melody so everybody can enjoy it?" Mikki asked Tammy as she helped her into a blue, sequined, after-five dress.

"I'm going to try it out tonight at the club."

"To test the waters so to speak. I can tell you right now they're going to love it. Sterling Phillips is one talented composer who knows how to reach the heart. He sure homed in on your voice when he wrote that song. But then, he had plenty of opportunity. I can't get over him being the mystery man. But when I think about it, everything fits."

"It does. With Sterling I feel exhilarated, rejuvenated. I've never shared that kind of rapport with a composer before. None has ever gotten it right until now."

"He's interested in you for more than singing one of his songs."

"I'm helping his son."

"That's not what I meant, and you know it. I've seen the way he looks at you. The man is clearly besotted."

"Mikki."

"You feel the same way about him, so don't try to tell me any different because I won't believe you."

"Isn't it time for me to go on?"

"What did I tell you? They loved it. You need a demo tape to present to producers. Sterling can help you there," Mikki said as she accompanied Tammy back to her dressing room. "He's got to know everybody who's anybody in the music business."

"Now, Mikki, don't you think you're taking a lot for granted?"

"No. Hasn't he mentioned anything about doing a demo? I would have thought… You've been holding out on me, haven't you?"

"Sterling said he wanted to work with me, but he hasn't mentioned doing a demo."

"It's the next logical step. He's probably just waiting for the right time. Oh, I'm so excited."

"Don't jump the gun. I've been down that road before, don't forget."

"Those dummies at Pacific Coast Recording didn't know what to do with you. Sterling Phillips has been around and knows his stuff. If he's willing to work on a demo with you… He should have been here tonight to see the audience's reaction to that song. I wonder why he wasn't?"

Tammy recalled what Sterling had told her concerning the man at the Inner Harbor.

"I'm sure he had his reasons."

"You know what they are, too, I'll bet."

"Mikki."

"You're going to be known as queen of the R & B charts one day, mark my words."

Anticipation began to build inside Tammy, in spite of what she'd said to Mikki. Could Sterling help turn her dream into reality?

Tammy's session with Kevin had gone well. What resistance he had to her was gradually crumbling, she concluded, after he'd gone upstairs. His acceptance of his father's presence was another thing entirely. She just didn't know what to do about that.

"The look on your face is priceless, Ms. Gibson," Sterling said as he watched Tammy gather her things in preparation to go home.

"What look?"

"The one that mountain climbers have when they gaze at a mountain, formulating their strategy for reaching the top. My son is every bit as tough to scale as the proverbial mountain."

"He's not unscalable, Sterling. I have to find the right tools and use the right strategy, that's all."

"You never give up do you?"

"No, I don't. And neither should you."

"Thanks."

"For what?"

Sterling drew her into his arms. "For being you, that's what." He kissed her.

"This isn't a part of my teaching assignment."

"No, only one of the fringe benefits."

"Oh, and you think there's more?"

"If I have my way, much more. I want you to consider doing a demo."

Tammy's heart lurched. "A demo? Does that mean you've written enough songs to float an album?"

"It does and I have. Lady, don't you know that you inspire me to greatness?"

"Oh, Sterling. Do you really think I can make it this time?"

"I don't think it, I know you will. I let a well-known producer hear that song we recorded, and he's impressed. When we've completed the demo, he wants to be the first to hear it." Sterling sensed the excitement Tammy was trying so hard to contain.

"When do we start?" she asked.

"You're still singing at the Black Pearl."

"Only for another month. They're closing for renovations, so they'll be ready to open for the summer season. I haven't signed to doing any more nightclub gigs yet."

"Then don't. By the time you're through, I'll have set you up with the best musicians in the business. I'm going to make you a star."

"Oh, Sterling." She slipped her arms around his neck and kissed him.

He groaned, deepening the kiss as he wrapped his arms

around her. Blood throbbed inside him, speeding through his system with alarming force and heat. When it poured hotly into his groin, he felt his lower body harden where it made contact with hers, and he shuddered.

The tips of Tammy's breasts tingled when meshed against Sterling's chest, and the tingling sensations didn't stop there. They streamed into her femininity. She felt his hands squeezing her buttocks, drawing her even closer. The friction of their bodies rubbing against each other heated her senses to the melting point.

Sterling eased his lips from Tammy's. "What you do to me, girl." He gently brushed her lips with his own.

"What do I do to you, Sterling?" she moaned, silencing his words before he could utter them.

"It's getting late, I'd better take you home or else you'll end up in my bed."

"Would that be such a bad place to be?"

"Are you ready to go there?"

Tammy hesitated.

"I didn't think so. I want you, Tammy, but the time has to be right for both of us. I care too much about you to rush what we have building between us. We'll know the right time when it comes. Then there will be no hesitation, just spontaneous combustion."

"Oh, so now I'm a car, and all you need to do is rev my engine."

Sterling laughed. "You do wonderful things for me, Tammy Gibson. And I intend to return the favor."

"I look forward to it."

CHAPTER FOURTEEN

"Let's run through it one more time," Sterling instructed the musicians and Tammy before resetting the recording equipment in his studio again. He wanted to finish the demo as soon as possible.

Tammy sighed, and as she did so, heard commiserating groans from the musicians. She'd worked hard on her other album, but never like this on a demo. Sterling Phillips was a precise, relentless taskmaster. They'd been working on this one song for a week, since she'd finished her singing gig at the Black Pearl.

Sterling smiled at Tammy's expression. They'd done some wonderful takes, but none of them were close to the perfection he knew he could draw from her. They were getting there, though. After recording another take, he called a break.

"Would you care to go for a walk with Simon LeGree?" he asked Tammy.

"You give that expression 'lift that bail, tote that barge' a different meaning entirely, Sterling Phillips." She laughed.

"Anyone who has ever worked with me refers to me as the S.D."

"S.D.?"

"Slave Driver. But I don't care. I always pull the best from my performers."

"That's why you've received so many Grammys and other music awards. You really feel that I can make it to the top, don't you?"

"Yes, I do. I told you that," he replied confidently as he guided Tammy through the garden door and down the path leading to the beach.

The sharp, salt smell of the ocean and the pungent odor of the seaweed filled their nostrils. Tammy heard the flapping of sea gulls as they wheeled overhead, along with the sound of waves washing over the sand. The sun splayed warm fingers over her skin. She brushed her fingers across the crystal-less surface of her Braille watch, imagining how the beach must look this time of the afternoon.

Sterling noticed the look on Tammy's face. He realized she was seeing the beach in a special way, with her other senses. But that didn't banish away any of the guilt and regret he felt, and would always feel, about that one reckless night all those years ago. He would see to it that Tammy got the respect and recognition she deserved. With his help, she'd reach the top of the charts in record time, he vowed.

Sterling was so quiet that Tammy couldn't help wondering what he was thinking as they walked arm-in-arm along the beach. She sensed that more was going on with him than anyone knew or he would ever reveal. Was he thinking about Kevin or maybe his wife?

"What was she like, your wife, I mean?" Tammy asked. She felt him tense, and when he didn't answer right away, she thought he wouldn't.

"What makes you ask about her?"

"Kevin has said a few things during our tutoring sessions. He and his mother were very close, I take it. I'm not trying to pry. I just want to know what kind of person she was."

"Kayla was a very energetic woman. She loved life and lived it to the hilt. It was one of the things I liked about her when we first met. We became involved, and she got pregnant before we really got to know each other and discover what we wanted and needed out of life. She craved attention, and I was so into my music that I failed to see that and give it to her. After Kevin was born, things went all right for a while, but then when he was no longer a baby and was in school, Kayla was at loose ends."

Tammy squeezed his hand, encouraging him to continue.

"All the unhappy signs were there, but I was too into my own world to pay any attention. Kayla grew more distant and more unhappy. She hired a nanny to see after Kevin so she could spend more time doing her own thing. Then I found out what her own thing was and where and with whom she spent most of her time." Sterling gritted his teeth.

"You don't have to tell me any more if you—"

"No. I need to talk about it." He paused before going on. "Needless to say, our relationship went to hell in a hand basket after that. Kevin was the only remaining link. I'm sure our son felt it was his responsibility to keep the family together, and it was totally unfair of us to burden him like that. He saw how unhappy his mother was and blamed me. It was my fault. If I'd paid more attention to her, maybe she would be alive today."

"Oh, Sterling." Tammy stopped walking and eased her hands up to cup his face.

Sterling slipped his arms around her waist and drew her close to his body.

"I've made so many mistakes, Tammy."

"You're only human."

"Oh, girl, I need you in my life."

"I'm here for you, Sterling."

God how he wanted to believe that. She might be here at this moment, but what about later when she found out the truth?

He glanced at his watch. "We'd better head back to the house. The gang is probably ready to get to work."

Tammy felt their moment of closeness disappear like a puff of smoke; the task master was back. At least they'd made some headway in getting to know each other, though. She smiled. After all, Rome wasn't built in a day. Relationships definitely took time and work and most of all, caring and love. If she wanted a relationship with Sterling, she would have to build it one brick at a time, one day at a time.

Sterling observed Tammy's facial expression and body language as she got into the song. This was the best take of them all. She was really pouring her heart and soul into it. Her memorable performances at the Inner Harbor came to mind. This incredible woman had more talent in her little finger than most singers had in their entire bodies.

"That's it. We'll go with this one," Sterling said with a feeling of satisfaction. He smiled when he saw the relief on the weary musicians' faces. He knew he could be hard-nosed at times, but he had to be that way to pull the best from them.

"I felt that we got it right this time, Sterling," Tammy chirped excitedly as she heard the musicians packing up their instruments to leave.

"I know I've been pushing you pretty hard the last few days. You don't have to tutor Kevin tomorrow if you're too tired," Sterling said to Tammy. "We can postpone it."

"I'll be here the same as usual. I'm not at all tired. In fact, I feel so exhilarated and confident, I'm almost conceited about it. I've never let myself go like that."

He'd love to see her let herself go in other areas, Sterling thought. He'd dreamed about it. Tammy's love was all the reward and accolade he would ever want or need.

"I'll have Marcus drive you home."

"Sterling, about the limo. I don't need to be chauffeured home."

"It's no trouble."

"I wasn't thinking that it was. It's your phobia about driving that concerns me." When she took his hand in hers, she felt him tense. "I know it's not a subject you feel comfortable discussing."

"I know what you're trying to say, but you don't understand."

"You're right, I don't, but I want to."

Sterling hesitated. "Every time I get behind the wheel of a car, I break out in a cold sweat, and my hands begin to shake. My heart races, and I feel like I can't breathe, let alone drive. I keep telling myself the accident was not my fault, but it doesn't matter. I still can't bring myself to drive."

Tammy smiled in sympathy. "I remember the first time I ventured out of my room after I'd lost my sight. I felt the same way. Then one day I decided to bite the bullet and open that door. I was never more frightened than I was at that moment. I kept telling myself it was something I had to do. It wasn't easy, but I did it."

"I know what you're trying to do, Tammy, but it's not the same thing."

"You don't believe you'll ever be ready, do you? The first step is always the hardest."

"You probably think I'm a coward."

"No, I don't. It's something you have to do for yourself. I can tell you what I did, and how other people have handled similar situations, but it's up you to do something about it. You have to want to do it with all your heart. There's nothing I can say or anyone else can say to make it happen for you. Concentrate your energy on overcoming your fears, and you'll be surprised at the results. That's all I'm going to say."

Sterling shook his head. His Tammy was some kind of woman, and he wanted her so very badly. He would do as she said. He would really give some thought to overcoming his problem.

"What's wrong, Kevin? You're not concentrating," Tammy gently scolded her pupil the next afternoon.

"I just don't feel like studying, all right?"

"Maybe we should pack it in for today. Maybe tomorrow you'll feel more like it."

"You been working in the studio with my father the last few weeks."

"And?"

"I was wondering, I mean..." His voiced trailed away.

"You want to know what's going on, don't you?"

"I—yes."

"He and I and some very talented musicians are working on a demo."

"I know that part. It's the personal thing."

How did she explain that? She could tell that Kevin was still worried that she would try and take his mother's place, not so much with him, but with his father.

"Your father and I have grown close. I respect him, and he recognizes my potential. He's easy to be with, and I've come to care for him and you."

"Has he asked you to be his lady?"

"No, he hasn't. But you think he will, don't you?"

Kevin rose to his feet. "I thought you weren't—forget it."

"We care for each other, Kevin, and we care about you."

"Yeah, right. You don't need me around."

"Kevin, have I done or said anything to make you think I didn't want you around?"

"No, I guess not. It's just that—"

"I know how hard it must be for you to adjust to your father's interest in a woman other than your mother. Your father is still a young man. It was bound to happen sometime. If not with me, then with someone else."

Tammy put her arm around his shoulder and squeezed. "I thought we were becoming friends. Friends trust each other, don't they?"

"I guess."

"What's going on?" Sterling asked upon entering the family room.

"Kevin and I were having a discussion about you, his mother and the three of us."

"I'm going to my room," Kevin said, easing from under Tammy's arm to exit the room.

"He still giving you a hard time?"

"Not really. He's concerned about your feelings for me and mine for you. He's wondering where he fits into the picture. He's a confused young man right now, Sterling. His world is changing, and he feels like he doesn't have much say about it. I'd say he was also having an attack of growing pains. It's always hard for a child to see their parents in a personal light. And it's harder for a boy Kevin's age."

"And because he's blind as well as motherless and still blames me for his losses. At least he doesn't display open hostility toward me anymore, only a kind of polite rudeness. Still, it's an improvement for which I have you to thank. You're a miracle worker, Ms. Gibson."

"I'm hardly that, Sterling."

"Never underestimate your power."

"Do I really have power over you?"

"You know you do." He smiled. "I just received a call from one of the record producers who has listened to your demo."

"And?"

"He loves it."

"Oh, Sterling." She reached out to find him. After doing so, she slipped her arms around his neck and kissed him.

"I'll have to give you good news more often if this is the reward I can expect."

"Sterling, I'm so excited. I can't wait to tell Augusta and Derek and D.J., not to mention Mikki."

"I'm still waiting to hear from several others. The only problem I foresee is which recording company to go with." He held Tammy close. He loved seeing her all fired up like this. If he couldn't give her her sight back, at least he could do the next best thing and fulfill her dreams of being a recording superstar.

Tammy was ready to jump out of her chair, her nerves were so sensitized as she and Sterling waited to see Jeremy Ward. She couldn't believe that *the* Jeremy Ward wanted to meet her and that he was actually considering her demo. He was one of the top record producers in the music business.

Sterling smiled. To know he would have an integral part in making her dreams come true was the best turn on in the world. He knew what she was feeling. He remembered the first success he'd had. He couldn't believe it either.

"Mr. Phillips and Ms. Gibson, Mr. Ward will see you now," Jeremy Ward's secretary informed them.

Tammy swallowed hard. "Oh, Sterling, I'm so nervous."

"I know," he said gently as he helped her to her feet and guided her into the producer's private office. He noticed the look of sympathy in the secretary's eyes. She didn't know that Tammy was a strong woman and didn't need it. When they entered Jeremy's office, Sterling noted his surprised reaction when he realized Tammy was blind.

Tammy also picked up on his involuntary gasp, and she tensed. She knew she should be used to that reaction by now, but she wasn't and never would be. She squared her shoulders and smiled.

"So what do you think, Mr. Ward?"

"Have a seat, Ms. Gibson, may I call you Tammy?"

"Yes, of course."

"You have an incredible voice. And please, call me Jeremy. As I told Sterling when I first heard the tape, I believe you should sign with R & B Records. You're exactly what we've been looking for."

Sterling locked gazes with Jeremy.

"Are you acting as her manager or agent?"

Before Sterling could answer, Tammy spoke. "Sterling and I need to have a word in private, Mr. Ward—Jeremy."

"Sure, go ahead, I need to speak with my secretary anyway."

"Thank you," she said, waiting to hear the door close. "We still have several other record companies to talk to, right? So what do you think?"

"I take it I'm acting as your manager/agent?"

"Was there ever any question about that?"

"I believe Jeremy is the best choice, but it would be a good idea to hear the others out. You may want to go with one of them."

"I trust you, Sterling."

Sterling winced. He'd longed to hear her say those words, but would she continue to trust him once she knew who he was?

Tell her, man.

"Tammy—"

Jeremy walked in. "I've taken the liberty of having my secretary record the gist of our usual contract on tape so you can listen to it privately, Tammy. And also a written one for you to look over, Sterling."

"We have several other companies who are interested in signing her with them. We'll have to get back to you, if that's all right."

"That's fine. I'm confident you'll decide to go with R & B. It's been an honor talking with you, Tammy, Sterling."

As they rode in the limo, Tammy took Sterling's hand in hers.

"The president of R & B Records wants me, Tammy Gibson. I can't believe it. He seemed really eager to sign me to a contract."

"You have an unbelievable talent, baby. Why wouldn't he?"

"You have so much confidence in me."

"It's well placed. After we've talked with the other companies and arrived at a decision, we should think about renting a studio."

"Won't yours do?"

"Others have more enhancement features and—"

"I don't care. I feel comfortable in yours."

"If we need more special arrangements, I guess we can take care of those details later. I want everything to be perfect for you, Tammy."

"And it will be. As I said before, I trust you."

Sterling leaned over and kissed her.

Tammy smiled. "The advantage of being blind is that you can surprise me like you just did. I love those spontaneous kisses."

"You're really something, Tammy Gibson."

"So are you." She kissed him back with enthusiasm.

CHAPTER FIFTEEN

"My dreams are firmly and finally on the road to coming true, Mikki," Tammy extolled excitedly.

"Look who you have going to bat for you. I'm telling you, that man really cares for you, girl."

"Don't get ahead of yourself, okay."

"Why shouldn't I? Why shouldn't you? Now if you're going to tell me he's only paying you back for helping his son, I don't want to hear it. The man has asked you out several times, for heaven's sake. Doesn't that tell you something?"

"Maybe. I only know how I feel."

"And how is that?"

"Mikki."

"All right, keep it to yourself. It's plain as the nose on your face that man is crazy about you."

Her relationship with Kevin and Sterling was growing stronger, and as a family unit they were growing closer with each passing day, Tammy thoughtfully admitted to herself. But for some reason, since the interview with Music Stars Recording Company, the last one on the list of possibilities, Sterling had grown more reserved. He was as attentive as ever, but there was something different about him. On the other hand, maybe she was reading more into it than she should.

"You have a meeting with Sterling tomorrow afternoon, don't you?" Mikki asked, breaking into Tammy's reverie.

"Yes, I do. After listening to everything all the other recording companies have said, it's decision-making time."

"Have you talked to Augusta and Derek about any of this?"

"Not yet. But Sterling and I are planning to this evening. We're having dinner with them."

"He's picking you up in the limo, no doubt. You always get the celebrity treatment, and you're not even a superstar yet."

"Now, Mikki."

"You're the only person I know who complains about being chauffeured around in one."

"I'm not complaining exactly, it's just that, never mind."

"Soon it'll be old hat to you, and you'll take it in stride."

"I don't think so."

"Sterling Phillips isn't just trying to impress you by the gesture, is he?"

"Don't get in my business."

"I'm just curious, that's all."

Tammy couldn't blame her companion. With the excitement of a possible album in the not-too-distant future, she hadn't been encouraging Sterling to fight his fears lately, but she would. She wanted to be as supportive as she could, but let him decide when he was ready to tear down that wall.

"D.J. has told us via Kevin about the album. We would have enjoyed learning first hand from the source," Augusta said to Tammy as she, Derek and Sterling sat out on the terrace after dinner.

"I meant to, but I've been so busy."

"Not too busy for your family, I hope?" Derek added.

"I'm never too busy for that. Sterling is acting as my manager."

Derek glanced at Sterling and smiled. "I'd say you couldn't be in better hands."

"Thanks for the vote of confidence, Derek."

"We both feel the same way," Augusta commented. "You sure this move and your work with Kevin won't be too much for you, Tammy?"

"Always the mother hen," Tammy muttered.

"Don't worry, Augusta, I won't let her tire herself out," Sterling affirmed. "Kevin has come a long way since Tammy has been working with him. I feel he's reached the point where he doesn't need personal tutoring anymore."

"Sterling is right. He's more confident and relaxed. Haven't you noticed that lately, Derek, when you work with him?" Tammy asked.

"I have. He's definitely toned down his attitude…"

"There's a *but* coming, right?"

"But he's still fragile where his father is concerned and also your relationship with Sterling. I think it would be a good idea if the three of you spent more personal recreational time together."

"That's a good idea," Tammy said to Sterling. "When we've decided which recording company to go with, I think we should plan on doing just that. What do you think?"

"I agree."

Augusta watched Sterling as they all partook of the buffet supper she'd prepared. She noted that he ate sparingly and popped antacid tablets before and after eating. She wondered if he was suffering from an ulcer.

"You can't stop being a doctor for one minute, can you, doc?" Derek teased.

"I'm busted as D.J. would say."

"You think there could be anything seriously wrong with Sterling?"

"I don't know. I want to suggest he see a colleague of mine who specializes in internal medicine."

"I think you should. Sterling is under a lot of personal stress, along with working so hard to help Tammy. It couldn't hurt. As much as we males believe ourselves to be indestructible, it's a fantasy."

"I can't believe I'm hearing the great Derek Morgan admit to such a thing."

Derek laughed. "All right, watch your mouth."

Just then, D.J. and Kevin came out on the terrace.

"You guys through playing all your new CDs?" Augusta asked her son.

"You heard us, huh?"

"I think half the neighborhood did," Derek quipped.

"I didn't think we were playing them that loud."

"You weren't," Tammy soothed. "Are you enjoying yourself, Kevin?"

"Yes."

Sterling waited for his son to add some sarcastic remark. When he didn't, he shook his head. Kevin's attitude had taken a

180 degree turn. Yes, they would take Derek's advice. Catching Derek alone fifteen minutes later, he asked for some more advice.

"You want to do normal everyday kinds of things with him, Sterling. Make him feel his blindness doesn't have to be a handicap, that he can see things by sharpening and using his other senses," Derek suggested.

"But so many things involve sight."

"When you do things and go places, explain what you see to him and Tammy. Give them vivid pictures they can easily visualize."

"You mean make him feel like he's actually seeing it. Take them to Monterey Bay and describe the porpoises leaping out of the water or the Napa Valley where he can smell the grapes, the earth, feel the sun. I get it. Thanks, Derek. I can take it from here. You have no idea how much you've helped me. I want so much to make my son's life bearable."

"I know you do. It's the way I felt when Augusta was blind."

"Maybe like Augusta, my son will one day get his sight back."

"Anything is possible."

"I wish Tammy could have gotten hers back."

"Me, too. If Augusta hadn't got her sight back, I don't know what I would have done," Derek admitted. "We probably wouldn't be together because my guilt feelings wouldn't have allowed it. You understand what I'm trying to say, don't you?"

"Yes, I do."

"Dr. Eekong didn't hold out much hope that Tammy will ever get her sight back, but he said the body has remarkably amazing regenerative powers and to never give up on its ability to perform miracles. And, of course, there could be a breakthrough at any time."

"Wouldn't it be wonderful if a new technique came along and she could see again?"

"Yes, it would, but if it doesn't happen, she's strong enough to handle it."

"You're right, she is. My Tammy is a survivor."

"You really love her, don't you?"

"With all my heart."

"Then you've got to tell her the truth, man."

❋

"You're so happy, Tammy. I love seeing you like this," Augusta said as she guided her foster daughter through the garden.

"It's all because of Sterling, Augusta. He knows me so well. We share the same love of music. I think we make an awesome dynamic duo, him writing the songs and me singing them. We have an incredible rapport. I don't think anything can hurt what we have together."

Augusta frowned. Sterling definitely needed to tell Tammy the truth. She hated to think about what could happen if he waited too long. She recalled the pain she'd felt when Derek revealed the truth about himself. She didn't want that to happen to Tammy, but some pain couldn't be averted. Tammy was bound to be hurt, no matter when she learned the truth.

"You're kind of quiet, Augusta. Do you have reservations about my decision to pursue a singing career?"

"No. I think it's what you need. I was just thinking of your personal relationship with Sterling."

Tammy smiled. "That's coming along. I have never felt this close, this connected, to a man. Not even David. Sterling is such a wonderful person."

"You love him, don't you?"

Tammy didn't answer.

"You do, but you're afraid to call it that. After what you went through with David, it's understandable that you'd be wary. To put your heart in someone else's hands can be scary, but it can also be a very beautiful thing, Tammy. With love there are no guarantees. You know that, don't you?"

"Oh, I do."

"I want you to stay as happy as you are right now. If Sterling Phillips is what you need, go after him."

"I feel that he could be, but I'm taking things slow, letting our relationship grow."

"I don't believe you'll have any trouble with Kevin. He seems to be adjusting to the idea."

"I think you're right about that. I've finally managed to convince him that I'm not trying to take his mother's place, that I just want one of my own. We still have a few problems to iron out, but on the whole I think everything will work out in time."

"I like being with your family, Tammy," Sterling said as they sat on the couch in her living room an hour later.

"I'm glad. Now about which recording company to sign with…"

"You know I'm leaning toward R & B Records, although the deal Ace Records is offering is pretty solid," Sterling said. "What do you think?"

"I feel comfortable with Jeremy. He seems more attuned to my feelings and my situation. Having his secretary record the contract so I could listen to it was a very thoughtful gesture."

"Jeremy is like that. I've known him for years. Another thing about him is that he doesn't mind spending money to keep his performers happy."

"Then I think we should go with him."

"I'll have my attorney look over the contract to make sure it covers everything. If it checks out, then I'll call Jeremy and arrangement for you to go down and sign the contract."

Sterling drew Tammy into his arms and just held her.

"I can picture you holding your first Grammy for best new vocalist, and after that, for best performer in the BET Awards, then—"

"Whoa. I know you have confidence in me, but aren't you getting a little carried away."

"No, I'm not. You just don't realize how good you really are, but I intend to open your eyes, lady." He started singing his own rendition of the song "You Gotta Be A Special Lady."

"You're crazy, do you know that?"

"Yes, crazy about you." Then he sang the words to "I'm Crazy About You," by Jeffrey Osborne.

Tammy stopped the flow with a kiss.

"You keep that up and I won't want to go home."

"It might be kind of nice to have you stick around for a while."

"How long is a while?" He kissed her eyelids, her nose and then the sensitive area behind her ear. He got even more aroused when he heard her little moan of pleasure. He cleared his throat. "I'd better go."

"Do you have to? Isn't Kevin spending the night with D. J.?"

"Yes, but do you have any idea what being here with you like this is doing to me?"

"I know what it's doing to me."

"Are you ready for the kind of relationship your actions suggest?"

Tammy was silent.

"I didn't think so. There's no need to rush what's developing between us. When the time is right, we'll make love."

"You're a special man, Sterling Phillips."

"Because I turned down your invitation to jump my bones?"

"You!" She laughed, punching him in the arm.

"I love hearing you laugh. I love quite a few things about you, Tammy Gibson."

"Do go on."

"Maybe another time. It's time you went upstairs and went to bed."

"Yes, sir."

"Don't think for a moment I wouldn't love to take you up those stairs and make wild, passionate love to you. When we make love, I know I'll lose all sense of control."

"I'm looking forward to that."

Tammy walked Sterling to the door. He kissed her one more time. She felt the tingling sensation down to her toes. That this man could really kiss there was no doubt. She could only imagine what it would be like to make love with him.

"You really blow a girl's mind."

"That's not all I want to do to a certain woman. Good night."

"Good night, Sterling."

"I'll call you when I know anything about the contract nego-tiations."

Tammy leaned against the door after Sterling left. They could have made love tonight. What was holding her back?

Like Augusta said, you're afraid.

Afraid of what?

Of yourself more than likely. Love means taking a risk. Are you ready and willing to do that?

I don't know.

You'd better find out pretty soon.

CHAPTER SIXTEEN

"The demo was just a warm up exercise, Tammy. Wait until we get down to business and really start working on the album," Sterling commented as they sat on the couch in his living room.

Tammy smiled, recalling how she'd felt when she signed the recording contract with R & B Records the day before. "I'm not a complete novice at this, you know. I have worked on other albums before. And I definitely remember what it's like."

"That may very well be true, but you've never worked with me on one before."

"You mean you're even worse than when we were working on the demo?"

"Tip of the iceberg, dear heart."

"I don't know if I like the sound of that."

"You may end up hating my guts by the time we're finished. I insist on perfection or as close to it as we can come."

"I've been warned. When do you think we'll be able to start working on it?"

"Next week if all goes as planned. I told Jeremy you wanted to work in my studio. He said if we need any special arrangements, he'll put his studio at our disposal at any time. He doesn't do that for just anybody. He's a stickler for schedules. You've evidently made quite an impression on him."

"Is he the only one I've made an impression on?"

Sterling turned to her and slipped his arms around her waist. "Most definitely not," he said huskily.

She smiled at him and snuggled closer. "Kevin actually seemed interested in what we're doing. He asked me if he could sit in when we record. You have no idea how that makes me feel."

"I think I do. Derek's idea that we do things and go places together like a family is a good one. What are your thoughts on taking a trip to the Napa Valley this weekend?"

"Sounds delicious. Kevin should enjoy that. I know I did when Augusta and Derek took me there a couple of years ago. The tart fragrance of grapes and the pungent smell of warm, sun-kissed earth is stimulating. To learn how they grow grapes and the process they use to turn them into wine should interest Kevin. I remember sampling quite a few varieties of grapes and wines."

"Did you get tipsy?"

"I won't answer that on the grounds it might tend to incriminate me." She laughed.

"I'd love to see your face flushed from the wine and taste your lips afterward. I know they'd be sweet."

"You do have a way with words, Mr. Phillips."

"Does that mean you want me to continue?"

"Hold that thought until this weekend."

"You're a cruel woman, Ms. Gibson."

"Not at all. The wait isn't going to be easy for me either. I'm really looking forward to spending time with you and Kevin."

Sterling liked the sound of that. She was imagining how it would be for the three of them if they were a family. His conscience pricked him. He knew he should tell her the truth about himself, but decided he would wait until he was sure she felt secure in their relationship. When that happened, maybe it wouldn't change her feelings for him when she found out. He knew her feelings for Kevin wouldn't change. But what about her feelings where he and she were concerned? He shuddered to think how he would feel if… He didn't want to even think about that possibility.

Who are you trying to fool? No matter when you tell her, she'll be hurt, and she may never want to see you again. You'd better face reality, man.

"Sterling."

"What were you saying?"

"You seem preoccupied. Is anything wrong?" she asked, searching for his hand.

"No, nothing is wrong. I was just raking over a problem, that's all."

"Does the problem have anything to do with the album?"

"It's a lot to think about. I can barely contain my impatience to get started."

"I have to admit, I'm more than a little anxious about that myself."

"Don't worry. You'll do just fine. I'll be there every step of the way to help you. Even in the times when you want to throw things at me for being such a tyrant."

"You think you'll be safe because I can't see you, don't you? You remember Luke Skywalker in *Star Wars*? Obi-Wan had him blindfolded when training him to be a Jedi."

"Yes, I remember. Are you warning me that you can find me under any circumstances?"

"I'm sure there are parts on you I'd like to zero in on."

"Like?"

"Like these." She found his lips and kissed him thoroughly.

He groaned. "Anywhere else?"

"You're bad."

"Not as bad as I'd like to be. When I make love to you, woman, I'm going to let you explore me until your little heart is content."

"That a promise?"

"You'd better believe it. Now, I've made tapes of the songs I've written for the album, and I want you to take them home and familiarize yourself with the words until you're humming them in your sleep. I want the music to feel as familiar to you as your skin, the beating of your heart, reaching deep into your very soul."

"You don't ask for much do you?"

"I don't ask for anything; I demand everything. I want you to know that about me."

"I'm beginning to."

"You didn't know what you were getting into when you got hooked up with me, did you?"

"I think I can handle it."

"I know you can." He kissed her. The taste of her was driving him crazy. "Oh, girl," he moaned when she kissed him back.

Tammy felt her insides melt. She realized for the first time how desperately she wanted this man. She hadn't trusted any man completely over the years. Only Brent Stevens had ever come close emotionally. It was different somehow with Sterling. Was he really different? Or was it that she wanted so badly to believe he was?

"Daddy?"

Sterling let Tammy go. "What is it, son?" he asked as he watched Kevin make his way into the living room.

"Miss Gibson."

"I'm here."

"I know, I smelled your perfume."

"Very good. You're really learning how to use your other senses. I'm proud of you."

Kevin smiled. Sterling observed his son's expression. He hadn't seen very many smiles on his son's face over the last three years. That Tammy was able to put one there so easily humbled him. She was important to him and his son. He wanted her in their life more than he'd ever wanted anything. The nagging feeling that he could lose her before he really got her made his heart ache. He knew he would have to tell her the truth and soon. But how could he when he knew it would hurt her?

"You gonna eat dinner with us this evening, Miss Gibson?" Kevin asked Tammy.

"Will you?" Sterling grazed Tammy's cheek with his fingers.

"If the both of you want me to."

"I do," Kevin said eagerly.

Sterling confirmed it with an, "I second the motion. It's unanimous. You stay."

"How can I refuse an invitation like that?"

"You can't, so don't even think about it."

"I won't," she said softly. A feeling tender and warm flooded her being. Had she at last found what she needed to be a whole woman? Only time would tell, and she intended to enjoy every minute of the discovery. "You can call me Tammy, Kevin."

Tammy instructed Kevin where the different foods were on the table using clockwise directions, reminding him that he had to do these things for himself, not wait for his father to fix a plate for him. She smiled when she didn't hear a single complaint. A few weeks ago, Kevin would have defiantly refused to follow her instruction and waited for his father to fix his plate.

Sterling nodded his head in approval. Tammy had indeed worked miracles with Kevin. She was the perfect buffer between father and son. Kevin didn't voice or display any hostility toward him when Tammy was around. He was also no longer as withdrawn or defensive with her anymore. In fact, he seemed genuinely fond of her now.

"It's time for me to go," Tammy said to Sterling later that evening. Kevin had already gone up to his room.

Sterling reached for the phone. "I'll call Marcus to—"

"There isn't much traffic this time of night. You could drive me home."

"Tammy—I—can't."

"If you took it slow and easy you—"

"No. I'll get Marcus to take you home. I know what you're trying to do, and I appreciate it, but I'm just not ready."

"What would it take to get you ready? A life-threatening emergency?"

Sterling was silent.

"You should be mentally preparing yourself for that possibility. Who knows, the decision whether to drive or not to drive may be taken out of your hands one day."

Sterling didn't say another word on the subject. He just picked up the phone and called Marcus. Within minutes, the driver arrived around front.

"I want you to know this is not the end of it. I'm not giving up on you, Sterling Phillips."

"I didn't think for a moment that you were."

The Napa Valley lay one hour north of San Francisco. As Marcus drove through the Carneros Wine District, Sterling regaled Tammy and Kevin with the history of the Napa Valley. He disclosed that the planting of grapes had begun big time when the Hungarian Colonel Agoston Harazthy started Buena Vista vineyards in 1857, and that the rivalry between vineyards was in full swing when Charles Krug introduced an easier, faster way to press grapes by using an apple press.

Just before they reached the turn off to Sonoma, Sterling had Marcus drive through the Buena Vista vineyards, where they stopped to taste several varieties of the Americanized sweet Tokay grapes that originated in Hungary. Then he described in vivid detail how the stagecoaches that traveled between the farms and Sonoma looked before they proceeded on to Sonoma's rival city of Napa.

Sterling had Marcus stop at Celadon's so they could feast on their famous Maine crab cakes. Then they toured the Firefighter's Museum. Sterling described how the old fire-fighter equipment looked and Kevin was allowed to touch the old relics when the tour guide realized he was blind.

Sterling enjoyed the look of pleasure that came over Tammy's face when she tasted a particularly good vintage of Chardonnay at the Napa Cellars later that afternoon. They also went to the Napa Valley Museum and several other wineries before heading back to San Francisco.

Kevin yawned and stretched when his father awakened him after they arrived home. The day had gone even better than Sterling had hoped it would.

"I'll be smelling grapes and dirt for the next six months."

"Me too," Tammy said. "What about you, Kevin?"

"I didn't know it took so many different kinds of grapes to make one wine."

"You enjoyed going to Napa, then?" Sterling asked.

"Yes. It was so cool. Miss Gib—I mean, Tammy made learning about grapes more like fun."

"It's exciting learning how to tell when grapes reach their peak of ripeness by smell. You don't need sight to do that. Mr. Angelino said you were a natural, Kevin," Tammy related.

"He did say he'd like to hire me for my keen sense of smell. It would be my job to let him know when the grapes were ready to be picked. He said that was one of the things the grape-picking machines couldn't do."

Sterling could see how positive the trip had been for Kevin. Thanks to Tammy and what Mr. Angelino had said, his son was really feeling good about himself and accepting that being blind wasn't the end of the world.

"I'm not going to get out," Tammy said to Sterling. "All that fresh air and sunshine has really done me in. Not to mention all the samples of wine I've tasted. All I want to do is go home, soak in a hot tub, then go straight to bed."

"Sounds like a good idea." Sterling helped a tired Kevin out of the limo and instructed Marcus to drive Tammy home.

"You like Tammy, don't you?" Sterling asked Kevin after the limo headed out the drive.

"Yeah, she's all the way cool, just like D.J. said she was."

"I'm glad you do."

"You thinking about marrying her?"

"It's too early for that. She may not even want to marry me."

"Oh, I think she'll say yes when you ask her."

"What makes you so sure?"

"I just know, that's all."

"How would you feel about it if she did?"

"I don't know."

"You're not still worried that she's trying to take your mother's place?"

"No. Like she said, she can't do that. Nobody can."

"You've come to accept your mother's death, haven't you?"

"It's not like I have any choice. She's gone and nobody can ever bring her back."

"How do you feel about the accident?"

"I don't want to talk about it."

"All right, I won't push you, but one day we're going to have to talk about it."

Kevin shrugged, unfolded his cane and headed toward the house.

CHAPTER SEVENTEEN

If she could see, Tammy was sure the man cracking the whip would look more like a troll than a man when she and the crew did "I'll Always be There for You," yet again. For the twentieth time that day, she was realizing Sterling hadn't been kidding when he'd said he was a relentless taskmaster. But what he'd failed to add was that he also happened to be a real honest to goodness tyrant.

"You missed the last cue, Tammy," Sterling said via the head set in a patient, child-to-parent voice.

He had warned her what he was like when he was working on an album. Now that she'd experienced it, she had to wonder if she really wanted him to always be there for her when he was like this. But when she recalled Sterling's thoughtfulness in having a special recording device installed in her head set which prompted the words in case she'd forgotten them, it deflated her exasperation. But later after they'd gone over the same song for what seemed like the thousandth time, Tammy was ready to throw things."One more time," Sterling said to Tammy then signaled to the background singers and the musicians. He had to smile. It was a good thing recording studios were soundproof. He was sure that if his nearest neighbors had heard all the times the music had been repeated, it would have driven them crazy, because he and his crew had redone this one particular piece countless times.

Tammy found her water glass, drank deeply, then readied

herself to do yet another take of that same track. A feeling that somehow this time would be the charm came over her, and she poured her heart and soul into the song like never before.

"Beautiful, Tammy," Sterling extolled, satisfaction adding sparkle to his words. "It's perfect. We'll go with this one."

"Hallelujah," shouted one of the musicians.

"Amen," chorused the background singers.

Kevin, who had walked in between recordings and had been listening intently for the last hour said, "That was awesome, Tammy."

She smiled. "I think so too, Kevin." Sterling was a perfectionist, and like Quincy Jones, had an uncanny ability for knowing when his singers had given him their best. Tammy felt lightheaded, and her entire being filled up with profound joy, secure in the realization that she had created several standout masterpieces so far.

Sterling had a buffet supper catered in, which they all dug into with relish. He watched the interaction between Tammy, the musicians, the background singers and Kevin. She never failed to include Kevin in the conversation. What a woman. God, he admired and loved her more and more with each passing day, if that were possible.

A dull ache started in his upper abdomen and radiated upward into his chest. Sterling reached inside his shirt pocket for his antacid tablets. He had begun to notice lately that they didn't work as well as they once had, and he was considering going to see a doctor. He wondered if he had developed an ulcer or the beginnings of one. As soon as they finished this album, he'd follow through and make that appointment.

Although Sterling and company were down to the last two songs on the album, the session was turning into a never-ending story. No matter how many times they recorded and re-recorded the next to the last track, it never seemed to turn out quite right.

"Sterling, I thought the last recording on 'Believe Me' was good," Tammy complained.

"It is, but it's not good enough, so we'll do it again until we get it right." He signaled the musicians and the background singers to get ready. "All right, Tammy, when you hear the prompt, give it all you've got."

Tammy sighed in frustration. Hadn't she been doing that? She started slowly counting to ten. If it wasn't perfect this time, she'd scream just before strangling a certain producer.

"Stop. The beginning notes on the chorus just aren't right. Let's run through it again."

"Sterling!"

"Again, Tammy," he commanded firmly.

They did it again and again and again before Sterling finally called a break. Groans could be heard among the musicians as well as the background singers as they filed out of the studio.

"Tammy," Kevin called to her.

"Yes, Kevin, what is it?"

He made his way over to the piano. "I want you to hear

something."

"All right, go ahead."

Kevin played the music and sang the words, rearranging the sequence of the notes as he did so.

"Do it again, son," Sterling encouraged. "I believe you've solved our problem."

"I think so, too. Thank you so much, Kevin." Tammy slipped her arm around his shoulder, giving it an affectionate squeeze. "Maybe I should have you join the background singers. Would you like to do that?"

"If you want me to."

"We do, Kevin." Tammy smiled.

After two more tries, they got it perfect, and Sterling praised them all, happy to see the satisfied smiles lighting their faces and triumph resounding in their voices.

"Only one more song to go and we'll be home free," Tammy shouted happily.

"Then we have to run it all by Jeremy," Sterling reminded her. To the musicians and background singers, he said, "You've all done a great job. Go home and rest up for tomorrow." To his son he said in a gentle, proud voice, "You were incredible, Kevin."

"I'd say musical genius runs in the family, wouldn't you?" Tammy remarked.

"I agree."

Kevin rose from the piano bench. "I can hardly wait to tell D.J. that I'm going to be singing with you on your album. He'll want to play his guitar with the musicians."

"And we just might let him." Sterling laughed as he watched Kevin leave the studio.

"Are you serious?" Tammy put her hand over his. "Would you, Sterling?"

"Your little brother is very good on the guitar. Yes, I would."

"You're the best, Sterling."

"You really think so? I could have sworn that not more than a couple of hours ago, I heard you mention something about committing violence on my person."

"Like D.J. would say, I'm busted."

"I'll let you make it up to me over dinner tomorrow night."

"I thought we'd be working on that last song all day tomorrow."

"No, I've changed my mind. I think you and the background singers need to rest your voices for a couple of days. I'm sure the musicians won't complain about the time off. Then when you come back, we'll wrap things up."

"I can't believe the tyrant that's been driving us so hard for the past few weeks is actually letting us off the hook so easily."

"Not off completely, it's only a stay of execution."

"That sounds about right." Tammy shook her head and laughed wryly. "Can you come to my house for dinner at, say, seven?"

"You're not going to lace the mashed potatoes with arsenic, are you? Or baste the barbecue chicken in hemlock sauce?"

"Those are some great suggestions. But no, I won't end your days just yet. You have to finish producing my album first."

"You mean you only want me for my music expertise and not my body. I feel crushed."

Tammy kissed him. "Does that make you feel better?"

"A little."

Tammy kissed him again, longer this time. "Better?"

Sterling drew her into his arms and kissed her until she was breathless. "Yes, much better."

Tammy thought her insides would melt when his lips moved over hers in yet another soul-shattering kiss. Mikki was right. Sterling Phillips was definitely a good kisser.

He's probably an even better lover. Do you intend to find out from hands-on experience? an inner voice taunted.

Sterling knew the exact moment her mood changed. He wondered what Tammy was thinking. Was she comparing his lovemaking to David's? Or some other man's?

It's your guilty conscience talking, man. You've got to tell her the truth.

Sterling eased Tammy out of his embrace. "I'd better have Marcus drive you home. I'll see you at seven tomorrow evening."

Tammy wondered what she had done to make him react this way. Had he sensed her apprehension? She had to learn to trust again, and come to grips with her feelings. Sterling would never hurt her the way David had.

"I'll be looking forward to it. Oh, and one other thing."

"Yes?"

"You have to leave your slave driving personality in the studio."

"All right. You got a deal."

"Would you please sit down and relax. You're driving me up the wall, Tammy!" Mikki exclaimed. "Everything is perfect.

Sterling will be here any minute. But you're not nervous, right?"

"Mikki, you don't understand."

"Oh, I think I do. For some reason, this evening is very important to you."

"Yes, it is if you must know."

"Why? Do you think he'll ask you to marry him?"

"No, of course not. It's too soon for that."

"Gotcha. You're really serious about him, aren't you?"

"I'm getting there."

"I'd say you've already arrived. And I also say Sterling Phillips has melted that icy wall you've built around your heart."

"Let's not go into that tonight, okay?"

"I'm glad for you, Tammy. I believe he really cares for you."

"You've said that before. Why do you think that?"

"What I saw in that man's eyes definitely wasn't gratitude."

Tammy shrugged in reply.

"I'll leave you alone for now, but I expect a full report in the morning. I'm spending the evening with Wiley, so don't expect me back until later, much later, if you get my meaning. Got to give you and the hunk plenty of time to, ah, get acquainted."

"Mikki, you're impossible."

The doorbell rang.

"That's probably Wiley. The table's set. All you need is to have Sterling light the candles. I'm sure you can take it from there."

Tammy felt butterflies fluttering in her stomach when fifteen minutes later she heard the bell. It was Sterling this time.

"I brought you flowers. I'm not going to tell you what they are, I'm going to let you guess, using your super powers."

"Super powers?"

"No more subterfuge."

Tammy breathed in the sent of lilacs, daisies and another flower she couldn't recognize. "This is not your ordinary garden variety bouquet, is it?"

"No, it's not. I knew if I gave you roses, you'd guess right away."

"And you love presenting me with challenges."

"But of course. What woman wants a boring, predictable man?"

"You're something else."

"And is that a quality you like about me?"

"What do you think?"

Sterling noticed the dress Tammy had on. With her bronzed brown skin and black hair, she looked beautiful in her peach sundress. His appreciative gaze lingered on her face, and he swallowed hard. She had the most kissable lips... He felt himself harden and his palms began to sweat. God, how he wanted to make love to this woman.

"The matches are on the buffet. Would you light the candles while I bring in the dinner?"

He wanted to tell her that the candles weren't the only thing he wanted to set fire to, or the dinner he wanted to taste and savor, but he didn't. She'd gone to a lot of trouble. And he knew she'd probably fixed it all herself. Derek had mentioned that Tammy had taken cooking classes at the Institute and that Mikki only helped her with difficult dishes. The smells drifting from the kitchen were delicious. He lit the candles.

He was glad she'd decided on baked chicken, mashed potatoes and green beans. He preferred simple dishes since he'd been having stomach problems. He patted his jacket pocket where he kept his antacid tablets.

"Would you like something to drink?" Tammy asked Sterling after they'd finished eating their dinner.

"No, the wine with dinner was enough for me, although I wouldn't mind getting intoxicated on you, Ms. Gibson. Care to dance?"

"Dance?"

"Do you remember when I asked you to dance at the fund raiser dinner? I told you I wasn't a Gregory Hines, but that I hadn't stepped on any ladies' toes recently."

"Yes, I remember." She laughed. "And as I recall, you didn't step on mine then, so I guess my toes are safe this evening."

"I hope you'll eventually trust me with much more than that."

"Why don't you choose some music while I clear the table?"

Sterling started to offer his help, but knew how defensive the blind got when they thought you didn't trust them to see to the simplest tasks. He'd learned a great deal from Derek, Tammy and his son on the subject.

He chose Jeffrey Osborne's recent CD, "That's for Sure," then an old one by Mariah Carey. He could tell by her music collection that Tammy liked slow jamming ballads. He noticed that she had several CDs by singers who'd recorded some of the songs he'd written like the one by Crecia, called "Lover Man." He hoped that one day Tammy would let him be hers.

As they danced, Sterling closed his eyes, reveling in the feel of Tammy's warm, soft body nestled in his arms as they swayed in time to the music. Her perfume wafted up his nostrils, completely intoxicating him. He loved holding her like this, and he wanted to do it for the rest of his life.

For that to happen, you have to tell her the truth.

"Tammy, it's as if I've known you all my life. We seem so perfectly attuned to each other."

"I feel the same way. I never thought it would happen again."

"You mean because you were hurt and disillusioned in the past?"

"Yes, but that was a long time ago."

"And have you really gotten over it?'

"I believe I have. When I fell in love with David, we were teenagers. And even though we were so young, I felt that we had a special bond. I was so sure that he loved me as much as I loved him."

"And he didn't?"

"Evidently not. He never came to the hospital to see me. I guess finding out I would be blind turned him off."

"Maybe he felt responsible and was afraid to face you."

"He still should have come to see me. I can forgive him for the accident, but I'll never forgive him for abandoning me afterward."

Sterling's heart sank. He couldn't tell her now; she would hate him. Maybe after he'd helped make some of her dreams come true, she could find it in her heart to forgive him. He would eventually have to tell her the truth. There was no getting around it.

"I don't want to talk about David or the accident. I'm sure talk of accidents still makes you feel uncomfortable since—you know what I'm trying to say."

"Yes. And you're right. When I think about Kevin—and Kayla…"

"I understand. Do you think we have a hit with the album so far?"

"I do, but then I'm the producer. After Jeremy hears it and gives his opinion, I'll decide. My gut feeling is this album will go to the top in record time, maybe even earn you a Grammy nomination for best new recording artist of the year."

"And I predict that you'll get nominated for best song-writer, and you'll deserve it, Sterling. I love the songs. I guess when you pushed me to put my soul into it, it's the reason the finished product sounds so perfect."

"You mean you take back what you said about me being a tyrant, a slave driver and so on and so on?"

"I don't know if I would go quite that far. You are both of those things and a few more you failed to mention."

"At least you're honest." He laughed. "No soft soap treatment. I've really enjoyed dinner, but I'd better call Marcus to pick me up. I know I should be trying to conquer my phobia, but I didn't drive myself over."

"I'm sorry I can't conquer it for you."

"It's something I have to do myself."

"And you will."

"You really believe that I will, don't you?"

"Of course. You'll do it in your own good time."

"I know you're right." He took out his cell phone and called Marcus.

While he waited, they talked about the next recording session and what they thought Jeremy's reaction might be to the finished product. Then they heard a car horn.

"That'll be Marcus. Walk me to the door."

Tammy did. "I'll report to your house at eight sharp day after tomorrow, ready 'to lift that bale, tote that barge.'"

"And I'll be happy to let you in so I can start cracking the whip."

"I hope you won't lash me too hard, Massa Sterling."

"You're crazy, you know that?"

"Yes, so you keep telling me," she replied before singing the first few bars of, "I'm Crazy About You," by Jeffrey Osborne.

Sterling drew Tammy into his arms and lowered his mouth to hers. When he heard her low sensual moan of pleasure, he deepened the kiss.

When he finally let her come up for air, Tammy said, "You're dynamite on a girl's senses."

"And when the right time comes, I'm going to look forward to watching you explode."

"And will you explode with me?"

"Oh, honey, yes." Then he kissed her one more time before heading down the walk to the limo.

Tammy frowned as she heard the limo drive away. She'd been ready to do anything he asked and was sure he was ready to follow through until they got off on the subject of accidents. Then his ardor had subsided. She knew he felt responsible for his wife's death. That had to be it. Well, the next time they wouldn't talk about anything close to that subject. She smiled because she knew there would be a next time with

Sterling and many more besides. She could feel it. It was only a matter of time before they made love.

CHAPTER EIGHTEEN

It was four o'clock in the afternoon, and Tammy, the musicians and the background singers still hadn't done a satisfactory track of the last song on the album. Tammy was so tired, she wanted to kill Sterling "the Slave Driver" Phillips. D.J. had joined them in this song as had Kevin.

When Sterling finally called a break, Tammy avoided talking to him and decided to hang out with the boys.

"I don't know what's wrong," Tammy complained. "The song is beautiful and the music—something about it when we do the chorus just doesn't gel, but I can't put my finger on it."

D.J. played the music part of the chorus on his guitar and Kevin sang the words.

"I've got it," D.J. said excitedly. "Before you come in, Tammy, I think there needs to be a build up to that high A. Listen while I play."

Tammy listened as D.J. played, and so did the musicians. They soon picked up on what he was doing and joined in. At the right time Tammy sang the chorus, and then Kevin and the background singers came in.

"That's perfect," Sterling said from the doorway. "I want you all to do it again just that way."

Later, after several more minor changes, they completed a track that satisfied Sterling.

"We're finally finished with this album. I don't think I want to step foot inside another recording studio for the next six years," Tammy rasped hoarsely.

Concern came into Sterling's voice. "You need something for your throat. "I didn't realize I'd pushed you that hard. I'm sorry."

"I'll be all right. That last track was beautiful, Sterling. Kevin, you sounded good doing the harmony. And D.J., you really have a good ear for note modulation. I'll have to put in a good word for you with Derek."

"You will?"

"And so will I," Sterling added. "Now I'm going to see that Jeremy gets these tracks this evening."

That night, Tammy was so excited she couldn't settle down to sleep and got up and played the copy tracks of all the songs on her album. They were outstanding. They were more than that; they were perfect. Jeremy had to like them, he just had to.

"Can't sleep, huh?" Mikki asked as she entered the living room.

"I didn't mean to wake you."

"That's all right. What's wrong?"

"Nothing is wrong. I'm just hyper about finishing the album. Sterling took the final tracks to Jeremy, and I'm waiting on pins and needles to hear what he thinks of the album."

"He'll love it if this song is any indication. I have to say, it's really something special."

"This is the song we had the most trouble with until my genius brother ironed out the bugs. D.J. and Kevin are so talented. That voice you hear in the background is Kevin's."

"Looks like this album is turning into a family affair."

"You're right, it is."

"If this Jeremy doesn't like it, there's something wrong with him. If the rest of the album sounds anything like this, you have a chart buster on your hands."

"Thank you for saying that, Mikki."

"It's only the truth."

"Now if only Jeremy agrees with us."

"This is fantastic, Sterling. Tammy Gibson has the voice of an angel. By the way, on the last couple of songs I heard a very unusual voice in the background."

"That was my son."

"He has a voice that stands out, but doesn't overpower Tammy's. I think with a few lessons, he could be great. We can only hope that once his voice changes, it mellows and enriches the quality. I'm getting ahead of myself. I don't know if you even want him to embark on a music career."

"If it's what Kevin wants, I won't stand in his way. About the album," he said anxiously.

"There are a few places that need enhancing, but only a little. I like it now as it is, but with the additions I have in mind… You've done it again, Sterling. You've written at least seven stand-out hits on the album. And you thought you'd never write again."

"All I needed was Tammy for my inspiration."

"You're in love with her, aren't you?"

"Is it that obvious?"

"I'm afraid so. Have you told her how you feel?"

"Not yet. There are problems."

"Aren't there always? From what I've observed when the two of you are together, she has deep feelings for you."

"You really think so?"

"Yes, I do."

"I hope you're right."

"When are you going to tell her?"

"I don't know, man. It's complicated."

"My money's on you. As for the songs, you're a genius with lyrics. I predict that by the time Grammy season rolls around, you two will be engaged or even married."

"Do you have gypsy blood, or are you psychic?"

"Neither, I just know love when I see it."

"I knew there was a reason why I've always liked you, Jeremy."

"I expect an invitation to your wedding."

"Don't worry, you'll get one. What day next week do you want me and the crew come to your studio?"

"Bright and early first thing Monday morning of course."

Waiting to hear how her album was faring was the longest month Tammy had ever lived. Though local radio stations raved about it, and she'd heard good reviews from stations in Los Angeles and Texas, she was waiting word from Nashville and New York City. One afternoon near the end of the month, her phone rang.

"Tammy, baby, are you sitting down?" Sterling asked when she picked up the phone.

"Sterling, tell me!"

"Jeremy just heard from Lance Cummings. He and his people want to work with you on a video."

"Oh, Sterling," she sniffed.

"Are you crying?"

"I can't help it. You know who Lance Cummings is. He's only the best when it comes to directing and producing award-winning music videos. And he wants to work with *me!*"

"It means you've arrived. The man's not stupid, he knows a good thing when he hears it."

"I'm so excited I can't stand it."

"Cummings predicts that your album will break or almost break all the records for the speed with which a new album reaches the top of the charts. It's being played on every major R & B station across the country. I think that calls for a celebration. I'm going to throw you one of the biggest parties this town has ever seen."

"The party I have in mind is a very private one."

"After the big one I'm going to throw, you mean."

"Before."

"Before? But I thought you'd want to have the big one first."

"We'll have that one because I can't deny you anything. And I do owe my instant success to you."

"Your talent is the real star. You have one hell of an incredible voice, Ms. Gibson."

"Without the fabulous songs you wrote for me, no one would know that. We make a great team, don't you think."

"I agree, we do."

"And since you've talked me into having a public celebration, I insist that we have our own private celebration tonight."

"Your place or mine? Since Kevin will be spending the night with your brother, the choice is yours."

"Are you trying to seduce me over the telephone?"

"Is it working?"

"Send the limo for me, or better yet, come and get me yourself."

"You don't give up, do you?"

"Never. You should know that about me by now. I predict that you'll be driving yourself and me around very soon."

"People are making a lot of predictions lately."

"Most of them have been coming true, haven't they? And this one will, too."

Sterling wished he could predict how she would take the truth once she knew it. He wouldn't worry about it today. Right now he had a lot to do before his lady arrived.

Tammy had Mikki take her shopping. She wanted to wear something special for this special night.

"Seeing you like this—I told you you'd have something to celebrate, and I don't mean your singing career either."

"I'll concede that you were right, Mikki. You've got to help me pick out a dress. I want you to describe each one in vivid detail so I can imagine the look on Sterling's face when he sees me."

"Here's a mint green slip dress." Mikki moved Tammy's fingers over the material.

"There doesn't seem to be much to it."

"It's the way they're wearing them these days. Either that or down to the floor."

"Maybe I should make it a long dress. I don't have legs like Tina Turner, Mikki."

"You don't have to with a figure like yours. You're one of those rare people who look good in anything. I'm jealous."

"Yeah, right. Wiley is crazy about how you look. Isn't he coming over again tonight?"

"Yes, he certainly is. He's so much fun to be with, and he's fine to the bone on top of that."

"Can't ask for a better combination than that. Now back to the subject of what to wear."

✳

"Kevin, are you ready?" Sterling called up the stairs to his son.

"I'm checking to make sure I haven't forgotten anything."

"You're only going to be gone for two days."

"I heard you pacing back and forth. Everything all right between you and Tammy?"

"Yes, why do you ask?"

"I don't know. You just seem nervous or somethin'."

"This is a special occasion, and I want everything to be perfect, that's all."

"It's got to be. Those catering people have sure been busy. You're really going all out, aren't you?"

Sterling's eyes narrowed. "That doesn't bother you, does it?"

"No. I told you I think Tammy is cool."

"Yes, you did." Sterling glanced at his watch. Where in the hell was Marcus? He was supposed to be here to take Kevin over to the Morgan's and then pick up Tammy. Sterling let out a frustrated groan. He had to calm down or he'd drive himself crazy before the evening began.

He walked over to the window and glanced out. A few minutes later, he smiled and breathed in a sigh of relief when he saw Marcus drive up. After Kevin had climbed into the limo and was gone, Sterling checked to make sure everything was ready. He had in mind showing Tammy just how much he wanted her. And not for just tonight, but for always.

CHAPTER NINETEEN

Even though the idea for a private celebration was Tammy's, she couldn't understand why she was having a sudden attack of nerves when she heard Marcus cut the limo's engine after the short fifteen minute drive to Sterling's house.

Don't kid yourself, girlfriend. You know good and well why you're nervous.

Yes, she did know or had a pretty good idea where this party would most likely end: in Sterling's bedroom. Was that where she wanted it to end? End? It would hardly be the end, more like the beginning of a special intimate relationship. She had to ask herself if she was really ready for this. It wasn't as though Sterling's desire for her was in question; it wasn't, nor was hers for him.

She was sure he felt more than just simple desire for her. In fact, she believed he might even be falling in love with her. A sensual thrill shot through at the thought of that being true.

Tammy smiled. Sterling was a unique man. He was talented as well as sexy. And according to Mikki, was fine to the bone. And although he could play the role of slave driver for all it was worth, he could also be warm and gentle. He was a rigid perfectionist, and he could be tough and demanding, and a few other adjectives she could think of. But he could also be thoughtful and kind as well.

This special man had done something for her that no other had been able to until now. She owed her instant recognition to Sterling most assuredly, but it was more than that. He'd given her self-confidence a real boost and made her feel the urgent ambition to reach out and grab for the brass ring of success, something she hadn't felt inspired to do in the last three years.

While tonight's party was to celebrate her career, at the same time, it completely encompassed her personal life. When she heard his front door open and footsteps advancing along the walk, then caught the unmistakable scent of his cologne, she knew Sterling was coming to escort her inside to enjoy their private celebration.

Sterling's breath caught in his throat when Tammy stepped out of the limo. The mint green dress she was wearing clung to her body, giving the illusion of being painted on. The thrust of her firm breasts against the silky material made his male equipment harden with desire. Even the moonlight silvering her shoulders, bare where her shawl hadn't covered them, joined in the conspiracy to overwhelm his senses, for it gave her dark honey brown skin a tantalizing glow. Add to that the contrast of her glossy black hair and the titillating fragrance of her sexy perfume, and it set his heart racing at an alarmingly fast rate.

Sterling had to smile when a line done by a woman comedian on *Comic Review*, came to mind. She claimed a man had said to her that he was so aroused by her he could drink her bath water. At this moment, he could joyfully drink Tammy's with no problem. He shook his head at the absurdity of that particular thought. He hadn't felt this light-hearted in a very long time.

"Tammy, girl you look…" His voice faded.

"Just how do I look, Sterling?"

"Bewitching, beguiling, beautiful."

"The three b's, huh?"

"Yes, and if there are any more that will get my point across, I can't think of them at the moment. I hope you'll enjoy all the delights I have in store for you this evening."

"I'm sure I will," she whispered sultrily.

Sterling took her cane, wrapped her arm around his then led her into his house.

As they entered, the scent of jasmine and the soft, mellow sound of music greeted them.

"I've just added a few special touches for a special lady. You will have to let me be your guide tonight."

"I will, huh?"

"Yes, ma'am."

"Sounds intriguing."

"Only the beginning, sweet woman." He leaned her cane against the wall, slipped the shawl from her shoulders and guided her to the couch. Then he gently seated her on it.

Anticipation trickled through Tammy. She wondered what was next.

"To your left on the end table is a candelabra."

"Where the jasmine scent originates, no doubt. I can imagine the candles' soft glow and smell their sweet, exotic scent. You've certainly gone all out to create this romantic setting."

"Yes, I have, Ms. Gibson. And like I said, it's only the beginning. You remember where the bar is?"

"Yes, vaguely." She laughed.

"Tonight I've added a mini champagne fountain."

"Really?"

"I built it myself."

"So are you an artist, too? How fascinating. Can you describe this work of art to me?"

Sterling walked over to the bar and took a bottle of champagne from the ice bucket and popped the cork. "Picture a dozen champagne glasses, stacked in tiers, then listen for the sound of champagne bubbles popping as I pour champagne into the top glass on the tier. When it is filled to overflowing, you'll hear champagne spilling into the glasses beneath it, then on to the next tier, and then the next."

"I can hear it, and I can see it with my mind's eye. The picture you paint is definitely inviting."

Sterling brought a glass to her lips. "Taste," he softly commanded.

She did. "Delicious. Tart, dry, just the way I like it."

"And now I want to enjoy you." He tasted her sweet lips, and the champagne that lingered on them.

"You make drinking champagne a sensual experience."

"Only the prelude, my love."

"Oh, I can expect more?" Tammy asked.

To her right, she heard another male voice clear his throat.

"Dinner, monsieur?" the French-accented voice inquired.

"Yes, we are ready, Jean-Paul."

Tammy listened as he walked away. "Is he really a French waiter?"

Sterling laughed softly. "If he isn't, the food he's serving will be."

"Tell me how you look before we go in to dinner."

"You want to know that?"

"Of course. Describe what you're wearing," she sensuously entreated while taking tiny sips of her champagne.

"Everything?" he teased, taking sips from his own glass. "You mean down to the barest, most intimate detail?"

"Sterling! You're so bad."

He went on to describe his black tux, the black silk shirt and matching bow tie and the diamond-studded lapel pin molded into the shape of a musical note. Tammy reached out to run her fingers across his shirt front.

"Feels sexy." She walked her fingers up his throat to his chin, then on to his full lips.

She quickly replaced her fingers with her mouth.

He kissed her back with ardor.

"What you do to a poor woman's mind." Tammy sighed and then let go, allowing herself to really get into the kiss.

"I'll have to write award-winning albums for you all the time if this is the response I can expect."

"And if any of the private celebrations are anything remotely like this one, I'll certainly be looking forward to rewarding your efforts."

"Your dinner awaits, mademoiselle," Sterling whispered in her ear. Then he escorted her into the dining room.

When they were seated, the waiter cleared his throat. "We begin the meal with the soup julienne, salad Yvette, then the main course, filet of sole a la Orly. Your choice of wine, monsieur?"

"A dry, white Bordeaux, Jean-Paul."

"An excellent choice, monsieur."

Tammy smiled, imagining the waiter bowing in the traditional European manner. She was thoroughly enjoying her own private, five-star restaurant.

"The dinner was delicious. You really know how to party, Mr. Phillips."

"Dessert?"

"Didn't we just finish… Oh, you're wicked, Sterling Phillips."

"Pleasantly so, I hope. Do you wish to enjoy me further?"

"Enjoy you further? Like?"

"A question with a question. Very clever." Sterling drew Tammy into his arms and breathed in the scent of perfume and woman, almost immediately becoming intoxicated. Desire roughened his breathing, and he let out a low, sensuous growl.

Tammy heard and responded. "Oh, Sterling."

He lifted her off her feet and started walking.

"Where are you taking me?" she asked.

"To my palace of delights. My Casbah, if you will."

"Carry on."

"Oh, I will." Sterling nudged his bedroom door open with his shoulder, strode over to the rose petal strewn, satin sheeted bed then lowered Tammy onto it. He punched a few buttons on his wall stereo controller. A 70s collection of slow jams began to play, starting with the soft, sexy song "Always and Forever." He returned to Tammy and went down on his knees before her. Resting his weight back on his heels, he removed her shoes then lifted her feet onto his thighs. He caressed an ankle then eased his hand slowly upward, sensitizing her skin.

Tammy sucked her breath in sharply and reveled in the

decidedly sensual heat radiating from his fingers as they continued their journey up her calves.

Sterling felt her tremble when he kissed her knees then tremble even more when he brushed his fingertips against the sensitive skin behind them.

Tammy closed her eyes. Her body jerked when the moist heat from his mouth dampened her upper thigh through the filmy sheerness of her pantyhose. A delicious rush of desire surged into her femininity as she fantasized seeing his full, sexy lips kissing her there, imagining how his tongue would feel when it found the epicenter of her desire.

Sterling abandoned that pursuit, however, lowered her dress, then rose up and lowered himself down on the bed beside her. He cupped her chin and began planting kisses, first on her lips, then her cheek bones. The song "Oh Girl" began to play. He rasped the words, "I want you, Tammy," against her eyelids.

A knock at the door altered the mood. Sterling instructed the intruder to enter. Tammy heard the rattle of what she imagined were dishes on a food trolley as it was wheeled into the room. Moments later, she heard Sterling whisper instructions to the waiter Jean-Paul. When he dismissed the man, she waited eagerly for him to speak.

The scent of strawberries and chocolate filled the room.

"Sterling, what—"

"Open your mouth," he said in a low sexy voice.

"Why?"

"Just open your mouth."

She hesitated for a moment then did as he said.

"Taste."

She did. The tart flavor of fresh strawberries dipped in warm, rich chocolate delighted her taste buds, and a moan of decadent pleasure eased from her lips as she swallowed. She felt something warm dribble over her lips and down her chin, and moments later, gasped when she felt Sterling's tongue slide up her chin, removing the chocolate as he slowly inched to her lips. With each flick of that talented tongue, more of the warm sweet chocolate was removed, giving her senses the utmost pleasure.

While she was recovering from this onslaught, Sterling lowered the straps on her dress and eased the bodice down to her waist and then slipped the dress off.

"Another surprise awaits you. Open your mouth."

She did. This time the taste of strawberries and whipped cream courted her senses. Then she felt the cool froth on her breasts. Seconds later, a hot mouth covered a nipple, sucking the whipped cream off the tempting peak. The unbelievable sensation turned the other nipple into a hardened, aroused, cream-capped peak.

"Mmm." The moan of pleasure slipped from her lips.

"Tell me which combination you prefer?"

"I can't decide. Both have much to recommend them."

Sterling peeled her pantyhose from her body. "I'll make the decision easy for you. Open your mouth for me one more time."

When she did as he requested, he placed a strawberry dipped in honey onto her tongue. Before she could fully enjoy this different taste combination, he eased her back flat onto the bed and drew her legs apart. Then she felt something thick, warm and liquid roll slowly down her belly to the apex of her thighs, then drizzle into her femininity. Again, that wicked tongue found a pleasure point and dipped into her well of honey. Over and over again, it flicked the bud of her passion and delved beyond with light-ning strokes.

She gasped loudly. "Ooh, Sterling, you don't play fair."

He lifted his mouth. "I'm not playing."

"What are you doing then?"

"Luring a lady."

"Do I need to ask where and into what?"

"All you need to consider is, is it where you really want go or what you want to do? And am I the one you want to do it with?"

"If my answer is yes?"

"As Snoop Dogg said in 'It's a G thing,' 'then we move on to the next episode.'"

"And what is the next episode? I don't know if I can stand it if it's more provocative than this."

"First, we shower together."

Tammy never had a shower the likes of the one Sterling treat-ed her to. He rubbed the soapy washcloth repeatedly against her nipples until they ached with wanting, then he went lower to her still throbbing pearl of desire, dragging the cloth newly turned into an instrument of pleasure between her thighs until the fric-tion nearly drove her crazy.

Sensing he had pushed her as close to the edge as he dared, Sterling allowed the shower to rinse away the soap. He then quickly dried their bodies and carried her back into the bedroom.

"Now where did we leave off?" He removed the top sheet from the bed and let it drop to the floor. "Ah, this," he whispered before slanting his lips across hers and darting his tongue between her lips, eagerly laving the sensitive roof and walls of her mouth with his passionate onslaught while at the same time caressing her breasts.

Pleasure ignited into flame and raced through Tammy's veins like wild fire. He continued the sensual journey, slowly covering every inch of her womanly territory, heightening her arousal so she could fully receive the benefits of his intimate exploration.

Monitoring Tammy's reactions and then acting upon them gave Sterling a feeling of gratification he'd never experienced with any other woman. Watching the pleasure his touch brought her aroused him, turning his shaft hard as granite. The pleasure-pain sensation of her enjoyment sent his own senses up in flames.

The song "Love Won't Let Me Wait" began to play.

"Oh, Tammy girl," he groaned. "You aren't going to make me wait, are you?"

Tammy gasped at the touch of his skin caressing hers. And as he continued to arouse her, white-hot need consumed her body. And as her thought processes began a slow sensual meltdown, the remaining barriers disintegrated, obliterating the hold the past had on her emotions. She was truly free.

"Sterling, I want you to make love to me. I need you so badly."

"And I need you just as badly, my angel."

Tammy reacted to that name. David used to call her that.

What an eerie coincidence. Instead of turning her off, the opposite happened. Sterling was no immature boy. If he considered her his angel, he meant every word. Her being blind didn't faze him at all. She was no trial he felt he had to endure. He accepted her as she was.

"What are you thinking, Tammy?" he asked in a passion-husky voice.

"How much you've come to mean to me. How you and Kevin have enriched my life, made me feel alive again."

"We did all that?"

"Oh, yes, and more. Now, can we get on to the next episode?"

"An eager woman, I love it. The object of this evening is to delight your senses."

"I'd say you've done that with the strawberries, the chocolate, the whipped cream and, have mercy, that wicked honey."

He laughed. "Only the first among many episodes to come. You won't need sight, just your imagination and your passion."

"Imagination and passion. I like that combination better than the strawberries, the chocolate, the whipped cream or the honey."

"You do? I take it you're ready to explore other options."

"Oh, definitely."

"Your body is as beautiful as that of an ancient goddess. And what you do to this mere mortal man."

"You Are Everything" ebbed into the room.

He kissed her collarbone, one shoulder and then crossed over to the other and paid it equal worship before arrowing down to the valley between her beautiful breasts. He palmed the nipples until they peaked. He flicked his tongue across her sweet skin. Then drawing the stiffened peak deep into his mouth, he sucked strongly.

Mewling pleasure-torture sounds erupted from her throat while surge after surge of rapture undulated through her body. She shuddered violently as lightning bolts of ecstasy sank their sensual points deep into the bubbling core of her womanhood.

When Sterling began to massage her mound of Venus with his fingers, Tammy nearly flew apart as passion assaulted every inch of her highly inflamed body.

"I want you now, Sterling, right now, this minute," she cried as the friction of his movements sent her to the edge.

When he stopped moving his fingers, she felt bereft of their warmth, but not the fire or the desire that continued to build between them.

Sterling teased the excited nerve ending between the damp velvety folds of her womanhood until he felt it swell and throb. When her body began to shudder as she neared her climax, he stepped up his campaign to bring her exquisite pleasure.

Tammy groaned and cried out as her aroused flesh swelled and throbbed even more. Then her senses shattered, sending her soaring through a vortex, suspended in time for seemingly endless moments.

Sterling could hardly keep his eyes off the euphoric expression he'd put on Tammy's face as her climax slowly ebbed into contended sighs.

He wanted her world of darkness to be filled with the sensual light of love, joy and the promise of complete fulfillment. Their joining would be more than physical. It would be cerebral, soulful, every kind of gratification she could ever imagine.

Sterling slid his body over Tammy's and let his warmth seep into her. The moment he felt her hand encompass his hardened male flesh, he nearly leaped off the bed. With shaking hands, he reached inside the nightstand for their protection and opened the foil packet to retrieve the condom.

"May I?"

He reversed their positions. "I don't know if I should, considering what your touch on that particular part of my anatomy does to me."

"I'll be brief, I promise," she said, easing back a fraction. When her fingers rasped against his hot, hardened manhood as she slid the condom over it, she heard his sharp intake of air and a moan escape his lips. She slid her body back over his then lowered herself onto him, urging his hardness hilt deep inside her softness. She stayed still for long moments, letting the wonder of him filling her reverberate through her being. "Stairway to Heaven" played.

Sterling could stand it no longer and began to move restively beneath her.

Each movement of his hips rocking against Tammy built the fire hotter and higher. She responded with a cry of bliss as she began to ride him. Moments later, she heard staccato groans of ecstasy pour from his lips as he neared his completion. She was with him every step of the way. When rapture overtook them both, their wondrous celebration burst into an indescribable pleasure that seemed to go on and on forever.

CHAPTER TWENTY

From his position on the bed where he laid spoon fashion behind Tammy, Sterling raised himself onto his forearm to gaze into her face while she slept. He lovingly brushed a sleek, black lock of hair away from her cheek. He couldn't believe she was here with him like this and that he'd made love to her for most of the night. In his wildest fantasies he'd dreamed of, waking up and finding her lying in his arms, but doubted it would ever become a reality.

You need to tell her the truth, man, today, the voice of reason entreated.

Sterling frowned. Yes, he knew he would have to tell her one day, but not now, not while he was this close to…

Close to what?

Tammy was close to falling in love with him, he could feel it.

You can't continue to deceive her this way. That love could easily turn to contempt. Is that what you want to happen?

No, he didn't want that, but there was no guarantee that once she knew the truth, she would understand and forgive him.

What he had right now might be all he'd ever have. He was a selfish man when it came to Tammy. He wanted all of her, for as long as he could have her. A lifetime wouldn't be long enough.

You're afraid to risk it, so you keep procrastinating, but you must know that you have no choice. You'll have to tell her sooner or later. Suppose she finds out from someone else?

He hadn't thought of that. Then he remembered the nosey

celebrity reporter at the Black Pearl. He had been suspicious. If he somehow remembered Sterling and put two and two together and started digging around in his past or Tammy's, he would surely find out what he had done and ruin everything.

"Sterling," Tammy moaned sleepily.

"I'm here, darling girl."

Tammy smiled lazily and eased from her side onto her back. "I want you over me, inside me." She brought his hand to the dark triangle at the juncture of her thighs.

"You're an insatiable wanton, aren't you?"

"Only with you. Now, no more procrastinating."

Sterling covered her mouth with his own, slowly, thoroughly, exploring it, learning the intricacies with his tongue. When he finally let Tammy come up for air, her body was pulsing with desire.

"No more procrastination did you say, my hot little wanton?" he murmured huskily. Without further preliminaries, he proceeded to make long, slow, passionate love to her.

Tammy studied Sterling with her fingers and listened to his deep, even breathing as he dozed. It was unusually heavy, as if he were winding down after having run a race. She smiled. She had practically worn the man out with her demands, she thought, remembering how it had been between them last night and earlier that morning.

She lightly traced her fingers over his nose, his full lips, his strong chin, features that vaguely reminded her of… She quickly shoved the thought from her mind. She slid her fingers down his throat, then on to the slight smattering of hair on his chest. She proceeded downward to his ribs and stopped to feel the strong thudding of his heart. As she continued her exploration, she encountered a flat stomach, trim waist, and lean, narrow hips. When she came to his manhood and began to move her fingers up and down his length, she felt him squirm restively under her touch as that very male part of him sprang to life. She couldn't resist brushing her lips against him.

"Ooh, you're playing with fire, woman," he rasped out in a low, sexy growl.

"Maybe I'm eager to get burned. Are you going to make me go up in flames?" she challenged.

"Never let it be said that I ever disappointed a lady." He pulled Tammy on top of him and lifted her onto his aroused, aching flesh. As her wet heat took him deep inside, he closed his eyes and let stream an urgent, savage mating cry.

As she rode him, the friction from the movement of her body on his hard shaft rendered her speechless with exquisite ecstasy. But not Sterling, he was very vocal. Tammy heard the sounds of unbridled pleasure tear from his throat as again and again her hot, throbbing sheath rose and fell on his virile maleness. The fire spread, and their frenzied joining sent titillating flames of sensation rising higher and higher, until they reached the final, ultimate blaze of rapture and the all-consuming fire burned them into oblivion.

Tammy touched Sterling's face one last time before sliding from the bed to search for something to slip into. She cautiously felt her way around the unfamiliar room and bumped into the trolley, making her regret having left her cane downstairs. She stifled a pained response, not wanting to awaken Sterling. She smiled in triumph when she finally found the sliding door of his closet, claimed a robe hanging there then pulled it on and left the bedroom.

The house was silent as she carefully made her way down the stairs, counting each step, grasping the special rail Sterling had installed for Kevin. Jean-Paul and company had left the night before, after having served that sumptuous dinner and later the decadent feast in the bedroom.

Tammy felt her way along the wall until she came to Sterling's studio door and pushed it open and entered. She slowly inched her way over to the piano. Finding it, she sat down on the bench and began to play and sing the song "Killing Me Softly." It brought back memories of the time just before Augusta had become her foster mother. That wonderful lady and Derek had help guide the course of her life. The three of them had connected in a way that up until then she'd only done with David. Now she shared that special rapport with Sterling. She stopped playing and hugged that knowledge to herself.

"Tammy, are you all right?" Sterling asked from the doorway, a hint of concern in his voice.

"I'm wonderful, thanks to a certain composer, producer, lover."

"Slave driver, etc, etc," he added wryly.

"And a few other names I could come up with if I really put

my mind to it."

"Lover is good," he remarked, walking over to where she sat and easing down on the bench beside her. Then he drew her close, encircled her shoulders and rested his chin on the top of her head.

"I agree." Tammy smiled. "I love that word best of all, especially when I think about the marvelous things you did to me."

"I'm sure I can think of a lot more if you're willing."

"Oh, I'm willing, all right. Are you sure you're up to it? Sure I haven't tired you out?"

He rose to his feet and swept her up into his arms and headed for the small bedroom just off the studio.

"I'll show you tired. I'm going to make love to you until you beg me to stop."

"Sounds like words to a song."

"You inspire me to greatness, woman."

"As you inspire me," she whispered in his ear then grazed it with her teeth.

He groaned, slanting his mouth over hers, drinking of her sweetness. "If I were to die tomorrow, I would be the happiest man on earth."

"You're not going to do that because I intend to extend your happiness well beyond tomorrow, well into a lifetime."

"Ooh, baby, I want you to get started right now."

"It must be true what they say about great minds thinking alike."

"I don't know about that, but I can hardly wait for our bodies to respond in unison."

Sterling started the love making process with a deep, arousing kiss.

Having given Marcus the weekend off, Sterling called a taxi to take them to her house so she could change for their evening out. They'd skipped lunch, opting instead to make love in the afternoon. By early evening, they were ravenous.

It was seven o'clock when Sterling and Tammy stepped out of the taxi. She smiled at the sound of a train whistle and commented on it.

"You're about to enter the Dining Car."

"As in train?"

"Yes."

"How did you come to know about this place?"

"Oh, the Dining Car has been here forever. It's exactly the way you'd expect a dining car on a train in the Gay Nineties to look. The waiters are dressed in white jackets, and the waitresses are sporting their gingham dresses and wearing their hair in the Gibson girl style. No pun intended, Ms. Gibson."

"You certainly know how to create a mood whether it be in bed or other places."

"Thanks for the compliment."

"Tell me a little of the history surrounding this place."

"It was originally a luxury train car on one of the railroads in 1897 San Francisco. The owners who bought it after the railroad's heydays had it restored, painted red and gold, then had a length of track lain. Every hour the Dining Car moves up the hill, goes through a tunnel, swings around a curve, then back down. And, of course, the whistle blows. Now that I've given you the particulars, let's hurry up and order so you can do your duty as my own personal Gibson girl in a more private setting."

"You're not very subtle about your intentions or expectations, are you?"

"You have no idea how grand my expectations really are, and how very unsubtle my intentions once I get you alone, my darling girl."

"But you're going to enlighten me, right?"

"I'll make it my greatest pleasure in life."

"Now that we've had our, ah, private celebration, when are we going to have the public one?"

"Next weekend."

"It'll be kind of anti-climactic, don't you think?"

"Only to us. We get to share your success with family, friends and well wishers." He smiled at Tammy, but moments later, his smile dimmed when he saw an all-too-familiar face staring at Tammy from a table further down the aisle. Sterling's heart leaped into his throat. It was that nosey celebrity reporter, Hunter Bryant.

Sterling swallowed his uneasiness at seeing the man. Hopefully Bryant wouldn't remember. Maybe he had just enjoyed Tammy's performance and was staring because he had recognized her. Sterling could only hope that was true, because if the man ever connected him to the mystery man, he would…

"Is anything wrong, Sterling?" Tammy asked. "You've gone awfully quiet all of a sudden."

"I'm fine, just eager to have you all to myself."

Tammy smiled, taking his hand in hers. "Is that all. In that case we can leave right now."

"You have the look of a well-loved woman about you this morning, girlfriend," Mikki teased Tammy as they ate breakfast. "Mikki, I'm in love with Sterling," she admitted.

"And you're a little afraid. I can relate to that. Being in love can be scary. Do you think he feels the same way about you?"

"I know he cares, but as for love, I'm not so sure."

"I believe he does. That man treats you like a queen, maybe even better, more like a goddess. You're so lucky, Tammy. But you deserve it."

"I think so, too."

"I can hardly wait until the weekend to go to your party. Maybe your man will pop the question."

"Don't you think you're kind of rushing things?"

"Not at all. Men like him don't waste time with long drawn out courtships or engagements."

"What do you mean, men like him?"

"Men of beautiful words and blazing passion. You have to admit, he is one of those. I wish Wiley were more like him as far as the beautiful words go, although I can't complain when it come to the blazing passion department."

"Mikki, you're terrible!"

"You want to go shopping for a dress for the party?"

"I guess."

"That private party has kind of spoiled you for the public

one, hasn't it?"

"A little."

"You'll get over it. Girl, you are going to be officially launched Saturday night as an up and coming diva, and it won't be long before they put you in the same category with greats like Lauryn Hill, Mariah Carey and Mary J. to name a few."

A kind of excitement at the thought rose inside Tammy. Her career was finally on track, and the party would help it along.

"You're right, let's go find that one special dress."

"I love seeing Tammy like this," Augusta said to Derek as they watched their foster daughter charm her many guests at the party celebrating her intro into the music business.

"Me, too. Sterling certainly can't keep his eyes off her."

Augusta frowned. "I'm worried about him, Derek. You're his friend. Can't you convince him to see a doctor? He shouldn't be popping antacid tablets all the time like that. And he's beginning to look tired, too."

"You think he could have an ulcer?"

"I don't know. It could be a warning sign of any number of physical problems. Will you talk to him?"

"Yes. Here they come."

"Are my two favorite people in the whole world enjoying themselves?" Tammy asked, her voice ringing with happiness.

"Seeing you get the recognition you deserve is enjoyment enough for us," Derek answered.

"Are you going to sing for us?" Augusta queried.

Taking Tammy's hand in his, Sterling answered, "Of course she is. Jeremy insists that she perform a mini concert this evening."

"And we have to keep him sweet, don't we?" Tammy laughed.

"Do I hear someone taking my name in vain?" Jeremy quipped as he walked up.

Tammy introduced him to her parents. "Augusta and Derek Morgan, I'd like you to meet Jeremy Ward, the president of R & B Records. Jeremy, my parents."

"You have a very talented daughter, but then you already know that."

"Yes, we do indeed," said Augusta, pride accentuating her words.

As they all made their way to the tables set up in front of the bandstand, Sterling observed the array of media people attending the party. Jeremy had invited one that Sterling wished he hadn't.

Jeremy defended his invitation. "I know how you feel about Hunter Bryant, but he can be very helpful in spring-boarding Tammy's singing career."

Sterling knew he was right, but he worried about this particular reporter. He could be as relentless as a dog digging for a hidden bone. Sterling didn't want Tammy or himself to become this dog's dinner.

Sterling sat staring in awe when Tammy started singing the title song from her album. He played her songs before he went to bed every night. He was completely caught up in the rapture of this woman he loved so desperately.

"Man, you didn't eat much tonight. Are you feeling all right?" Derek asked Sterling.

"I feel fine. It's just that the food is a little rich for my taste."

"You sure? I saw you popping quite a few antacid tablets, considering the small amount of the food you'd actually eaten."

"I'm okay, Derek. Tonight is not about me, it's about Tammy's and what's right for her. I want to do it up right and tight."

"A composer to the bone." Derek laughed. "I don't know how you managed to do it so fast."

"I owe it all to Tammy. She started my creative juices flowing again. I didn't think that would ever happen. She's my life, Derek."

"I understand completely. Speaking of sweet women, here comes the love of my life." Derek's eyes lit up as he watched Augusta approach.

Sterling smiled. "We're lucky sons of a gun."

"We are indeed."

"Ms. Gibson? The same Ms. Gibson who recently finished a singing engagement at the Black Pearl?"

"The very same," Tammy exclaimed with a smile.

"I'm Hunter Bryant, from *Variety Entertainment Magazine*."

"I take it you've heard me sing there?"

"Indeed I have, and I thought you were fantastic. You have an incredible voice, Ms. Gibson. It never occurred to me that I'd be afforded the opportunity to say I knew her when," he said charmingly.

"Thank you for saying that, Mr. Bryant."

"Call me Hunter. It's only the truth. And I'm dedicated to reporting all of the facts."

Sterling tensed as he walked over to where Hunter Bryant and Tammy stood talking. His tension increased when he heard the reporter's last words.

"Sterling," Tammy called out, recognizing his scent, a unique mixture of his cologne and maleness.

"Yes."

"I've just been talking to Hunter Bryant, from—"

"*Variety Entertainment Magazine.* I know of him and the magazine." Sterling wondered what Tammy had been telling the man.

"Didn't I see you and Ms. Gibson at the Dining Car a week ago?"

"You probably did," Tammy answered. "We did dine there one day last week."

Maybe the man hadn't remembered seeing him that last night at the Black Pearl, Sterling thought as he listened while the reporter asked Tammy some more questions. It had been dark. Sterling was relieved when Bryant finally concluded the interview and politely excused himself and walked away.

"You don't like Hunter Bryant very much, do you, Sterling?" Tammy asked.

"The man is a ruthless newshound."

She laughed. "It's his job to sniff out the facts and report them, isn't it?"

"That man goes above and beyond the call of duty."

"Did he write something bad about you?"

"He wrote a lot of things about me, and all of them were bad.

I bet the bastard doesn't even remember all the cruel innuendos he printed about me—about what he believes happened the night Kayla died."

"I'm sorry if he's hurt you, Sterling."

"It's in the past, old news. You're new meat for him to chew on. Let's forget about him. Are you enjoying your night?"

"I prefer our other celebration actually."

"When this one is over, we can take up where we left off."

"Have I told you I love the way you think?"

"You have, but I'll never tire of hearing it."

"I hope not."

"I know not."

CHAPTER TWENTY-ONE

"I was hardly aware that you were at the party, Mikki," Tammy remarked as they sat having coffee at the kitchen table Sunday morning.

"Well, Wiley kind of kept me, ah, occupied." She giggled.

"I'll just bet he did. He's crazy about you, you know."

"And the feeling is mutual. He's finally gotten around to asking me to marry him. We got engaged last night."

"I'm so happy for you, Mikki. He hasn't been as slow on the uptake as you thought."

"No, I have to admit, he hasn't."

"When's the big day?"

"We haven't decided on one yet."

"I want to be one of the first to know."

"You will be. I'll bet Sterling asks you to be his wife before too long."

"We have a ways to go before we reach that stage. He hasn't said that he loves me yet, Mikki."

"A mere technicality. What are your plans for this afternoon?"

"Sterling is taking me, Kevin and D.J. to Monterey Bay."

"You guys going to visit the aquarium and the old cannery row?"

"Probably. I told him we needed to do more things with Kevin."

"The kid used to be a real pain, but since knowing you, he's changed."

"I'm glad. He used to treat his father badly, and it really hurt Sterling."

"I know. I saw the pain in his eyes every time Kevin rejected his overtures of fatherly love and concern. I felt so sorry for him when that happened."

"Me, too, but things are a lot better between them now."

"Thanks to you."

"We decided to invite D.J. along so Kevin would have somebody his own age."

"Your little brother is a good friend to Kevin. He has more patience than most boys his age. Kevin's old attitude was enough to try the patience of a saint."

"I admit that D.J. is special. And not because he's my brother. He was raised by two very special parents. Maybe if Kevin's mother had lived, he would be different."

"You're probably right."

"You and Wiley are welcome to join us."

"Thanks for asking, but we have other plans."

"D.J. should be ready to go in a few minutes, Kevin," Augusta told him as she led Sterling, Tammy and Kevin into the living room. "You can go on up if you want to."

"I think I will."

Augusta watched Kevin make his way up the stairs. When he had safely made it to the top, she turned her attention to Sterling and her foster daughter.

"Derek is on the phone with the parents of one of his pupils.

He shouldn't be too long," she explained. "In the meantime we can go out on the patio."

As he and Tammy followed Augusta, Sterling's mind drifted away from the conversation and back to what he'd read that morning in the newspaper. Hunter Bryant had a Sunday byline in the local newspaper. In his column, he'd alluded to the mystery man and wondered how he fit in with Tammy's sudden rise to success. He went on to praise Tammy's voice, but he had made his point. He was curious and intended to pursue the question. Damn him.

"Sterling."

He shook himself free of his momentary reverie. "Derek, I didn't know you'd come out here."

"Because your mind was somewhere else."

Sterling looked around. "Where are Tammy and Augusta?"

"They went out to the kitchen to get the drinks. You really were in another world, weren't you?"

"Did you read this morning's paper?"

"I read it. And?"

"Hunter Bryant."

"He's quite taken with Tammy, it would seem."

"On the surface maybe, but I don't trust him. He practically crucified me after the accident. I saw how interested he was in Tammy when she sang at the Black Pearl."

"What do you think it means?"

"He doesn't know that I'm the mystery man, but if he were to ever find out..."

"He would put two and two together and start digging. Sterling, you'd better tell Tammy the truth before that happens.

You can't put it off any longer."

"I know you're right. I'll tell her tonight."

"It may not be as bad as you think."

"No, it'll probably be worse."

"She cares for you, man."

"I know she does, but…"

"I understand where you're coming from. Living under this kind of tension can't be good for you. Is that the reason you look so tired?"

"I can handle it. What I can't handle is losing Tammy."

"There's hope that she'll forgive you. Augusta forgave me."

Tammy and Augusta joined Derek and Sterling, putting an end to the conversation.

"What were you two talking about?" Tammy inquired.

"The two most beautiful women in the world. What else?" Derek answered.

"The question is, what were you saying about us? Right Tammy?" Augusta let out a good-natured chuckle.

"It was all good, I can assure you," Sterling quipped. "Where are Kevin and D.J.? We need to get going if we want to catch all of the aquarium tour."

"They should be down any minute," Augusta reassured him.

"Monterey Bay is south of San Francisco. The Monterey canyon was discovered in 1890 by pioneer scientist George Davidson," Sterling read from the brochure to Kevin, Tammy and D.J. as Marcus reached the turnoff that wound into

Aquarium road.

"The aquarium sits on the rocky shores of the southern side of Monterey Bay," Sterling went on, attempting to create a mental picture of the scene around them. "The aquarium looks like an industrial building with its two smokestacks."

"Why does it have smokestacks?" Kevin asked.

"Because it used to be a cannery before it was dismantled. The aquarium has giant exhibit tanks that are 216,000 square feet. Monterey Canyon itself is thirteen miles wide and a mile deep canyon off the coast of Monterey. It's like an undersea Grand Canyon."

"I remember how it looked," Kevin said thoughtfully. "You took me and Mama there once when I was little."

Sterling hadn't forgotten that trip either. It was one of the few they'd gone on together as a family before the relationship between Sterling and Kayla started to disintegrate.

Sensing the tension, Tammy strove for a change of subject. "Describe what you remember, Kevin. I want to be able to picture it through your eyes."

"You really want me to?"

"Yes, I do."

Sterling breathed a sigh of relief. Tammy was the perfect buffer between father and son. She seemed to know all the right things to say and the right time to say them.

"My mother and father took me to see the Grand Canyon when I was little," D.J. commented when Kevin started describing the Monterey aquarium as he remembered it. "I mostly remember how hot it was."

Sterling smiled, glad Tammy had suggested bringing D.J.

with them.

Twenty minutes later found them at the aquarium, listening to the tour guide.

"There are now more than 300,000 plants and animals housed in two wings of the aquarium since it first opened its doors in 1984. There is a sixteen-foot-high kelp forest, sandy shores, and outer reefs surrounding the aquarium. The second floor houses rotating specialty exhibits. A third floor observation deck overlooks Monterey Bay."

Sterling watched the interested look on his son's face as the tour guide told them more about the aquarium. During the next leg of the tour, a marine biologist guided them to where visitors could pet the sea creatures.

Kevin petted a bat ray. "Its skin feels kinda silky-like," he said in a pleasantly surprised voice.

When they walked over to the indoor tide pool, Kevin and D.J. took off their shoes and socks and went into the water.

D.J. giggled. "Something just tickled my leg."

"It's probably a sea star," the biologist explained. Monterey Bay is also a whale sanctuary and..."

The biologist's voice droned on about the other exhibits. When they finished the tour, their heads were filled with information. Sterling suggested going somewhere to eat, then doing some beach walking afterward.

They ended up eating at the Sardine Factory in the Captain's Room, which had a fireplace and walls that were lined with portraits of sea captains.

Right after they arrived home, Sterling watched Kevin and D.J., tired from their excursion, head upstairs to Kevin's room to, as D.J. said, veg.

"I think the day went very well. What do you think, Tammy?"

"You've still got a ways to go with your son. One excursion and a visit to wine country do not a father and son relationship make," she said as Sterling guided her into the living room, and they sat down on the couch.

"With your help, maybe it won't be so long in coming. You've completely entranced at least one of the Phillips men, Ms. Gibson."

"I hope I entranced one Phillips man in particular."

"Oh, you have. And I'd love to show you how much."

"There is always later when you take me home."

"What will Mikki say?"

"She's otherwise occupied this evening. She's spending the night at Wiley's place."

"In that case, I'll stay a while."

"You driving me home? There's hardly any traffic this time of the evening. I'm sure Marcus is as tired as the boys, probably more so since he did all of the driving."

Sterling stiffened. "We can take a taxi."

"But if you stay late—"

"Tammy, I know what you're trying to do."

"But you're not ready to chance driving, right? There will never be a perfect time, Sterling. You just have to take the plunge."

That statement brought home the other thing he needed to

do.

"Tammy, I can't..." His voice faltered.

Tammy took his face in her hands and kissed his lips. "You can do it. I have every confidence in you."

"I know you do," he answered absently, his mind dwelling on an even more important dilemma. How could he begin to tell her the truth? By saying, "Oh, by the way, Tammy, I'm the bastard who caused you to lose your sight and then abandoned you afterward." How could he tell her something like that?

Sterling urged Tammy to her feet. She realized he was deliberately evading the subject and wondered if it were the real subject he was trying to avoid. But if not that, then what could it possibly be?

"Where are you leading me?"

"To my den of pleasure, where else?" he teased, guiding her in the direction of the family room. He'd had it redecorated, taking a few of Tammy's suggestions, and it was now a pleasure going in there. He deposited her on the L shaped sectional before stepping over to the wall and programming the stereo.

The voice of Brian McKnight singing "Back At One" flowed into the room. "He conveys my sentiments exactly," Sterling whispered into Tammy's ear when he joined her on the couch.

"You don't need to list those things. I'm already in love with you, Sterling. I hope I can be your dream come true."

"You are," he said huskily. "And for the record, I happen to be madly in love with you, Ms. Gibson." He kissed her lips, not giving her a chance to reply, then lowered the strap on her sundress and caressed first one sensitive nipple, then the other. When he heard Tammy's moan of pleasure, he murmured, "Oh, how I want to make love to you."

"The boys might come down."

"I know," he said, a frustrated sigh blowing from his lips.

"I'd better call Marcus and have him take you home." He kissed her bare skin before lifting the strap back over her shoulder.

Tammy snuggled closer. "I love being close to you like this. We don't have to make love. Just hold me."

"You're one hell of woman, Tammy."

"I'm glad you think so."

"I want you to know how much you mean to me." He cleared his throat. "The last years of my marriage were hell, and since Kayla's death, and until I met you, I've been lonely and desolate. When Brian McKnight mentioned throwing out the life-line in the nick of time, it was as though he was speaking to me, because that is exactly what you did. You virtually saved my life. I never thought I'd compose again. Songwriting was my life, but my emotions were so irrevocably entangled in guilt, bitterness and pain that I had no hope of ever loosening their stranglehold. You, my darling girl, have freed me."

"I'm glad. I wouldn't be enjoying the success I have now if not for the beautiful words you composed just for me."

"Your voice gives them life, makes them beautiful. We make one hell of a team, don't you agree?"

"Yes, I do." She slipped her arms around his neck and tugged, bringing his lips down on hers. A sigh of pleasure eased from her lips when Sterling gently urged them apart and delved his tongue inside.

Moments later, he raised his head. "Oh, Tammy girl, what

you do to me."

"If it's anything close to what you do to me, you're ready to melt in your underwear."

"Forget the underwear. I'm melting, period. I don't want you to go home."

"I don't want to leave, but I think I should before it gets too late."

CHAPTER TWENTY-TWO

At that moment, Sterling felt frustrated as hell. If he drove her home, he could stay and make love to her as long as he wanted to. But the thought of how he'd felt the last time he'd been behind the wheel of a car came back to haunt him, and he sought to quickly squelch the idea. But it wouldn't be so easily wrestled into submission.

Tammy had an idea of what Sterling was thinking. She sensed that his desire to take her home and make love to her warred with his driving phobia. She smiled. Maybe her plan to have him behind the wheel of a car again had a chance of succeeding.

"You're a crafty one, Ms. Gibson," Sterling said, accurately reading her smile. He drew her back into his arms and hugged her tight.

"I care about you, Sterling."

"I know you do, as I care about you." He kissed her ear then her neck.

"I'll never get home if you keep that up."

Sterling wrapped Tammy's arm around his own then headed for the front door. Once they were outside, he gazed along the drive to the garage. His midnight blue Navigator was parked behind the left door, waiting for him to climb in and conquer his fear. Could he conquer it? Tammy was sure that he could.

Beads of sweat popped out on his forehead, and his palms felt clammy. He swallowed hard, his heartbeats coming in erratically fast jerks, pretty close to being physically painful. He shot a quick glance at the limo and up the stairs to Marcus's apartment. All he had to do was call him.

Sterling delved into his pocket for his keys. When he heard them jingle, he realized his fingers were shaking. The next moment, he forced himself to walk to the garage. Sweat rolled down the sides of his face with each step.

"Sterling, baby, you don't have to do this if you're not ready."

He didn't think he'd ever be ready. Suddenly, flashes from the night of the accident streaked across his mind's eye. He, Kayla and Kevin were living in L.A. then. It had begun to rain hard. Lightning scored the sky and thunder rumbled, shaking the ground beneath them. He was driving on a treacherous stretch of PCH. He wanted nothing more than to pull over on the danger-ously slick highway and wait out the storm, but couldn't find a place to do it. He was desperate to get his family to safety. Kayla panicked when they came to a particularly winding curve.

Sterling heard her screams then felt her nails as they dug into his hand as she viciously struggled to wrest control of the wheel away from him.

"Give me the wheel, damn you," she had screeched.

"Kayla, stop it before you kill us all. I can handle it." He finally managed to wrench her hands from the wheel. She start-ed beating at his hands with her fists. When that didn't work, she slammed her fist into his temple. Pain exploded in his head and bright spots of color danced before his eyes and for a crucial few seconds he couldn't see.

Under her hands, he felt the car swerve, then careen to the right on two wheels. At that moment, his vision cleared and he shoved Kayla aside, grabbed the wheel, fighting to regain control.

Kevin's frightened voice flooded the interior of the car.

The rain started coming down in blinding sheets, making it almost impossible to see out the windshield. But he finally could. Just a few hundred yards ahead of them, there was a shoulder wide enough for him to pull over and wait out the storm. But before he could reach it, the car went into a skid. He tried veering it to the right by applying easy pressure on the brakes, but they wouldn't hold and the car lurched out of control, sliding across the road. Headlights from an oncoming car flashed, momentarily blinding him. Then came the loud, nerve-destroying sound of screeching tires. Sterling swung the wheel sharply to the right to avoid hitting the car, but in doing so, slammed his own car into a wall of solid rock. He felt pain, terrible excruciating pain lance through his brain, then a floating black nothingness.

"Sterling, are you all right?" Tammy asked frantically.

"It wasn't my fault. It wasn't my fault!"

"What?"

"The accident! Kayla—oh my God. I finally remember what happened in the seconds just before the crash. I tried to prevent the accident. The rain and the slickness of the street and an oncoming car made it impossible."

He grabbed Tammy and hugged her tight, closing his eyes in blessed relief.

Tammy sensed that Sterling was on the edge of conquering his fears, but he needed to go that one step farther.

"Sterling, are you ready to drive me home?"

"I don't know if I can."

"You can do it, baby. I believe in you. Please, believe in yourself."

He suddenly felt numb. Knowing he wasn't responsible for Kayla's death was one thing, but getting behind the wheel and driving was another. That accident wasn't the only one plaguing his conscience.

Sterling took a deep breath then proceeded forward.

Tammy held onto him.

He activated the buttons on the garage door, and the light came on and the door opened. The insurance company had replaced the vehicle that had been totaled in the accident, and Marcus took the new Navigator in for servicing every few months and occasionally borrowed it. He kept it in tip-top running condition. The condition of the car wasn't what concerned him. The question was whether he was ready to take it out. That was the real kicker. He glanced at the woman standing beside him, and he saw no sign of fear on her face, only the trust she had in him. That she could trust him so completely humbled him. He could do no less than what she asked of him.

Drawing on courage he didn't know he possessed, Sterling took a step, then two, until he reached the passenger side of the Navigator. He unlocked the door, helped Tammy inside then walked around to the driver's side. He eased his body behind the wheel. His fingers shook at first when he touched the steering wheel. He inserted the key in the ignition, started the SUV and turned on the lights. He adjusted the mirrors, lowered his hands back to the steering wheel, put the Navigator in reverse then backed it out of the garage. The lights in the garage apartment came on and the window opened.

"It's all right, Marcus. Keep an eye on Kevin and D.J. I'm

driving my lady home."

He heard the chauffeur's astonished gasp before he acknowledged his instructions and closed the window. Sterling eased the Navigator out of the driveway and drove tentatively for a few yards. When he got his bearings, any residual fear remaining slipped away, and he picked up speed and confidence. When they reached Tammy's house, Sterling parked the Navigator in front of it. He reached across the seat and pulled Tammy onto his lap and kissed her deeply.

"God, how I love you," he said after releasing her lips.

She captured his in a soul-burning possession. "I think you'd better come inside so we can finish this, don't you?"

"Your wish is my command." He unlocked her front door and then let her lead him up the stairs to her bedroom. He'd never ventured past her living room when he'd been there before, and he was curious to see it. Once inside the bedroom, Tammy turned and finding him, wrapped her arms around his waist.

"No negative thoughts are allowed tonight, Mr. Phillips."

"How did you know I was doing that?"

"I'm psychic."

"You are?"

"Of course. I predict that in a few minutes you'll start thinking of all the many ways you want to make love to me."

"I'll be damned if you aren't psychic." He cupped her face and kissed her lips, promising her ecstasy, his tongue stroking, caressing, expecting an equally passionate response. And he wasn't disappointed.

Tammy hungrily answered, drinking from his lips as though drinking a special nectar from the gods, touching him as if he were the most precious thing in her world, breathing in his masculine scent as if it were the breath of life. To her it was. Her entire world was reduced to this room and this man. She lost all concept of time and place in his arms.

A song of love and yearning so profound it took his breath came to mind, tugging at his heart and encompassing his soul and it came pouring out of him. "Oh, Tammy, you are my love, my hopes, my dreams, my everything."

"Those are the most beautiful words I've ever heard. They are so true because you are my love, my hopes, my dreams, my everything."

"You are the music of love. Play on, play on."

"You pick the best times to be creative."

"I don't pick them, they just happen. As I've said before, you inspire me to greatness."

"Prove it."

"I thought you'd never ask." He swept her up in his arms and carried her over to the bed, his lips never breaking contact with hers. He wordlessly undressed her, savoring every inch of her beautiful body as each piece came off. "You're finer than wine," he murmured against her mouth. When she was completely naked, he added, letting his fingers trail down to her breasts, "And oh so incredibly soft and sexy." He squeezed gently and circled his thumbs around the aureole, turning her nipples into pebble-hard peaks.

Sterling felt her quiver as he kissed a path down her stomach. When he parted her thighs and his lips reached the door to her desire, he flicked the knob with his tongue. Tammy gasped, and her hips arched involuntarily against his mouth.

"What are you doing to me?" she rasped.

"Proving that you inspire me to greatness."

"Only greatness? Is there more to come?"

"Do you want more proof?"

"Oh, yes. God, yes."

Sterling returned to her mound of desire in his quest to elicit more proof. His tongue delved and retreated, delved and retreated, until he felt that nub of flesh throb and swell.

The friction of his tongue was driving Tammy crazy. Again and again that wicked instrument of pleasure flailed the throbbing bud. Her heartbeat quickened, and then she exploded into tiny particles of delight.

As she slowly floated down from oblivion, Sterling quickly undressed and joined her on the bed.

"Watching you come apart like that inspires me to even greater heights."

"Greater?"

"Oh, yes." Starting from her feet and moving on up her legs, he caressed her sensitized skin, rekindling her desire to fever pitch. By the time he reclaimed her mouth, she was writhing beneath him.

"Sterling, I want you to be a part of me now." She moved her body in the persuasive way of a woman wild for the intimate act of joining her lover's body to her own. Her soft whimper was one-fourth plea, three-fourths demand.

He was not ready to give her release; he wanted her pleasure to be complete. He moved his mouth and his hands over her body; his tongue darting, licking, devouring; his fingers probing, stroking, caressing.

Tammy thought she would lose her mind as he played her like a fine instrument, sounding every possible note of passion within her. If she inspired him to this degree of greatness now, what pinnacle of greatness could she expect him to reach in the future?

Before she could utter even a restive sigh, he pulled her on top of him. He could feel her inner muscles ripple along his sex as he filled her with all of himself. He could hold off no longer and eased her onto her back and gave himself up to the need strumming through his body.

As the music of love played on, their senses reached for each and every high note, delved for the very lowest one, then together played every chord to perfection, rising and falling in passionate harmony until ecstasy consumed them in one last burst. It was like a clashing of cymbals as the song slowly ebbed away.

As Tammy lay with her fingers splayed across Sterling's chest as he slept, her brows arched in concern. He'd fallen asleep so quickly after making love, as if doing so had completely wiped him out. She didn't know why that should bother her so much. It was probably a combination of the strain of reliving the night of the accident, then the joy of conquering his driving phobia. But maybe it could be from something else. Or maybe she was just being paranoid.

The soft, early morning sun streaming through the blinds tickled Sterling's eyelids, gently awakening him. He smiled, gazing into Tammy's face. She was beautiful inside and out, and he loved her so much. He owed her the truth, and he intended to tell it to her today.

"How long have you been awake?" Tammy asked sleepily, slipping her fingers over his manhood, instantly arousing Sterling. He groaned aloud. Before he could do anything, she slid her body over his, completely enveloping him in her womanly heat.

"We have no need for words, Sterling."

"But I have to tell you—"

"Later. Enjoy what I have in mind to do to you."

And he did.

CHAPTER TWENTY-THREE

For the next two weeks, Sterling and Tammy were busy making guest appearances on national talk shows, local radio and TV programs. And the week following that, Sterling watched Tammy work on the Lance Cummings video. Cummings was a first-rate professional, Sterling had to admit as he observed the way he cleverly incorporated Tammy's blindness into the scenes. The song "I'll Always Be There For You" was certainly apropos. Cummings had the male love interest show his devotion to the woman he loved, her blindness no deterrent to that love. Sterling breathed a sigh of relief that Hunter Bryant seemed to have lost interest in Tammy.

Don't let it go to your head, man. It doesn't absolve you from the responsibility of telling her the truth, came the prick of his conscience.

"What do you think of the video so far?" Tammy asked Sterling.

"You were great in it of course. I didn't know you had hidden acting talents in addition to possessing a fantastic singing voice."

"I'm a woman as well as a singer, Sterling," she said in a that's-explanation-enough tone of voice.

"I'll testify to that on both counts, especially the woman part."

"You know what I meant."

"I do, and I'm more interested in the woman part right now."

"You would be."

"You've totally enchanted me, Miss Gibson. I'm completely under your spell."

"More great words for a song."

"I agree. Pretty soon I'll have written enough songs to paper my entire house, let alone my studio, if it's left up to you. You are great for my ego as well as other parts I could name. By the way, when are you going to take care of those other parts, woman?"

"Not so loud. Do you want everyone to know our business? Lance wants me to fly to Galveston and tape the rest of the video on location. You could come with me. Since Kevin will be staying with Augusta and Derek, maybe when we get to Texas, I can do something about satisfying the other parts you mentioned."

Sterling saw Lance Cummings heading in their direction.

"I should have had you in the video instead of Montel, Sterling. I wouldn't have to pull emotions from you."

"You sure wouldn't because where this lady is concerned, my responses come naturally whenever I'm anywhere near her."

Tammy smiled, feeling the aura of Sterling's love surrounding her like a cocoon.

Sterling watched with longing as Tammy did the beach scene on Galveston Island. He could picture himself and Tammy enjoying the sunset with him describing the colors as the warm Gulf breeze whispered against their skin. Then, suddenly, the scene of a windswept rainy night replaced the sunset. The sound of screeching tires replaced the calls of the sea gulls. If not for him, there would be no reason to describe the sunset to her. She would be able to see it for herself.

You have to stop beating yourself up about that and tell her the truth, man, or you're going to drive yourself crazy with these guilt trips.

"Sterling, are you all right?" Tammy asked. "I've been calling your name for the last few minutes."

"I'm fine, just deep in thought."

"About me I hope."

"Always about you."

"That's a wrap," Lance called to the players, camera crew and technicians several hours later. "Sterling, you can have this lovely lady all to yourself."

Tonight he would tell her the truth, but first he was going to make love to her like there was no tomorrow because this could be his last time with Tammy.

The flowers Sterling ordered came, and the fabulous dinner would arrive at the pre-arranged time. He wanted everything, the evening and the night of loving, to be perfect. He wanted Tammy to never forget how it was between them if… No. He wouldn't think negative thoughts tonight. This was an up occasion. He would be spending precious time with the woman he loved more than his own life.

"What is the special occasion?" Tammy asked.

"Do I need one to show you how much I adore you?"

"You adore me, do you?"

"Oh, yes. I more than adore you, Tammy Gibson, I love you

to distraction."

"As I love you."

"Are you going to let me show you in a thousand and one little ways?"

"I might. How long will I have to wait?"

Sterling pulled her into his arms and kissed her breathless.

"Talk about a fast worker."

"Oh, baby, for you I'll be Speedy Gonzales."

"As lines go, that's pretty whacked."

"It gets my meaning across."

"Yes, it certainly does." Tammy studied his face with her fingers. For some reason a mental picture of David surfaced in her mind. She immediately shook it off. Why had thoughts of him come to her at that particular moment?

"What's wrong?"

"Nothing. It was just something you said that reminded me of a time years ago. Kind of like *déjà vu.* It's nothing. I want to concentrate on loving my man right now."

"And I want you to. Let's go for a walk on the beach and really work ourselves into the mood before we go inside."

"I don't need a walk on the beach to heighten my mood."

"Just humor me, okay?"

"You have something else planned, don't you? Is that why you don't want to return to the suite just yet?"

"I always said you were a genius." He laughed.

Tammy quirked her lips for a moment. "Yeah, right. If you say I look like Einstein one more time, I'll kill you. I remember what he looked like. Okay, I guess I'll let you take me on that walk. The sooner we do it, the sooner we'll get back, and I can find out what you're up to, Mr. Phillips."

"You know, you're beginning to look more and more like Einstein."

"I'm going to get you for that."

"Promise?"

"You're so impossibly sexy, Sterling. I love you so much."

"I hope you never stop."

"I told you there's not a chance of that ever happening."

Sterling smiled thinly. He hoped she was right. If Tammy only knew how desperately he wanted to believe that. Nothing negative, he reminded himself as he led her across the deck and down the steps to the beach.

Tammy loved the feel of the warm, humid subtropical breeze swirling around her, combing its gentle yet invigorating fingers through her hair, blowing the cool spray of water against her face.

"It's so lovely here. It's at times like these that I wish I could see."

Sterling's heart lurched at her innocently voiced remark.

"I'll be your eyes, Tammy."

"I didn't mean that you should feel you had to."

"I want to. You taught me how important it is for the blind to visualize their surroundings. I do it for Kevin most of the time now."

"Anything new where he's concerned?"

"I'm waiting to hear from Dr. Hastings. He's been trying to set up an appointment for Kevin with a specialist who's had amazing success with cases like Kevin's."

"Ben's really good about that. He still does follow-ups on me, although it's probably a lost cause in my case. But he never gives up hope, and he won't let me."

"He's right, you shouldn't. You never know when a new treatment breakthrough could come along and help you see again."

"I have been duly pepped up and bolstered, Dr. Phillips."

"Then you will do as the doctor ordered. Now let's get on with our visual excursion, Ms. Gibson."

"You're the doctor."

"And don't you forget it."

"If I do, I'm sure you'll enjoy refreshing my memory."

"As the sun is making its descent, the gold, yellow and red rays seem to be magically gilding the Gulf, giving the waves a goldish-red cast as they roll across the sand. Can you hear them?"

"Yes, I can picture it just as you've described it. No wonder you're such a brilliant composer."

"You think I'm brilliant, huh? Flattery will get you anything."

"Anything?"

"Is there anything in particular you want?"

"Yes."

"And do I know what that anything is?"

"You'd better."

"Sounds like a challenge to me, but then I'm not a genius like you."

"I think you go way beyond genius level when it comes to knowing what I want."

"Glad to hear it."

Just then a wave washed over their bare feet.

"It feels wonderful."

"As wonderful as I can make you feel?"

"Close."

"I think you need a refresher course."

Tammy stopped walking, turned toward Sterling, then eased her arms around his neck and kissed him full on the mouth, teasing his lips with her tongue until his breath sucked in.

"You don't need a refresher course, just more practice. And I'm eager to continue your training."

"But you're the one who wanted to take a walk on the beach."

"I think I've had enough of Mother Nature, thank you."

"And now you want to do what comes naturally, right?"

"Don't you, Einstein?"

"I don't have to be a genius to answer that question."

Sterling held her tighter in his embrace, not ever wanting to let her go. If he could only hold her like this forever and not have to hurt her. But he knew it was impossible.

When they reached the steps of their beach suite, they stopped. Sterling turned Tammy so that she was facing the sea, then wrapped his arms around her waist.

"It's so peaceful and quiet here, yet still vibrant and full of life. You are my life, Tammy. Please don't ever forget that."

"I won't. Why are you getting melancholy all of a sudden?"

"I'm not. I just don't want anything to go wrong between us."

"It won't, baby. I love you and nothing will ever change the way I feel about you. Now show me how much you love me. You did promise to help me stay in practice."

"Yes, I did. By the time we're ready to leave Galveston, you'll have advanced into expert status." He pulled her into his arms and guided her inside.

"I like the sound of that. After all, practice does make perfect. Right?"

Sterling closed the door, then answered, "Yes, it does. Oh, Tammy," he whispered against her ear then slid his mouth over hers.

Tammy was drowning in his kisses. And then he eased his fingers slowly down her throat and beyond. By the time they reached her breasts, wave after wave of pleasure washed over her, the overflow spilling into her belly, pooling in the heated core of her femininity.

"We've got to get you out of these clothes," he rasped. "You have on way too many of them." Sterling lowered the bodice of her dress to her waist and for a moment, gloried in the sight of her aroused nipples.

When Tammy felt Sterling cover her nipple with his mouth and flick his tongue over it again and again, that familiar wave of sensation engulfed her, reminding her of how close and yet how far she was from reaching the edge of rapture. She was eager to share that special moment of joy with him.

Tammy helped him finish undressing her. Then she practically tore his clothes off him. That sensual throbbing he'd set in motion within her was almost more than she could bear. Her body desperately craved the satiation only he could give it.

"I do believe you are as wild for me as I am for you."

"You only believe? Don't you know for sure?" She strummed her fingers along the firm hard length of his shaft until soft savage sounds erupted from his throat. She possessively closed her hand around him. She reveled in her power when she heard his sharp intake of breath.

"I think you've definitely proved your case." He let his breath go with a sound that was part sigh, part groan.

He moved her hand away from him. "Now it's your turn."

She felt the erotic brush of his fingers across her nipple, reawakening that urgent throbbing between her legs. His caresses stole her strength, leaving her legs feeling heavy and languorous, threatening to buckle her knees. The ecstasy of his touch made her lose all thought except one. She wanted him inside her.

God, how she needed him. "Please," she whispered urgently, her body eager to become one with his.

"Not yet, I've only just begun to prove *my* case," he said, half-teasing and half-meaning it.

"Is the taskmaster back?"

"The kind of work I have in mind will be a labor of love."

Sterling's fingers tormented the secret source of pleasure between her thighs then stopped. The soft sound that left her lips was more than a plea; it was an urgent need, encouraging him to continue.

His lips trailed slow, heated little kisses from the base of her ear along the line of her jaw and then to her lips. When he reached her breast and worshiped her nipples with his tongue, she quivered, and a passionate sigh escaped her throat. He blazed a trail of kisses down her body to her stomach then went lower still until he found what he sought. Then over and over again, he flicked his hot tongue against the pearl of her desire. She cried out, pulling him closer, glorying in the sparks and delicious shudders he sent rushing through her femininity.

Sterling lifted her in his arms and carried her over to the bed, slid his body over hers, and in one powerful thrust, was inside her sheathed deep, endlessly deep. A wail of pleasure shrieked from her lips as the friction of their joining swept her into a glorious climax.

Sterling closed his eyes, delighting in the feel of her warm damp sheath pulsing around his hard, throbbing column of flesh. The feeling was unbelievably wonderful.

Tammy gasped as Sterling began to move rhythmically within her, each thrust filling her more fully than the last. She wanted him to fill her entire being with his love. The hot sliding movement of his manhood in and out, in and out, drove her to the brink and over and an explosion of sensations burst over her.

He opened his eyes and watched her passion fracture, reveling in the feel of her wet, heated inner muscles contracting around him. It sent him over the edge. In that very moment, he knew he'd lost his soul.

❋

Sterling paced back and forth in his studio. He felt torn apart by his inability to bringing himself to tell Tammy the truth, even though he'd tried over the last week since they'd been back from Galveston.

Tried? Is that what you're calling it? his conscience taunted unmercifully.

It was true that he hadn't "tried" very hard because he dreaded the outcome. But not telling her was stressing him out. He rubbed his chest. His antacid tablets were completely useless against this burning, scorching sensation. He'd hardly eaten anything, so he knew it wasn't a simple case of heartburn. He had begun taking pain killers, which he deplored doing, but he'd had no choice because the pain was unbearable.

He picked up the phone book and searched through the physician section. He stopped when he came to internist Paul Stanford and punched in his number and made an appointment.

Sterling felt like a piece of ground meat after his examination. There was no doubt in his mind about Paul Stanford's thoroughness.

"Mr. Phillips," Dr. Stanford said, entering to his private office, "your symptoms indicate a serious condition known as bacterial endocarditis." He glanced through Sterling's medical history. "According to this, you had rheumatic fever as a child. It probably precipitated the endocarditis. What I want you to do is see a colleague of mine, Augusta Morgan."

"Augusta!"

"You know of her?"

"The woman I'm in love with is her foster daughter."

"What a lucky coincidence. She's the best heart surgeon around."

"You think I'll need surgery!"

"Not necessarily. But I'd like her to examine you. She may know of new alternative treatments I'm unaware of."

Sterling had never imagined it could be that kind of serious. He'd thought that a few pills and a strict diet would do the trick.

"The symptoms of endocarditis usually appear in a person's late twenties or early thirties. Physical exertion and/or stress usually triggers the onset of the physical manifestations. Are you stressed about something, Mr. Phillips?"

"I have been extremely busy lately."

"Is that all?"

"I have some personal issues I need to resolve."

"I must warn you that stress can exacerbate your condition markedly, possibly bringing on heart complications if the tension is not alleviated."

"What kind of complications?"

"I think you should let Dr. Morgan counsel you about them."

CHAPTER TWENTY-FOUR

On the drive home from the doctor's office, Sterling was in a subdued frame of mind, mulling over what Dr. Stanford had said about complications. By complications, did he mean a heart attack? Stroke? Or worse? Sterling considered himself to be a fairly young man and couldn't begin to envision any of those things happening to him at this stage in his life. All this time he'd thought it was heartburn, indigestion or possibly an ulcer. He had to admit that after he and Tammy made love, he was completely drained and usually slept like a stone for hours.

He needed to make an appointment with Augusta as soon as he could arrange it. He had every reason in the world to want to be healthy. His life was finally going in the direction he wanted it to go. He had the woman he loved in his life again. The relationship with his son was evolving into a—if not a completely loving one—at least a respectful one. His career was back on track. He had it all. Well, maybe not quite all.

After Kevin went up to his room, Sterling headed for his studio. Once inside, he picked up the phone and punched in Augusta's home phone number.

"Hey, Sterling, what's going on?" Derek said when he recognized Sterling's voice.

"Is Augusta at home by any chance?"

"No, she's still at the hospital."

"Could you give me her number?"

"Sure. Is anything wrong?"

"I just need to talk to her."

Derek gave Sterling the number. "Your heartburn is something serious, isn't it?"

"I won't know until after I've seen her. The doctor I went to today recommended her."

"It's all the stress you've been under, isn't it?"

"That's part of it."

"You still haven't told Tammy the truth, have you?"

"No. There never seems to be a right time."

"And there never will be. You might as well face it. You're just going to have to flat out tell her."

"I know," Sterling groaned. "Putting it off is only making it that much harder."

"You call Augusta. If after the examination you feel like talking, I'm here."

"Thanks, Derek. I appreciate it, man."

"Can you come to my office after you drop Kevin off at the Institute?" Augusta asked Sterling when he phoned.

"That'll work. He's taking summer craft classes and won't be out until one. I'll be there."

Sterling's nerves were a jangled mess by the time he arrived at Augusta's office.

"Sterling, have a seat, I'll be right with you." Augusta put down the papers she'd been poring over, buzzed her nurse and instructed her to ready an examining room for her new patient.

"I received a call from Paul Stanford right after you called," Augusta told him. "He was pleased that you moved on his recommendation so fast. Tell me about your bout with rheumatic fever. How old were you?"

"Seven. I don't remember very much about it. I was in the hospital a while though."

"What did the doctors do for you?"

"I remember taking a lot of medicine and shots."

"Probably antibiotics. I've sent for your childhood medical records. Right now I want to examine you."

The nurse came to show Sterling to the examining room. Minutes later, he felt wired for sound with all the wires hooked to him that led into the EKG machine. He was given an ultrasound and x-rays were taken. He was also given a battery of tests he couldn't begin to pronounce the names of.

When Augusta returned to her office with the x-rays and other test results, Sterling noticed that she had the neutral doctor-to-patient look on her face most doctors used when they were about to give their patients bad news.

"What's the verdict, doc?"

"Dr. Stanford was right. You do have bacterial endocarditis, which is an inflammation involving the lining and valves of the heart." Augusta put the x-rays on a lighted screen unit on the wall. "The endocarditis has severely damaged a valve in you heart." She pointed to a shaded area.

Sterling was quiet for a few moments. "What does that mean?"

"It means you're going to need surgery to replace the damaged valve."

"How soon do you suggest I have the surgery?"

"As soon as possible. There's a sixty-five percent chance of success if we do it right away."

"What you're saying is if I wait it may be too late."

"You're young and healthy, and that's in your favor. But I know the stress you've been under. You have to tell Tammy the truth and relieve the pressure."

"Do you think she'll forgive me?"

"She loves you, Sterling. And love is a powerful force. Never underestimate it."

"It couldn't have been easy for you to forgive Derek."

"No, it wasn't. But my love for him was stronger than my resentment and anger at what he'd done. What bothered me the most was that he didn't feel he could tell me the truth. I could understand why he couldn't right after the accident. But what I found so unforgivable was how long he continued deceiving me after I told him I loved him. Please, don't let someone else tell her. She needs to hear it from you. Now, about your surgery. When do you want me to schedule you for it?"

"I don't know."

"Sterling, this is serious. I can't stress enough how serious."

"Serious, as in I might die if I don't have it soon?" he said jokingly.

"It could come to that."

"I'll have to get back to you about this."

"Sterling—"

"Kevin is scheduled to see a specialist in Los Angeles this weekend. After that I'll have it."

"I know how concerned you are about Kevin. But you have to take care of your own health. Maybe you can reschedule the appointment. You need that surgery yesterday, Sterling."

"I understand what you're saying." He rose from his chair and headed for the door. "I'll get back to you."

"Tammy. I'm glad you called," Augusta exclaimed at hearing her foster daughter's voice. "You're sounding good. The video went all right, I take it?"

"Oh yes, it did. Lance wants me to do another one for one of the other songs on the album. Look, Augusta, I need to talk to you about something. Can you come over after dinner?"

"Are you feeling all right?"

"It's not me I want to talk about. I'll explain when you get here."

"All right. I'll be there at seven."

"Now what's this all about?" Augusta asked Tammy after arriving at her house at exactly seven o'clock.

"I'm worried about Sterling."

"Why?"

"It's hard to explain." Tammy felt her face heat up. This wasn't something a daughter discussed with her mother. "You know that Sterling and I are, ah, close."

Augusta laughed. "I know how close two people in love can become, Tammy. How do you think D.J. was conceived?"

Tammy had to laugh. "You're a modern mom. I keep forgetting that. I should have known I could discuss anything with you."

"Yes, you should. Now what about Sterling is bothering you?"

"When, or should I say after, we make love, Sterling seems to almost go into a coma and sleep for hours. Is it normal for a man to be so completely wiped out after making love?"

"It depends on the man."

"I'm serious, Augusta. I'm worried about him. His breathing changes, and it's as though his heart races a long time after it should have calmed down. Do I sound paranoid?"

"No. Only like a woman concerned about her man. I don't know what to tell you. Maybe he's just exhausted from the excitement of jump-starting his career and helping you with yours and his concerns about Kevin."

"I guess that could be it, but somehow I think it's more than that."

"He'll probably settle down once he gets some much needed rest."

"You're probably right. It's just that I love him so much, and I worry about him."

"I understand where you're coming from. I feel the same way about Derek. I think we women are natural-born worriers."

Augusta hoped her daughter accepted her explanation because she couldn't reveal any of the details of Sterling's condition.

Sterling drove around for a while, thinking about all that Augusta had said. He called Marcus on the cell phone and instructed him to pick Kevin up from the Institute. He had some more serious thinking to do before he told Tammy the truth. It would have to be tonight. After another hour of trying to prepare himself, he headed for Tammy's house.

Tammy heard the doorbell and went to answer its summons. "Sterling, what a wonderful surprise."

He took her in his arms and hugged her tight. "You feel so good in my arms, girl."

"It's where I belong. Come on in. I'm so excited."

"What's going on?"

"Lance Cummings wants me to do another video for one of the other songs on the album. He wants to film it on location in Costa Rica on Friday. I can hardly wait. Mikki's coming with me of course. Do you think you'll be able to come?"

"I'd like to, but I can't. I have to take Kevin to see a specialist in Los Angeles this Friday. Dr. Hastings recommended him. The man specializes in hysterical blindness cases in children and adolescents. This Friday is the only time he'll be able to fit Kevin in. If I don't keep the appointment, it could be six months or a year before I can get another one. I'm sorry, baby. I'd like nothing better than to be with you."

"Kevin is more important than any video. If I hadn't committed myself to this weekend, I'd postpone it and come with you. Is there a special reason you came over?"

"I just wanted to spend my last night before we leave for L.A. with you."

"It's all yours. What about Kevin?"

"He and D.J. want to hang out at my house. Kevin's grandmother is flying down from Portland to spend time with her grandson. Kayla's mother hasn't seen much of him since the accident. Getting over Kayla's death has been hard on her. She said seeing Kevin used to upset her because he favors his mother so closely."

"The poor woman. I'm glad she's decided to spend time with her grandson. Is she going to go with you to see the specialist?"

"Yes."

"That's a good idea."

"I love you."

"I love you, too."

Sterling kissed her. It was more than a communion of lips. Every time he kissed her it was like a new awakening. She was so precious to him.

"Wow! What a kiss. Any more like that and I'll crash and burn on the spot."

"I want you to know that no matter what happens I love you."

"You expecting something to change that?"

"No. Don't pay any attention to me. I just love you so much I don't want to lose you."

"You're never going to lose me. You're everything to me. I happen to love you very much, Sterling Phillips."

"I hope you never stop."

"That's an impossibility."

Tammy studied Sterling with her fingers as they lay together after making love. He had seemed unusually glad to see her, as if it would be his very last chance to do so. He had been so intense, as if he wouldn't let her go in the next hundred years. She felt so loved and cherished. He was her true soul mate.

She crinkled her brows in concern. Sterling hadn't so much as moved a muscle since they'd finished making love. He'd fallen into a deep sleep. She shook him. When he didn't move, she tried harder. He groaned.

"Couldn't wait for another taste of me, could you?" He reached for her, his voice thick with desire and sleep.

"Conceited beast."

"You're the one who woke him up." He kissed her and lowered her back down on the mattress and slipped over her body and thrust deep inside her. And they were soon lost in their lovemaking.

Tiredness dragged at Sterling that next morning when he left Tammy's house. Augusta had said it would only get worse until he had the surgery.

Sterling waited in the hall for Derek's last class to end. When it did, he walked inside.

"Derek, I need to talk."

"Have a seat."

"Augusta told me that it's imperative that have heart surgery. According to her, yesterday isn't too soon. I need a heart valve replacement. I intend to have the surgery, but there are some things I have to do first. Number one, I need to tell Tammy the truth. And two, I need to take Kevin to Los Angeles to see a specialist. About Tammy: after my appointment with Augusta, I went there to tell her the truth, but she was in seventh heaven about flying to Costa Rica to do another video. She was so excited, Derek, that I just didn't have the heart to do that to her. As it turns out, she'll be in Costa Rica for at least a week, maybe longer. By that time I'll be back from Los Angeles. Then I can tell her the truth."

"If Augusta says you need the surgery right away, couldn't you reschedule Kevin's appointment and fly down to Costa Rica with Tammy and after she's finished doing the video tell her the truth?"

"I want Kevin to see the specialist now. If I cancel this appointment, there's no telling when the specialist will be able to see him. It could be six months to a year. That's too long to wait. If this man can help Kevin see, I don't want to wait. The only thing that worries me now is Hunter Bryant. No telling what he could be up to."

"He hasn't written anything about Tammy or you in weeks. Maybe he's lost interest and moved on to someone else."

"Or maybe he's biding his time."

"You have problems, man. And I thought I had it bad. So what are you going to do?"

"Since Kevin's grandmother is going with us to see the specialist, I can fly down to Costa Rica after we see the doctor."

"Sounds like a plan."

CHAPTER TWENTY-FIVE

"I don't know if I want to see the specialist. None of the others have been able to help me get my sight back," Kevin complained to Sterling.

"Dr. Hastings wouldn't have recommended him if he thought he couldn't help you."

"Your father is right," Zetta Cochrane, his grandmother, said.

"You coming with us if we go?"

"Yes, if you want me to. I know I haven't been much of a grandmother the last few years."

"You mean since Mama died. I don't understand why you didn't come see me."

"It's hard to explain, Kevin. You see, you remind me so much of your mother. You look the way she did at your age."

"Seeing me makes you sad?" he said incredulously.

"Not anymore. I'm sorry I haven't been there for you. Can you forgive me?"

"I guess." He sounded uncertain.

"Kevin, people have feelings that don't always make them do the things they should. Your grandmother's grief was so painful, she couldn't come to terms with it," Sterling explained.

"And now she can?"

"I'm trying, Kevin," Zetta said hopefully. "Your mother would have wanted you to see this doctor. I know you want to see again, don't you? If you don't go, you'll never know if he was the one who could have helped you."

"All right, I'll go."

Sterling smiled at Zetta and breathed a sigh of relief. After they saw the specialist, he intended to fly down to Costa Rica and be with Tammy. His smile faded when he thought about the reason he would be going.

He left Kevin and his grandmother to get re-acquainted in the family room and went into the studio. He sat down on the piano bench and the words for a song flooded his mind. He wasn't really in a down mood about his decision to tell Tammy the truth. In fact, he felt strangely relieved. He would finally have it out in the open, and he and Tammy could deal with it together.

Will you understand, will you forgive me
No matter what life throws our way,
I just want to say, I'll always be your man
And you'll always be my woman…

Sterling took his music composition book from its place on top of the piano and started writing down the words to the song. He needed to polish it a little, but the rough draft expressed how he was feeling. He hoped that Tammy would understand and forgive him. He didn't want to think about what his life would be like if she didn't.

When Sterling, Zetta and Kevin arrived in Los Angeles, they learned that Dr. Fayland had been called out of town by a crisis of one of his patients and would be delayed getting back to see Kevin.

"We can take Kevin to Disneyland and a few of the museums

while we wait for Dr. Fayland to get back," Zetta suggested.

"Do you want to do any of those things, Kevin?" Sterling asked.

"Yeah, that'll be cool since we have to wait."

Sterling could tell that Kevin was frustrated by the delay. But he wasn't nearly as frustrated as his father. He would have to put off seeing Tammy.

Tammy tried to get in touch with Sterling to tell him that the video shoot had been wrapped up earlier than planned, but found out from Marcus that he, Kevin and his grandmother would be staying in Los Angeles longer than they'd planned. He had probably left his cell phone at home or forgotten to turn it on as he sometimes did. Tammy was disappointed, but made the best of it.

According to Lance, the video had gone well. The man he'd chosen for the lead character was a wonderful actor and made everything go smoothly. Mikki had even managed to snag a small part in the video and couldn't wait to brag to Wiley about it when they got back to San Francisco.

After several days passed and Sterling didn't get back to her, Tammy began to worry that things might not have gone as well as he had hoped. Finally she got a call.

"Baby, I was so worried. Is Kevin all right?"

"I'm sorry for not calling you sooner. We haven't seen the doctor yet. Something came up, delaying him from examining Kevin. He should be back in another day or so. In the meantime,

Kevin and his grandmother are getting to know each other. How did your video go?"

"Fine, but I missed you."

"I missed you, too, girl."

"I can't wait for you to get back."

"Me either. Being without you is hell."

"Jeremy has set up an interview for me."

"With whom?"

"*Variety Entertainment Magazine's* Hunter Bryant."

Sterling's insides knotted. "I wish you would put it off until I get back."

"I can't. Jeremy has gone to a lot of trouble. I know you don't like Hunter Bryant, baby, but he can help promote my career. Besides, I know how to handle people like him. Don't worry, everything will turn out all right. You'll see."

"I want you to remember how much I love you."

"I won't forget. And don't you forget how much I love you."

"Never." Sterling was resigned to the fact that he couldn't do anything over the phone. Hopefully Bryant hadn't stumbled onto the truth.

Dr. Fayland arrived the next day. Sterling was impressed by the man. He knew exactly how to handle situations with children Kevin's age. After examining Kevin and running a battery of psychological tests, he called Sterling and Zetta into his private office for a conference while the nurse kept Kevin occupied.

"Mr. Phillips, I'll be blunt with you."

"I don't want you to be any other way. Can you help my son?"

"Kevin is holding in a lot of rage toward you about the accident. He said you told him you didn't remember what happened before the crash."

"That was true until recently. I blamed myself for his mother's death, but now I know what really happened…"

"Have you told Kevin?"

"No. I didn't know how to bring it up. Every time I've tried to talk to Kevin about that night, he's refused to discuss it."

"You weren't responsible, were you?"

"No, but Kevin won't believe it."

"I think he already does. From the things he's said, I think he blames himself more than you. He said he heard you and his mother arguing just before the accident. Evidently, she said that if it weren't for Kevin, the two of you wouldn't have stayed together. Is that true?"

"Yes, I'm afraid it is." He glanced at Zetta. "I'm sorry, but it's true."

"I knew there were problems, but…"

"It was mostly my fault. I let my career get in the way and never paid her the attention she thought I should have."

"I know about the other men," Zetta said softly. "Kayla always craved to be in the spotlight. She was the middle child out of five children. She was sandwiched between two older brothers and two younger sisters. She felt that she never fit anywhere." Zetta looked down at her hands. "She thought when she married you, she'd get the attention she craved, but instead, your career put you in the spotlight, and she couldn't handle it. I think that's why she turned to other men."

"I should have spent more time with her and Kevin."

"Do you think Kevin knew about the other men in his mother's life?" Dr. Fayland asked.

"I don't know."

"I have an idea that he did and that's another reason to blame you for making his mother unhappy and him as well. What you have to do is get him to open up about his feelings. He needs to know that you love him, Mr. Phillips. He needs to demolish the wall of hatred he's built to protect himself from getting hurt."

"I'd never hurt him."

"In a way, you already have because for so long you blamed yourself for causing the accident. And in doing that, you fed his resentment. It's time for him to let go of it. When he comes to terms with it, then and only then will he get his sight back."

"You can't give us an idea of when it might happen?"

"I'm afraid not. Is there anyone else he feels close to?"

"The woman I plan to marry has become like a mother to him. I believe he trusts her enough to do that."

"She might be able to help. Does she know the truth?"

The word truth made Sterling flinch inwardly. "She knows that I remember what happened that night."

"If she could get Kevin to talk about that night… The key to healing him is locked in his subconscious."

"You don't think he'll resent her?" Zetta asked.

"No, because she had nothing to do with the accident. His feelings toward his mother are complicated. He loved her, but he also hated her for not trying to keep his family together. Although he's protective of her memory, he's also angry that she left him."

"But she had no choice about that," Zetta said sadly.

"It doesn't matter. He believes she abandoned him long before she died when she turned to men other than her husband."

"You learned all this in one session?"

"The questions I asked made him reveal things that he didn't know he felt. Guilt is a heavy burden to carry, especially when you're as young and troubled as Kevin."

"But he doesn't have anything to feel guilty about."

"He believes he does. We have to make him see that none of it was his fault and that grown up relationships break down for reasons other than their children."

The nurse guided Kevin into the room.

"Can you help me, Dr. Fayland?" he asked.

"I hope so. The key to your getting your sight back is within you, Kevin."

"But I want to see again."

"I know you do, but the mind is a strange thing. It tries to protect us from things we aren't ready to face, the pain we aren't ready to deal with."

"I don't understand. I'm not feeling any pain."

"Maybe physically you're not, Kevin, but the emotional pain is still there."

"That don't make sense. Not seeing doesn't hurt."

"It does in a way. When you're ready to face the truth, you'll get your sight back."

"Can't you tell me when that'll happen?"

"It's all up to you, Kevin."

"I told you he couldn't help me," Kevin said bitterly to his father.

"In a way, he already has, Kevin." Sterling knew his son didn't understand what he was talking about, but with Tammy's help, he would someday soon.

"How long have you been blind, Ms. Gibson?" Hunter Bryant asked Tammy as he sat in her living room interviewing her.

"Since I was a teenager."

"How and where did it happen?"

"In Philadelphia. I was a passenger on a motorcycle, the person driving lost control of the bike and we crashed through a department store window."

"Was the other person hurt?"

"Only cuts and bruises."

"Who was the other person, Ms. Gibson?"

"I really don't want to talk about this anymore, Mr. Bryant. It happened a long time ago."

"I'm sorry if talking about it upsets you. How long have you known Sterling Phillips?"

"For about six months."

"You know about his past, I take it?"

"Yes. And I know that he doesn't trust you to tell the truth as it is."

"Is he still pissed about the way I handled things three years ago?"

"You got it."

"I was only telling it the way I saw it. Getting back to your relationship with him. Are you two involved?"

"I love him if that's what you want to know."

"He's done a lot to further your career, hasn't he? He's almost obsessed about it. It makes me curious as to the reason why, not that you aren't talented, Ms. Gibson. From what Jeremy Ward has told me, he has great plans for you with his company."

"I can't say it makes me unhappy." Tammy smiled. "Is that all, Mr. Bryant? I'm tired from doing the new video and would like to get some rest."

"You've answered a lot of my questions, but you've also raised a lot more. I'll be in touch if I need to know anything else. I'll do all I can to help you reach the top of the charts. Your voice is as special as you are."

"Why thank you, Mr. Bryant. I appreciate that."

After he'd left, Tammy wondered what he meant when he said she'd raised other questions. What kind of questions was he referring to? Something about Hunter Bryant made her feel uneasy. It was as though he were examining her very soul, looking for flaws. If he went digging around in her past, he'd find out her mother had been a crack addict and had abandoned her and her sisters and brother. But the public always had sympathy for the children in such tragic circumstances. Surely, he wouldn't try to use that in some way.

She was letting Sterling's feelings about the man color her opinion, she decided. With a weary groan, Tammy opted to go to bed. The interview was over, and in a few days, Sterling would be home, and they could get on with their lives. She was anxious to know if the doctor had been able to help Kevin.

Sterling heard a knock on his bedroom door and went to answer it. He had reserved a three bedroom suite for himself, Kevin and Zetta at the Hilton.

"Zetta!"

"Can I talk to you?"

"Sure, I'll be right out." He reached for his robe, pulled it on and headed for the living room.

"I'm worried about you, Sterling."

"Me? But Kevin is the one—"

"I'm concerned about my grandson, but I've noticed you taking pain killers. Are you sick?"

"I need surgery. I have a condition called bacterial endocarditis."

"Is it serious?"

"I need a heart valve replacement."

"What are you chances for recovery?"

"Sixty-five percent."

"Does Kevin know?"

"No. I haven't told him."

"Don't you think you should? He's already lost one parent, Sterling. I don't know what would happen if you…"

"The way he feels about me now, I don't know if he'll be sad or glad."

"I agree with Dr. Fayland that he loves you even though he blames you. You need to tell what you remember."

"I'm not sure he's ready to hear it."

"You don't know that. I know my daughter was no saint, and you need to tell Kevin how things really stood between you and his mother so he can get rid of that resentment he feels toward you."

"You think he'll really understand?"

"If you and Ms. Gibson do it together, I think he will. He likes her a lot from what he's told me."

"He does, and it wasn't easy in coming. He fought her tooth and nail at first, but she managed to earn his respect. He's all for me marrying her. And I never thought that would happen."

"You really love this woman, don't you?"

"Yes, I do." He smiled. "That doesn't bother you, does it?"

"No. I'm sorry things didn't work out for you and Kayla, but she's dead and you're alive. Kevin needs a family. If this woman is what you both need, you won't have a problem with me."

"Thanks, Zetta."

"Something is still bothering you, though, isn't it?"

"You're very perceptive. Yes, but I'll take care of it as soon as we get back to San Francisco."

"If I can do anything for you or Kevin, please let me know. When you and Tammy get married, I'll take Kevin to live with me while you go on your honeymoon."

"I wish Kayla had been more like her mother."

Sterling smiled as he watched Zetta go to her room. The burning sensation in his chest and stomach was becoming unbearable. He would have to have that surgery soon, he thought, reaching inside his robe pocket for the pain killers. Just as soon as he told Tammy. They'd be leaving for San Francisco in the morning. By tomorrow evening, he would have told Tammy the truth. Would she forgive him for deceiving her for so long? He knew she loved him, but would love be enough? It had to be. He walked over to the bar and poured a glass of water to take the pills.

Sterling sat down on the couch and reached for the phone. "Tammy."

"Oh, Sterling! Are you and Kevin back from L. A.?"

"No, that's why I'm calling, we'll be back at noon tomorrow. I want to see you as soon as we get back. God, I've missed you, girl."

"I'm happy to hear it because I've missed you, too. I'll be waiting for you at your house."

"That's the best news I've heard all year."

"How did it go with Kevin?"

"I need to talk to you about that. Dr. Fayland thinks you're the key to Kevin's getting his sight back."

"He does!"

"Kevin is comfortable with you, more comfortable than he is with me right now. Dr. Fayland feels that Kevin respects you and may be able to open up to you. We'll talk about it when I get back. I love you, Tammy."

"And I love you. I can hardly wait to get you in my bed for good, Mr. Phillips."

"That's exactly the place I want to be. Until tomorrow."

"Tomorrow."

Tammy sat down with Mikki at the kitchen table the next morning, poured herself a cup of coffee, then found the knobs on the radio and turned it on. She was eager to hear Hunter Bryant's Sunday morning radio program since he hadn't contacted her again about another possible interview.

"The new singing sensation, Tammy Gibson, is some kind of woman. Or maybe she's a saint. Despite what the man in her life did to her in the past, she forgave him and they are back together. At age fifteen in Philadelphia, she was blinded in a motorcycle accident. David Dixon, a.k.a., Sterling David Phillips, renowned R & B composer and the love of her life, was driving. I guess they must have had their own forgive and forget session. Eat your heart out, Mother Love.

"Jeremy Ward, her producer has a lot planned for Ms. Gibson and Mr. Phillips. They appear to be the perfect composer/singer dream team. R & B records—"

Mikki turned the radio off. "Tammy, I'm sure he—"

"Told the truth." Her mind was whirling like a spinning top. Hunter Bryant couldn't have said what she thought she'd heard. Surely Sterling and David couldn't be one and the same person. He wouldn't have deceived her like that. He would have told her who he really was, if he…

Tammy remembered when she found out Sterling was the mystery man. He'd only admitted it because he had to. All this time and he hadn't told her the most important truth. Why? He'd had plenty of opportunity. How could he have kept this from her? He'd let her fall in love with him and come to care for his son as though he were her own. He'd written songs for her and had made tender sweet love to her. Damn him. Was it all done

281

out of guilt, and he really didn't love her? Did he even know how he truly felt about her?

"Tammy, you need to talk to Sterling about this."

"It won't change anything, Mikki. He deceived me."

"But he loves you, surely you know that."

"I don't know anything right now. All I know is that the man I love couldn't bring himself to tell me the truth. Is it me? Am I that unapproachable?"

"It's not that at all. You know who you are. Don't take it like this. Give Sterling a chance to defend himself. You know those celebrity reports color the truth to sell their stories."

"In this case, he didn't have to do very much coloring to accomplish it, did he?"

"Don't talk like that."

"It's the truth, Mikki." Tammy rose stiffly to her feet and stumbled.

"Tammy, let me—"

"No. I'm going to my room. You don't have to stay here with me. Go somewhere. I'm sure you have plans."

"I can't leave you like this."

"I insist. I want to be alone."

"And do what? Brood? Tammy, why don't you call Augusta and talk to her about this."

Tammy's breath sucked in. Did Augusta and Derek know the truth about who Sterling was? He and Derek were close. Had he confided the truth in him? Now that she thought about it, Augusta had been evasive when she'd voiced her concerns about Sterling's health. She and Derek had probably known for a while. Had Sterling ever intended to tell her the truth?

"I don't want to talk to anyone right now. You go and spend time with Wiley."

"Tammy, I don't want to leave you like this."

"I insist. Go. I want to be alone to think."

CHAPTER TWENTY-SIX

Sterling was glad when the plane landed at the San Francisco airport. Their flight from L.A. had been delayed. He was glad he'd conquered his driving phobia and had the Navigator waiting in the airport parking lot because he didn't have the patience to wait for Marcus to come drive them home. He knew Tammy would be there. God, how he'd missed her. Today he'd tell her the truth and get that out of the way…

And then what, Phillips?

Tammy would forgive him and they could get on with their lives.

You should prepare yourself for the worst.

I won't have to.

You hope. What you have to say is going to devastate the woman.

I know, but she loves me.

And you love her, but there are some things a woman can never forgive. Deceit is one of them.

We'll work it out.

Sterling called Marcus from his cell. "Is Tammy there?

"Yes, she's in your studio. You want me to tell her you're on your way home?"

"No. Don't do that. We'll be there in a few minutes."

Sterling smiled when he heard the piano as they drove up.

God, he could hardly contain his impatience to see the woman he loved.

"I can't wait to see Tammy!" Kevin exclaimed. "I mean, talk to her."

"I know, Kevin, but she and your father need some time alone," his grandmother answered.

"You mean to kiss and stuff like that."

"Kevin!"

Sterling laughed. "It's all right, Zetta. You're right, I do want to do those things because I love her, Kevin."

"You gonna marry her?"

"I hope she'll say yes when I ask her. What do you think about that?"

"She's cool. If I'm gonna have a stepmother, I want it to be Tammy."

"I'm happy to hear you say that, son. She really cares about you."

"And I care about her."

"Kevin and I will just say hi to Tammy then we'll leave you two alone to talk." Zetta smiled knowingly.

After they entered the living room, Kevin and Zetta followed Sterling, down the hall to his studio. When they entered the room the music stopped.

"We're back, Tammy!" Kevin made his way over to the piano.

She hugged him. "I'm glad you're back. Later we'll talk about what the doctor said. Okay?"

"I guess you want to talk to my father and do what most grown-ups do."

"And what might that be?"

"You know," he said, sounding the slightest bit embarrassed by the subject matter.

"It's good to see you again, Tammy." Zetta smiled. "I'll take Kevin into the family room so you and Sterling can talk."

Sterling walked over to the piano and put his hands on Tammy's shoulders. He frowned when he felt her stiffen at his touch. A frisson of fear slithered up his spine. Something wasn't right.

After Zetta and Kevin left the room, Tammy eased her shoulders from beneath Sterling's fingers.

"Let's go out in the garden," she said emotionlessly.

"Tammy, is something wrong?"

"I'd say everything is wrong. I found out what you've been trying so hard not to tell me."

"What do you mean?"

"You know damn well what I mean. For starters, your real name is Sterling *David* Dixon. The same David Dixon I knew when I was fifteen. The same David Dixon who abandoned me after the accident when he knew I'd be blind."

Sterling's heart lurched with pain. He'd waited too late, and his house of cards had come tumbling down.

"I was going to tell you, Tammy, honest I was."

"Honest? You haven't been that since we met at the fund raiser. No. Even before that when you sent me flowers as the mystery man. I bet you wanted your secret to remain a mystery for the rest of your life. Did you ever really intend to tell me the truth?"

"I did, you've got to believe that."

"No, I don't have to because it's not true. You had to know when I found out what it would do to me. Why didn't you tell me yourself, Sterling?" she asked, her voice cracking from the strain.

"I meant to, my darling girl. I'm sorry now that I didn't." He put his arms around her shoulders and hugged her tight while she cried.

Tammy pulled away from him after she regained her composure.

"How did you find out?"

"It's not important."

"I think it is. Was it Hunter Bryant?"

"Yes. He said it on the radio this morning. Does Derek know?"

He didn't answer.

"How could you tell him and not me, Sterling?"

Sterling sighed heavily, his heart breaking at the pained sound in her voice. He'd done this to her. God, he hoped she'd forgive him. He wasn't sure he'd ever be able to forgive himself for hurting her like this.

"Why did you abandon me after the accident?"

"I didn't, Tammy. I was there when the paramedics came and took you to the hospital. After the doctors operated, I waited to see you. You were like a broken doll all wrapped in bandages, and so still I thought…"

"You never came to see me. I remember waking up and asking for you, but you never came."

"I was there, but I felt so damned guilty about you losing your sight, I couldn't say a word."

"What about later when you knew I would be all right? Why didn't you come then?"

"I thought you'd be better off without me. I'd already messed up your life. I knew you'd never forgive me."

"But I forgave you about the accident. It was just that, an accident. I remember how hard you had tried to slow the bike down and how the icy rain on the street prevented it. You couldn't help what happened. What I can't forgive you for is not being there with me when I found out I'd be blind. I felt so alone, Sterling. You were all I had. When I lost you, I wanted to die."

"Baby, I'm so sorry. I'll make it up to you, I promise."

"I don't know if you can. All these years I thought you didn't care. It warped my viewpoint about men, made me afraid to trust completely. Then I met Sterling Phillips, a man I could believe in, one who believed in me, believed that I could make it to the top of the charts. A man with a troubled son that I've grown to love.

"Kevin reminded me so much of myself. I understood his pain, his frustration at losing his sight. How ironic that in accidents where you were doing the driving we both…"

"Don't say it. I know what I did, and I've paid, believe me."

"What really hurts is that you couldn't bring yourself to tell me the truth. You knew how much I'd come to love you."

"I know, but the right time never came."

"I can't believe you deceived me like this for so long. All that you did for me was all out of guilt, wasn't it? Hunter Bryant said you seemed almost obsessed about helping me gain success. And now I know why."

"I ruined your life, and I wanted to make up for what I'd taken from you. I couldn't give you your sight back, but I could make you a star."

"Do you really love me or is it guilt?"

"You can't believe that I don't love you."

"I'm not sure I can believe anything you say."

"Darling, please let me—"

"Let you what? Convince me? Or convince yourself?"

"I don't need to convince myself about my feelings for you. I love you, damn it."

"If you did, you would have been honest with me from the beginning."

Sterling felt a dull ache in his chest. He had to convince her that all he'd done wasn't just out of guilt. He had to convince her that he loved her and always would.

"All those times you made love to me. Were they also out of guilt?"

"No, never."

"I feel so betrayed. If you love me like you say, why couldn't you have trusted in my love and just told me the truth?"

"I did trust you, but I wanted—never mind what I wanted. Can't you find it in your heart to forgive me?"

"I don't know. I want to."

"You can't just give up on what we have. Maybe after the pain has—"

"I can't talk about it anymore. I'm going home."

"You can't leave things like this between us. I love you and want to marry you."

"I can't think about marriage right now."

"Daddy, you've got to make her change her mind," Kevin pleaded from the open sliding glass door. He'd obviously been standing there long enough to figure out what was happening.

"Tammy, I want you for a stepmother."

"Kevin, I don't know what to tell you."

"Say you'll change your mind, please."

"I can't. I know it's hard for you to understand."

Kevin turned on his father. "It's all your fault. You made Mama stop loving you. Now you're doing the same thing to Tammy."

"Son, I—"

"I hate you."

"No, you don't, Kevin," Tammy said and then walked over to him and hugged him. He pulled away.

"You hate him, too, or else you'd marry him and we could be a family."

"It's not that simple. But I don't hate him."

"But you won't change your mind about marrying him."

"Oh, Kevin. I'm so sorry, but no, I can't, not right now. I don't know when or if—I have to go."

"Please, don't go."

"I have to. You can still—we can still be friends, can't we?"

"It won't be the same."

"I know, but…"

"I'll get Marcus to drive you home," Sterling said. "And after you've had time to absorb everything maybe you'll—"

"Right now I can't make any promises."

Sterling walked into the studio and called Marcus to bring the car around. Zetta came into the room after Marcus and Tammy had left.

"Kevin, I know its hard for you, but—"

"It's his fault that Mama is dead, and now he's made Tammy

go away."

"Things happen, but we shouldn't cast blame."

"But it is his fault."

"Your mother's death was an accident."

"He was driving."

"Kevin, I didn't want your mother to die. Don't you remember what happened before the accident?"

"I remember hearing you and mama fighting."

"Don't you remember anything else?"

"It doesn't make any difference. She's dead and she's not coming back. And now Tammy... I wanted her to come live with us."

"I did, too. I still do. Maybe when she—"

"You hurt her just like you hurt Mama." Kevin started crying.

"You'd better help him to his room, Zetta."

The woman shot Sterling a look of sympathy, then, nodding her head, did as he'd asked.

Sterling stood looking out over the garden. He'd procrastinated too long, and now he might lose the woman he loved. Derek had pleaded with him to do it sooner, but he hadn't wanted to risk losing Tammy. What an irony. By not telling her himself, he'd lost her. It was no wonder that she couldn't bring herself to trust him.

He'd been living with this guilt and uncertainty too long, and it was telling on him. He suddenly felt dizzy and sick to his stomach. And the dull pain that he'd experienced in his chest earlier returned with a vengeance, squeezing as tight as a vice around his heart with each breath he took. He stumbled over to the desk and was searching for August's phone number when Zetta came back into the room.

"Sterling, what's wrong?"

"Dr. Morgan's number—call—" Sterling gasped, clutched his chest, then crumpled to the floor. His last thought before blackness descended was that he loved Tammy and wondered if he would ever be able to tell her again.

CHAPTER TWENTY-SEVEN

The phone rang and Tammy picked up the receiver.

"Tammy, it's Derek."

"Derek, you sound so—is anything wrong?"

"The reason I'm calling is—"

"Is it D.J. or Augusta? What is it?" she asked, her voice frantic.

"No. It's Sterling… Oh, God, how do I tell you this."

"Derek, please!"

"Sterling collapsed and was rushed to the hospital. Augusta is operating on him as we speak."

"What? Sterling? What happened?"

"He's been seeing Augusta professionally."

"But she's a heart surgeon. That means he has a heart condition."

"Augusta will have to fill you in on that. Can you get Mikki to bring you to the hospital?"

"She's not here, I'll get a taxi. How is Kevin?"

"His grandmother called Augusta. She and Kevin are probably at the hospital."

"It's all my fault. He and I had—I found out who he was and we—"

"He needed surgery before this, Tammy."

"Why didn't he tell me? I knew he'd been—I don't know—tired lately. He's going to be all right, isn't he, Derek?"

"I don't know, Tammy."

"Oh, God, he has to be. I love him."

"Did you tell him that?"

"I was so upset about finding out he'd deceived me all this time that I didn't tell him so."

"Just get to the hospital. My prayers are with you and Kevin. Sterling is young and strong. He has that in his favor. D.J. and I will get there as soon we can."

Tammy was in a state of shock by the time she reached the hospital. She found Kevin and his grandmother in the waiting room. Sterling had been rushed into surgery an hour earlier.

"He's got to be all right, Tammy," Kevin cried. "I said some real bad things to him. It's my fault if he dies. It was all my fault that Mama died, too."

Tammy took him in her arms. "No, it wasn't, honey. Can't you remember anything about what happened the night of the accident? If you did, you'd remember that it was your mother who struck your father, momentarily dazing him. Kayla wrested the wheel from him, causing the accident."

A strangled cry left Kevin's throat as the memories bombarded him. He shuddered then collapsed in tears against Tammy.

"How do you know?"

"Your father told me."

"Why didn't he tell me?"

"I don't know. Maybe he felt that he couldn't. Maybe he wanted you to remember on your own. If anyone is to blame for putting him in here, I am," Tammy went on. "I should have told

BEVERLY CLARK

him that I still loved him, enough to forgive him anything, but I let my injured pride get in the way. I know he loves me and never meant to hurt me."

"Both of you stop blaming yourselves," Zetta said sternly.

"Sterling wouldn't want either of you doing that. He loves you both."

"But I was so mean to him when he tried to talk to me about Mama," Kevin sobbed.

"He knew you were upset."

"But I told him I hated him. I didn't really mean it."

"He knows you didn't, Kevin."

Tammy closed her eyes, trying to stave away the pain of her own guilt. She loved him, and yet she hadn't been able to tell him the words of forgiveness he had needed so desperately to hear.

"We came as soon as we could," Derek said, entering the waiting room with D.J.

"Are you all right, Kevin?" D.J. asked.

"I don't know, man. I feel so bad, D.J."

D.J. walked over to his friend and gave him a bear hug.

Derek was proud of his son. He had his mother's compassion when dealing with the pain of others. He took Tammy's hand and guided her over to the seats by the window.

"We need to talk."

"Oh, Derek," she cried, "he's got to be all right. I'll never forgive myself if he…"

"Stop talking like that. He's in the best of hands, you know that. If anyone can pull him through this, Augusta can."

"I know you're right. If I'd only—"

"Those are the two most overused words in the universe. You

295

had to come to grips with your feelings and sometimes we need more than a few minutes to do that, so stop blaming yourself."

She smiled a watery smile. "You're right, they are overused."

"What was it you couldn't bring yourself to forgive him for? The past or the present?"

"I thought it was the present. Now I'm wondering if it isn't both."

"You know what Augusta and I went through because I couldn't bring myself to tell her the truth. When Sterling comes out of this, I want you to make up with him."

"If I get the chance."

"Put your trust in God. He'll give you the strength to see you through this."

Tammy squeezed his hand. "As my father is helping me to do right now."

The swishing sound of the operating room doors opening down the hall alerted them all that the operation was over. It had been seven hours since the surgery began. It was now two o'clock in the morning.

Derek saw the weary look on his wife's face as she headed in their direction, still in her surgical scrubs. He tensed, wondering how the surgery had gone. He took Tammy's hand in his.

"Sterling's being transferred to Cardiac ICU," Augusta explained.

"How is he, Augusta?" Tammy asked worriedly.

"He came through the operation. I had to replace a valve in

his heart. Now it's up to him and God if he survives. If he'd only agreed to have the surgery when I first suggested it… Since he didn't, we'll have to wait and see."

"How long before you'll know anything?" Zetta asked.

"I can't say, Mrs. Cochrane."

"My daddy isn't going to die, is he?" Kevin rasped brokenly.

"We'll do everything we can to keep that from happening, Kevin," Augusta reassured him.

Tammy gave Augusta a pleading look. "When can I see him?"

"Not for several hours. He's heavily sedated. You'd better take Kevin home, Mrs. Cochrane."

"I don't want to go home," Kevin cried.

"There's nothing you can do, son," Derek told him. "D.J. will go with you."

"As soon as we know anything, I'll call you," Augusta said, sympathy lacing her voice.

"I can't go, so don't tell me I have to, Augusta," Tammy said strongly.

"I knew you wouldn't, so I've arranged a bed for you."

"If Tammy's staying, so am I," Kevin blurted.

Augusta conceded defeat, knowing it wouldn't do any good to insist that the boy go. "There are two beds in the room."

Tammy sat beside Sterling's bed, listening to the beeping of the heart monitoring equipment, imagining how he looked hooked up to the many wires she'd touched leading to his chest. The other mechanical sounds in the room frightened yet comforted her all at the same time. She eased her hand over Sterling's. He was so still.

She remembered how animated his voice had sounded when he was cracking the whip during the recording sessions. He was a perfectionist when it came to his music. He'd taught her to be one, too.

Augusta came into the room to check Sterling's vital signs and to see if he showed any signs of regaining consciousness. It had been thirty-six hours since the surgery. Still, no change. It wasn't unusual, considering the damage his collapse had caused and the seriousness of the surgery. It took time for the heart to adjust to the new valve. And there was always a chance his body might reject the valve.

She'd tried to talk Tammy into going home for a few hours, but she had refused. She'd had Mikki bring her a change of clothes. At least she'd managed to get Kevin to go home with his grandmother. The child was completely exhausted.

"Tammy, you really should go home for a while. You know I'll call you if there is any change."

"I know you would, Augusta, but I just can't leave him. I want to be there when he opens his eyes. I want my face to be the first thing he sees."

Augusta quietly left the room. "I tried," she whispered to herself.

"You've got to wake up, Sterling. We belong together, baby. Who else will be there to whip me into shape?"

Tammy heard the door open and Kevin's cane tapping the floor as he entered the room.

"Kevin?"

"I'm here, Tammy. Has he—"

"No, I'm afraid not."

"But he has to. Daddy, please wake up," Kevin pleaded, making his way over to the bed. "He can't die, Tammy."

"He's not going to. We just have to be patient and let his body heal itself. When it has, then he'll wake up."

"I have so much to tell him. I have to tell him how sorry I am."

"I'm sure he knows, Kevin."

"You really think so?"

"Yes, I do. I'm going to get some coffee. You take my seat." She unfolded her cane and headed for the door.

Outside the hospital room, Tammy leaned wearily against the wall for a moment before heading down the hall to find the coffee machine. She began to imagine what it had been like for a seventeen-year-old boy waiting to hear if his girlfriend would live or die, then to discover that she'd be blind and know that he was responsible.

It had to have been hell for the sensitive boy he'd been back then. Even then he'd been obsessed with writing songs. Was his attention to making her a success an atonement for what he considered were his sins? Was his procrastination some kind of self-punishment? Oh, Sterling, how you must have suffered. And she hadn't made it any better.

Tammy returned to Sterling's room and had a nurse bring in another chair which she moved next to Kevin's.

They waited as the nurse checked Sterling then left the room.

"When do you think he'll wake up?" Kevin asked.

"It could be today, tomorrow or—"

"Never!" Kevin cried, grabbing his father's hand. "Please wake up, Daddy. I remember the night of the accident. I know it wasn't your fault."

"Sterling, baby, I love you," Tammy said. "I hope you can forgive me, I've forgiven you." Tears streamed down her face.

Sterling groaned, groggily opening his eyes and saw Tammy. "Too pretty to cry."

"Daddy!" Kevin cried.

Sterling looked at his son. "Kevin?"

"You're going to be all right."

Sterling watched his son's face and knew the moment his sight returned, and he smiled.

"I can see!" Kevin threw his arms around Sterling's neck and cried.

Sterling's tears blended with his son's. He hadn't thought he would ever see this day or that look in Kevin's eyes. He also saw the joy and relief on Tammy's face. He wished with all his heart and soul that she would one day get her sight back.

"Tammy, I—"

"You don't have to say anything. My answer is yes."

"Yes?"

"Yes, I'll marry you. Yes, I love you. Yes, I adore you."

EPILOGUE

Tammy would never forget the day she saw her baby daughter's face for the first time. It was through a haze that cleared a little more each day, but sight was no less beautiful for lack of perfect vision.

Dr. Eekong, the eye specialist who had helped Augusta regain her sight, had a breakthrough with optic nerve surgery, using the special laser he'd created. He'd been able to reduce the scarring near the optic nerve, relieving the pressure. That allowed light to travel through the narrow passage to the center of the eye.

Tammy smiled when she saw her husband's handsome face as he tossed his daughter up in the air. Two-year-old Samantha squealed with pleasure.

"Her squeals of pleasure remind me of her mother's when I make love to her."

"Sterling!"

"Samantha doesn't understand what I'm talking about. Or know how impatient I am to get her mother into bed."

Since his recovery from his surgery, Tammy had to practically beat him off with a stick. Sterling was insatiable, and his endurance was to be admired.

"You can't call me a tired old man anymore."

"I certainly can't. You'll have to write me another award-winning album right away."

"Don't tell me you're going to be like a certain singer who puts out an album with each child?"

"The doctor says spring, just before Kevin's graduation from junior high school. Think you can have enough songs written by then to float an album?"

Kevin came out of the house and walked toward them. He was a changed boy since getting his sight back, and his relationship with his father was finally on an even keel. They continued to grow closer every day. There were still mini blowups, but that was normal for two such headstrong males. Tammy was the buffer between them.

"You want me to take Samantha, Tammy?" Kevin asked.

"You mean you're volunteering?"

"I am, but don't spread it around. D.J. will never let me hear the end of it." He hoisted his sister onto his hip.

"It's already too late," D.J. teased as he, Augusta and Derek walked up, "'cause I heard it all."

Kevin groaned.

Sterling and Tammy laughed.

"I'm glad to see you both so happy, Tammy." Augusta smiled.

Seeing her foster mother's face for the first time had brought tears to Tammy's eyes.

"I'll add my sentiments to that."

Tammy smiled. Derek was every bit as handsome as she'd imagined him to be. The world around her was so precious. She would never take it for granted.

After the house was quiet and the children were asleep, Tammy and Sterling went downstairs to the studio. They'd been working on a duet. It brought back memories of when they were teenagers.

"We make a good team, as Hunter Bryant so aptly put it," Sterling commented. "I could have strangled him for what he did that Sunday morning."

"You're just upset because he beat you to the punch."

"That's not funny."

"On the contrary, he made me cherish the love I had. By the way, what are you going to name our song?"

"'Echoes of Yesterday.'"

"Any particular reason?"

"Our past echoes profoundly in our present and will in our future. I'm sure Augusta and Derek will agree with that."

"I know how I do. I love you, Sterling. You're my life." Tammy's eyes filled with emotion.

"And you are mine, and I love you and always will." With that, he pulled her to him for a kiss that spoke of the wonderful years still to come.

AUTHOR BIOGRAPHY

Working in the editorial department of the L.A. *Herald Examiner*, **Beverly Clark** was given her first exposure to professional writing. From there she wrote fillers for the newspaper and magazines such as *Red Book*, *Good Housekeeping*, and *McCalls*. She also wrote one hundred and twenty romantic short-stories with Sterlind/McFadden Magazines. Clark joined the RWA, a national writers organization that helps writers, published and unpublished, reach their writing goals. In order to gain more knowledge, she attended creative writing classes and other related courses at Antelope Valley College, and classes and seminars at L.T.U. This talented writer, who once managed a second-hand book store, The Book Nook, for two years, has since completed eight full length books. She is now currently working part-time for Walden Books. She also helps a group called Friends of the Libraries, encouraging children and adults to read and enjoy books. Beverly along with her daughter, Gloria, live in High Desert community of Lancaster, California.

Other Titles by Beverly Clark

1585710164   Bound by Love
Lesley Wells has made a new life for herself as a successful designer. Everything is perfect until Darren Taylor, her former fiance, plans to buy the company she works for and dredges up

the past. When he discovers that they share a child, he insists on her returning and marrying him. Lesley still loves him, but can she trust him?

1585710849   A Twist Of Fate

Camille was looking at building a beautiful full life with her jazz/saxophonist husband, until tragedy dashed those hopes. Holding on to one dream...having her husbands' child, she conceives through alternative methods.

1885478615   The Price of Love

Brenda Jackson has had it with men—until Gil Jackson walks into her life. His charm and good-looks win her over, but their love is threatened by a secret from her past.

1585710636   Cherish the Flame

Valerie Baker had left her hometown after graduating from college to find a job in her area of expertise in Detroit. She landed a position as an apprentice chemist at Price Industries. She also met and fell in love with Alexander Price, but Michael Price had his own plans for his son's future, and he tries to convince Valerie that she could never fit into Alex's world. When that ploy doesn't work, he uses information he'd gleaned from the private investigator to finally force her to break it off with Alex and return to her home in Quinneth Falls.

When Alex questions why Valerie has left him, lies are told

and secrets are kept. Alex is devastated to learn that the woman he loves has left him. Over the next eight years Alex turns into a wiser, but cynical man making Price Industries his life.

Upon hearing that Valerie was in need and extremely vulnerable, Alex couldn't pass up the chance to step in and bail her out. Now that he had her under his control, he would finally make her atone for her past sins as he saw fit.

1885478844   A Love to Cherish

Six years after their relationship ended, pro football star Cornell Robertson learns that Tracey Hamilton bore his twin sons. Now he wants her and his boys back in his life. What will Tracey choose?

1885478127   Yesterday Is Gone

Augusta Humphrey has a new life until an automobile accident turns her dreams of being a successful doctor into a life of darkness. Into the wake of this tragedy steps Todd Winters, whose endless devotion and abundant love make her altered life bearable. But he has a secret that threatens to break her heart all over again.

2005 Publication Schedule

January

A Heart's Awakening
Veronica Parker
$9.95
1-58571-143-9

Falling
Natalie Dunbar
$9.95
1-58571-121-7

February

Echoes of Yesterday
Beverly Clark
$9.95
1-58571-131-4

A Love of Her Own
Cheris F. Hodges
$9.95
1-58571-136-5

Higher Ground
Leah Latimer
$19.95
1-58571-157-8

March

Misconceptions
Pamela Leigh Starr
$9.95
1-58571-117-9

I'll Paint a Sun
Al Garotto
$9.95
1-58571-165-9

Peace Be Still
Colette Haywood
$12.95
1-58571-129-2

April

Intentional Mistakes
Michele Sudler
$9.95
1-58571-152-7

Conquering Dr. Wexler's Heart
Kimberley White
$9.95
1-58571-126-8

Song in the Park
Martin Brant
$15.95
1-58571-125-X

May

The Color Line
Lizette Carter
$9.95
1-58571-163-2

Unconditional
A.C. Arthur
$9.95
1-58571-142-X

Last Train to Memphis
Elsa Cook
$12.95
1-58571-146-2

June

Angel's Paradise
Janice Angelique
$9.95
1-58571-107-1

Suddenly You
Crystal Hubbard
$9.95
1-58571-158-6

Matters of Life and Death
Lesego Malepe, Ph.D.
$15.95
1-58571-124-1

2005 Publication Schedule (continued)

July

Pleasures All Mine
Belinda O. Steward
$9.95
1-58571-112-8

Wild Ravens
Altonya Washington
$9.95
1-58571-164-0

Class Reunion
Irma Jenkins/John
Brown
$12.95
1-58571-123-3

August

Path of Thorns
Annetta P. Lee
$9.95
1-58571-145-4

Timeless Devotion
Bella McFarland
$9.95
1-58571-148-9

Life Is Never As It Seems
June Michael
$12.95
1-58571-153-5

September

Beyond the Rapture
Beverly Clark
$9.95
1-58571-131-4

Blood Lust
J. M. Jeffries
$9.95
1-58571-138-1

Rough on Rats and
Tough on Cats
Chris Parker
$12.95
1-58571-154-3

October

A Will to Love
Angie Daniels
$9.95
1-58571-141-1

Taken by You
Dorothy Elizabeth Love
$9.95
1-58571-162-4

Soul Eyes
Wayne L. Wilson
$12.95
1-58571-147-0

November

A Drummer's Beat to
Mend
Kay Swanson
$9.95

Sweet Reprecussions
Kimberley White
$9.95
1-58571-159-4

Red Polka Dot in a
Worldof Plaid
Varian Johnson
$12.95
1-58571-140-3

December

Hand in Glove
Andrea Jackson
$9.95
1-58571-166-7

Blaze
Barbara Keaton
$9.95

Across
Carol Payne
$12.95
1-58571-149-7

ECHOES OF YESTERDAY

Other Genesis Press, Inc. Titles

Acquisitions	Kimberley White	$8.95
A Dangerous Deception	J.M. Jeffries	$8.95
A Dangerous Love	J.M. Jeffries	$8.95
A Dangerous Obsession	J.M. Jeffries	$8.95
After the Vows	Leslie Esdaile	$10.95
(Summer Anthology)	T.T. Henderson	
	Jacqueline Thomas	
Again My Love	Kayla Perrin	$10.95
Against the Wind	Gwynne Forster	$8.95
A Lark on the Wing	Phyliss Hamilton	$8.95
A Lighter Shade of Brown	Vicki Andrews	$8.95
All I Ask	Barbara Keaton	$8.95
A Love to Cherish	Beverly Clark	$8.95
Ambrosia	T.T. Henderson	$8.95
And Then Came You	Dorothy Elizabeth Love	$8.95
Angel's Paradise	Janice Angelique	$8.95
A Risk of Rain	Dar Tomlinson	$8.95
At Last	Lisa G. Riley	$8.95
Best of Friends	Natalie Dunbar	$8.95
Bound by Love	Beverly Clark	$8.95
Breeze	Robin Hampton Allen	$10.95
Brown Sugar Diaries &	Delores Bundy &	$10.95
Other Sexy Tales	Cole Riley	
By Design	Barbara Keaton	$8.95
Cajun Heat	Charlene Berry	$8.95
Careless Whispers	Rochelle Alers	$8.95
Caught in a Trap	Andre Michelle	$8.95
Chances	Pamela Leigh Starr	$8.95
Dark Embrace	Crystal Wilson Harris	$8.95
Dark Storm Rising	Chinelu Moore	$10.95
Designer Passion	Dar Tomlinson	$8.95
Ebony Butterfly II	Delilah Dawson	$14.95

Erotic Anthology	Assorted	$8.95
Eve's Prescription	Edwina Martin Arnold	$8.95
Everlastin' Love	Gay G. Gunn	$8.95
Fate	Pamela Leigh Starr	$8.95
Forbidden Quest	Dar Tomlinson	$10.95
Fragment in the Sand	Annetta P. Lee	$8.95
From the Ashes	Kathleen Suzanne	$8.95
	Jeanne Sumerix	
Gentle Yearning	Rochelle Alers	$10.95
Glory of Love	Sinclair LeBeau	$10.95
Hart & Soul	Angie Daniels	$8.95
Heartbeat	Stephanie Bedwell-Grime	$8.95
I'll Be Your Shelter	Giselle Carmichael	$8.95
Illusions	Pamela Leigh Starr	$8.95
Indiscretions	Donna Hill	$8.95
Interlude	Donna Hill	$8.95
Intimate Intentions	Angie Daniels	$8.95
Just an Affair	Eugenia O'Neal	$8.95
Kiss or Keep	Debra Phillips	$8.95
Love Always	Mildred E. Riley	$10.95
Love Unveiled	Gloria Greene	$10.95
Love's Deception	Charlene Berry	$10.95
Mae's Promise	Melody Walcott	$8.95
Meant to Be	Jeanne Sumerix	$8.95
Midnight Clear	Leslie Esdaile	$10.95
(Anthology)	Gwynne Forster	
	Carmen Green	
	Monica Jackson	
Midnight Magic	Gwynne Forster	$8.95
Midnight Peril	Vicki Andrews	$10.95
My Buffalo Soldier	Barbara B. K. Reeves	$8.95
Naked Soul	Gwynne Forster	$8.95
No Regrets	Mildred E. Riley	$8.95
Nowhere to Run	Gay G. Gunn	$10.95

Object of His Desire	A. C. Arthur	$8.95
One Day at a Time	Bella McFarland	$8.95
Passion	T.T. Henderson	$10.95
Past Promises	Jahmel West	$8.95
Path of Fire	T.T. Henderson	$8.95
Picture Perfect	Reon Carter	$8.95
Pride & Joi	Gay G. Gunn	$8.95
Quiet Storm	Donna Hill	$8.95
Reckless Surrender	Rochelle Alers	$8.95
Rendezvous with Fate	Jeanne Sumerix	$8.95
Revelations	Cheris F. Hodges	$8.95
Rivers of the Soul	Leslie Esdaile	$8.95
Rooms of the Heart	Donna Hill	$8.95
Shades of Brown	Denise Becker	$8.95
Shades of Desire	Monica White	$8.95
Sin	Crystal Rhodes	$8.95
So Amazing	Sinclair LeBeau	$8.95
Somebody's Someone	Sinclair LeBeau	$8.95
Someone to Love	Alicia Wiggins	$8.95
Soul to Soul	Donna Hill	$8.95
Still Waters Run Deep	Leslie Esdaile	$8.95
Subtle Secrets	Wanda Y. Thomas	$8.95
Sweet Tomorrows	Kimberly White	$8.95
The Color of Trouble	Dyanne Davis	$8.95
The Price of Love	Sinclair LeBeau	$8.95
The Reluctant Captive	Joyce Jackson	$8.95
The Missing Link	Charlyne Dickerson	$8.95
Three Wishes	Seressia Glass	$8.95
Tomorrow's Promise	Leslie Esdaile	$8.95
Truly Inseperable	Wanda Y. Thomas	$8.95
Twist of Fate	Beverly Clark	$8.95
Unbreak My Heart	Dar Tomlinson	$8.95
Unconditional Love	Alicia Wiggins	$8.95
When Dreams A Float	Dorothy Elizabeth Love	$8.95

ESCAPE WITH INDIGO !!!!

Join Indigo Book Club©
It's simple, easy and secure.

Sign up and receive the new releases
every month + Free shipping and
20% off the cover price.

Go online to www.genesis-press.com and
click on Bookclub or
call 1-888-INDIGO-1

Order Form

Mail to: Genesis Press, Inc.

P.O. Box 101
Columbus, MS 39703

Name _____
Address _____
City/State _____ Zip _____
Telephone _____

Ship to (if different from above)
Name _____
Address _____
City/State _____ Zip _____
Telephone _____

Credit Card Information
Credit Card # _____ ☐ Visa ☐ Mastercard
Expiration Date (mm/yy) _____ ☐ AmEx ☐ Discover

Qty.	Author	Title	Price	Total

Use this order form, or call 1-888-INDIGO-1	Total for books	_____
	Shipping and handling: $5 first two books, $1 each additional book	_____
	Total S & H	_____
	Total amount enclosed	_____
	Mississippi residents add 7% sales tax	

Visit www.genesis-press.com for latest releases and excerpts.

Order Form

Mail to: Genesis Press, Inc.

P.O. Box 101
Columbus, MS 39703

Name _____
Address _____
City/State _____ Zip _____
Telephone _____

Ship to (if different from above)
Name _____
Address _____
City/State _____ Zip _____
Telephone _____

Credit Card Information

Credit Card # _____ ☐ Visa ☐ Mastercard
Expiration Date (mm/yy) _____ ☐ AmEx ☐ Discover

Qty.	Author	Title	Price	Total

Use this order form, or call 1-888-INDIGO-1	**Total for books** _____ **Shipping and handling:** $5 first two books, $1 each additional book _____ **Total S & H** _____ **Total amount enclosed** _____ *Mississippi residents add 7% sales tax*

Order Form

Mail to: Genesis Press, Inc.

P.O. Box 101
Columbus, MS 39703

Name _____
Address _____
City/State _____ Zip _____
Telephone _____

Ship to (if different from above)
Name _____
Address _____
City/State _____ Zip _____
Telephone _____

Credit Card Information
Credit Card # _____ ☐Visa ☐Mastercard
Expiration Date (mm/yy) _____ ☐AmEx ☐Discover

Qty.	Author	Title	Price	Total

Use this order
form, or call
1-888-INDIGO-1

Total for books _____
Shipping and handling:
　$5 first two books,
　$1 each additional book _____
Total S & H _____
Total amount enclosed _____

Mississippi residents add 7% sales tax